KILLER OF KINGS

Other books by R. Wright Campbell

Where Pigeons Go to Die
Circus Couronne
The Spy Who Sat and Waited

KILLER
OF KINGS

R. Wright Campbell

The Bobbs-Merrill Company, Inc.
Indianapolis/New York

KILLER OF KINGS

1

The life of Harry Smiley had been a sorry one of broken dreams, lost hopes, crippled desires, petty failures, and a busted knee acquired while playing second-string halfback for his high school football team. The knee bothered him in damp weather. He limped a bit at other times because he believed it lent him a mysterious and romantic air.

Most people thought him likable enough. Most people didn't take the time to get to know him. Those who did were vaguely disturbed by him; a touch afraid, despite—or perhaps because of—the fact that he grinned a lot.

His mother thought he should have been a doctor because he'd once brought home a wounded rat and nursed it back to health. When it nipped him on the finger, he smashed its skull in, calling it an act of mercy.

His father claimed—sarcastically—that he'd have made one hell of a lawyer: he was all mouth.

One of his aunts expected him to be an actor. She was called the crazy aunt by the rest of the family.

His grandfather said he'd be unremarkable in every way unless he turned out to be a felon. Harry stole his watch and pawned it for a jug of guinea red and a carton of smokes. He considered that a profitable lesson for the old man.

He grew up as though practicing to be antisocial, on the lookout for any cause that might harness vague but powerful feelings of rage. He wanted desperately to stand out from the crowd, was depressingly aware that he didn't have the means to do so. He thieved and engaged in petty brutalities against the weak.

In spite of the bad knee, he was inducted into the army during the Korean action and probably saved from an early imprisonment. He spent two years in the dry hell of Camp Hood, Texas, where he avoided work, ate off the public, and developed a glutton's appetite for historical romances and revolutionary essays.

Such disparate tastes were reconciled in the story of Vera Zasulich, the young Russian socialist who seriously wounded General Trepov, the despotic prefect of the St. Petersburg police, in the year 1878. Her act had been in protest against the brutal flogging of her lover, who had been taken up as a political prisoner.

Later Harry placed himself in the role of one of the jurors who, outraged by the beating and sympathetic to Vera's action in the name of human dignity, acquitted her at the risk of czarist fury. In his daydreams it was Harry who spirited Vera out of the country before the police could arrest her.

Extravagant fantasies, carefully documented, frustratingly unreal.

After his discharge he went to San Francisco, where he hung around bars, telling lies about combat and the rare sexual talents of the girls of Pusan.

When his unemployment ran out, he decided to live off the people for yet a while longer and enrolled at the University of California, Berkeley, which had been one of the principal factories of student unrest. He majored in history and political science.

His big mouth had developed into a small but flashy gift for rabble-rousing. He became a minor celebrity on campus when he organized a demonstration protesting a speaking engagement by Senator "Tail-Gunner Joe" McCarthy. He was routinely placed on the sentinel lists of the Sheriff's Office of Alameda County, the Berkeley Police Department, and the University Security Force. Harry knew that his brief moment of glory was meaningless and quite ordinary. It was nothing compared to the deeds of the *agent provocateur* Mr. Verloc in Conrad's *The Secret Agent*. He was struck by the "theory of the absurd," an "act of destructive ferocity, so absurd as to be incomprehensible, almost unthinkable: in fact, mad." But he hadn't yet developed the stomach for random, bloody terror. Neither did he have the passion or the energy for it.

Harry left school and went on the bum. He landed in Little Rock, Arkansas, in the fall of '57, right in the middle of the integration riots. He mouthed off in favor of the black students and got the hell kicked out of him by the cops, who convinced him he ought to change his tune or serve ninety as a vagrant. So he was among those who yelled "Nigger!" into the faces of nine small black children. He was again taken into custody by the police because Governor Faubus had decided momentarily to pretend cooperation with the Federal court order; was kicked to hell again and run out of town. Harry drifted north, working one odd job after another, never well, never for long. He read a lot and daydreamed a lot.

In '60 he worked for the election of John F. Kennedy to the presidency. After the victory he wrote letters of advice to Kennedy and received form replies signed by machine. He wrote a letter telling the President that he'd "better pay some careful attention" to what people like Harry had to say or he'd get his "comeuppance," an old-fashioned word but threatening all the same. His name was entered on still another list.

In the same year Harry kept the death watch, with other protestors, outside San Quentin when the "Red-Light Bandit," Caryl Chessman, finally walked into the gas chamber. His attendance was duly noted.

In '63, eighteen days after Kennedy's assassination, Harry Smiley went to MacArthur Park in Los Angeles, erected a cardboard tombstone crayoned with the martyred President's name and date of death, and proceeded to urinate on it before a gathering of locals, who promptly called the cops.

Harry was kept in county jail while the DA's office searched through the lawbooks for a statute that would make such an act of desecration, even in facsimile, a hanging offense. Finding none, they remanded him into the custody of the Mental Health Authority and the State Hospital at Camarillo. He was studied for a year. One doctor theorized that Harry had been trying to express his grief and his willingness to have died in the young President's place, his urine a symbol of martyr's blood. Another doctor took the opposite view and called the act a declaration of the most outrageous hate and contempt. The facility was overcrowded and Harry was released, his name on the star sentinel list of all at Secret Service. He was unaware of it. He was a revolutionary spirit without a cause, a toilet without a flush.

He married a hooker with a fifty-dollar nose. She

hustled for rent, food and cocaine—not in that order. She was quiet and passive. Harry talked to her for hours and read her passages from such works as those written by the anarchist Bakunin as she nodded away, smiling sweetly.

Harry got a job as a stacker in a supermarket. His wife graduated to heroin. Harry was promoted to assistant manager. One day she got a hot-shot and killed herself by miscalculation. He quit his job. There was nobody to listen to him anymore.

Between January and May of '69 he spent a lot of time outside the courthouse during the trial of Sirhan Sirhan. His name was checked out on the Secret Service list.

In '72 he read with fascination and envy of the terrorist massacre of innocents at Lod airport, executed by three Japanese terrorists in the service of the Popular Front for the Liberation of Palestine. Commentators and analysts, seeking logic and rational motive, found it impossible to understand the shocking, almost casual, commitment of the stoned young men who'd killed people at random for a cause not even remotely their own. Harry thought he understood them very well. Impotent fury will accept any target.

In '73 the Secret Service sentinel list of forty-seven thousand names was revised and Harry's name deleted. He was living in a small clapboard cottage in a small court in West Hollywood and working as a part-time guard at 20th.

At the age of fifty he was as plain and unremarkable-looking as a bottle of nitroglycerin.

2

Michael Nordland was an actor. The stories about him in the magazines and press are generally not to be believed. What follows is the truth—sort of.

He was born out of wedlock to one Elvira Belcher in Ovett, Mississippi, product of a single night of cheap and casual passion with a traveling salesman who left his name but not his address. Elvira named her son Hartley, took the name Pragerman for herself without benefit of clergy or the law, then apprenticed herself to a bawdy house in Hattiesburg.

She was allowed to keep her infant until the boy was about seven and then was asked by the madam to make other arrangements, since he was either getting underfoot or trying to crawl under the covers with the girls.

Elvira was about fed up with the life anyway, so she accepted an offer of marriage from a rather thrifty farmer who figured it would be cheaper to buy the cow. Trouble was, he didn't want any half-grown pup around the place.

At that time Elvira's sister Phoebe, living up in New Jersey, lost her own seven-year-old boy in a street accident. She went into shock and refused to accept the reality. Every couple of hours she stuck her head out the window of her ghetto flat and called her dead son Michael in for supper.

Elvira, in a burst of sisterly affection, decided to give Hartley to her sister. At the very least she figured that when a blond-haired blue-eyed boy came in to supper instead of a black-haired brown-eyed one, Phoebe might be shocked right the hell out of her dream world. A double whammy for the sake of mental health.

It worked in an unexpected way. When Hartley walked in on his mother's hand, Aunt Phoebe called him Michael, told him to wash up, and sat him down to eat at the kitchen table. When Elvira left, telling him to call Phoebe "mother," he accepted it calmly, already possessed of the super-cool that was to become his acting trademark. Besides, he preferred the name Michael to Hartley.

His uncle didn't much like the idea of Elvira's dumping her brat on them, but if it made Phoebe content, he reckoned he would put up with it.

The new Michael Foley was a charmer and a winner in school right from the start. He knew how to push buttons and pull strings. When he graduated from grade school, he was chief of the security patrol, student representative to the Red Cross, editor of the paper, president of the debating team, and captain of the track team, and had been laid three times, once by a girl of twenty-two.

Phoebe was excessively proud of her "son," which didn't do her relationship with her husband any good. He got fed up and took off one day, tired of feeding the cuckoo dropped into his nest. If Michael saw a pattern of abandonment, he didn't let on.

He was a proper wonder in high school, breaking track records, maidenheads and cash registers with equal skill. He spent a good deal of time on the streets hustling. One night he returned late to the flat he shared with Phoebe. He knew she'd be waiting up for him, ready to scold in her weak and whining voice. For a moment, as he noiselessly slipped the key into the lock, he was shaken by the savage hope that she was dead. He slipped through the open door and silently closed it behind him. Strange noises were coming from her bedroom. He tiptoed along the hall and peered into the room illuminated by the faint glow of the streetlamp shining through the stained window shade.

Terror leaped and twisted through him, stealing the strength from his legs. He slid slowly to the floor in the hallway as he watched a hulking, shadowy figure raise its fist again and again, striking a smaller body cowering on its knees before the attack.

Michael wanted to cry out, but his throat was thick with fear and he had no voice. He may have whimpered. The intruder half-turned toward the hallway, struck his victim a final blow and escaped through the window, down the fire escape.

His aunt was dead. He felt an overpowering regret, a shattering sense of guilt. It would be a long time before he would succeed in burying it in his subconscious. Even then it would be awakened from time to time.

Phoebe hadn't been raped. Nothing had been stolen. After the funeral Michael left school and got a job on the docks. He wasn't that big, but he was broad in the shoulders, strong and willing. It was wartime and jobs were plentiful. After six months he found a berth on a freighter going to Murmansk. The ship was torpedoed and he was fished out of the icy waters more dead than alive. He was sensitive to cold from that time on and gave up any idea of a life at sea.

He hooked up with a stripper ten years older than he who was happy to keep his feet warm. She got him a job as a "talker" in a tent show where she danced summers. He left her after a time, took work in a burlesque house and added a few jokes to his patter. He loved it. There was something in the tinsel and gaud that moved him. The people got under his skin. The girls complained of tired feet, their pants were soiled, the flesh of their thighs was like orange peel, but they were brave. The comics were has-beens or never-weres, but they were brave as well, rattling off worn-out old gags, chewing over the same old material, sweating and capering. They called themselves actors, and Michael determined to really become one.

He joined the Neighborhood Playhouse and was cast in a small part but was called into the army two days after the play opened. He took basic training at Fort Dix and combat training in Japan and was tossed into Korea. He fought for thirteen months and was awarded the Silver Star for an act of valor he couldn't recall. All he could remember of that hero's day was crouching at the bottom of a hill, watching blood belching from his buddy's mouth and, later, standing over seven dead Chinese and their machine gun in a farmhouse. That and a terrible sense of nameless guilt.

He was discharged in due course, a quiet man, capable and cool. Without clearly understanding why—perhaps because he was alive and his comrade dead—he took the name of his fallen friend.

Michael Nordland went to New York and worked at the Neighborhood Playhouse until he was signed for the road company of *Angel Street*, which was touring to California. He was scouted, tested by Warners, and signed to a stock contract with six-month options. He was dropped after a year.

He got the part of a killer in a low-budget quickie.

He looked great in a trench coat. It got him a TV series that lasted three years and made him rich. When it was over he waited for a shot in a feature.

In '66 he made a small, lovingly crafted film about a stove-in cowboy trying to make a comeback after a year in the hospital. He had insisted on learning as much of the real thing as he could handle: he rode a few broncs, roped some calves, busted a few ribs, and earned the respect of the real cowboys, who shared their whiskey and women with him. They remained his friends, and he'd meet them from time to time in beer joints out in San Fernando Valley or in the hills of Calabasas.

The rest of his rise to fame and his most notable film, *Mute*, can be read about in fan magazines or in a recent book, *Michael Nordland—His Films*. At the age of forty-seven he had the world by the sneakers.

The two men, nearly of an age—one riding high, the other just plodding along; one at a beginning, the other nearly at an end; one looking ten years younger than his years, the other looking a decade older than his—had very little in common.

Except.

One hated and feared violence and death; the other had an unhealthy fascination with it.

3

The Secret Service is the shield of the president's body. Whenever he steps out of the White House, the agents get the willies. They disapprove strongly of chief executives who take pleasure in "pressing the flesh," who consider public exposure sacred to the traditions of American politics. They hate all presidential travel, because they know that one of their number may be called upon to throw himself in front of a gun. No one but a damn fool takes a bullet in the belly if he can avoid it, and Secret Service agents are a long way from being damn fools. They tend to be conservative, cautious, even colorless men determined to live into old age.

If possible they move into any city marked for a visit well in advance. They ask the cooperation of the nearest FBI field office and the local police. They plan several routes and deploy their forces to create a "sanitized zone." Even so, they are aware that a determined assassin—even a casual, inept one— might, with deceptive ease, blow their careful security to hell and pull the trigger on the "Man."

In January they went into Los Angeles to prepare the way for just such a presidential visit. FBI agents and four men from LAPD Intelligence joined them.

Detective Sergeant John Metzler was assigned the job of making a preliminary check of sentinel records for all persons considered potentially dangerous to prominent figures. The files on such crazies and politicals went back ten years. Harry Smiley's bizarre protest in the park fell outside the limit; his name didn't show up.

Harry had a girlfriend. Alice Belmont was an ex-hoofer, failed actress and Hollywood discard who'd ended up waiting table in an all-night coffee shop on Hollywood Boulevard. She had her own apartment but spent a good deal of time at Harry's, cooking his meals and warming his bed.

One day when she arrived at his place at noon she found him staring at himself in the hallway mirror. He was dressed in his old University of California athletic jacket. His concentration was so great he hadn't even heard her let herself in. She cleared her throat to announce herself. He quickly thrust the hand away from her into his pocket and turned his head slowly to look at her.

"Where you off to?" she asked, bright as a canary.

"The President's making an appearance at Century City," he said. "Four o'clock. I mean to be there." He pushed her aside and went out, leaving her standing there wondering what the hell was eating him. Wondering if she'd really seen a gun before he'd stashed it away.

Michael had a girlfriend whose true name was Sheri Silver. She spent nearly all her time with him.

About the same time on the same day she watched Michael get dressed. She admired the style, graceful and catlike, he brought to it.

"What's the occasion?"

"This country boy's going to have breakfast, lunch, brunch—whatever—with the President of these here United States," he drawled in humorous exaggeration.

She grinned up at him from where she sat on the bed.

Michael went to her and kissed her lightly at the corner of her mouth. She put out her tongue, licked the place and smiled.

"Mouthwash," she said, standing up.

"After-shave. Fifty bucks a bottle."

He kissed her full on the mouth, felt himself stir against her pelvis. "You think the President would understand if I called to say that more pressing demands had come up?"

"Get the hell out of here."

Michael left, feeling good, feeling hungry, excited that this "good ol' boy" was going to break bread with the "Man."

There were maybe three thousand people gathered in the mall at Century City. Harry arrived at the fringe of the crowd out of breath and grumbling to himself.

"The joker in the blue and gold jacket's talking to himself," John Metzler said to Coolidge, FBI.

"Looks a little old to be a student," Coolidge said.

They watched Harry elbow his way through the rear ranks of the crowd as it suddenly surged toward the building.

In a moment the first Secret Service agent appeared at the glass doors of the main building, opened them, and made way for a dozen uniformed cops moving out to force a passage. The crowd shifted away like a dumb beast.

Harry felt hot and miserable. The people in the crowd wouldn't move aside for him, making it difficult for him to get to the front. He shoved right and left, cursing them in a low voice. Some turned to glare at him, opened their mouths to scold, but thought better of it when they saw the rage in his florid face. He broke free of the front rank just as the President and Michael Nordland swept out the door.

Harry gripped the automatic in his pocket, thumbing off the safety. His legs felt cold and numb, his left arm leaden. His breath came in short, shallow bites. Only his right arm and the hand that held the gun felt alive.

The President stopped suddenly and plunged into the crowd to shake outstretched hands. Secret Service agents moved in and tried to cut him out and separate him from the crowd, like cowhands herding a straying steer. The President smiled and moved on.

It seemed to Harry that the President was coming to him at his call. His hand began to ease out of his pocket. The President was standing there right in front of him, no more than half a dozen steps away. Harry tugged at the gun. The forward sight snagged on a bit of frayed cloth. Harry's eyes flickered away from his target. He saw a pie-faced woman with red hair force her arm and hand between two people in the crowd. She held a gun.

"No!" Harry screamed.

Metzler, who'd been watching Harry, saw him cry out in rage and then saw the woman with the gun.

A man next to the red-haired woman lashed out at her arm, driving the gun above her head. A shot went off. The woman looked at Harry and seemed to smile softly at him before she was borne to the ground under the weight of heroes.

Only Metzler had been witness to the curious look that had passed between Harry and the foiled assassin.

4

Harry felt hands clapping him on the back as he watched the police hustle the woman out of the area. People were congratulating him for something. At first he didn't understand what they were going on about; then he realized they thought he'd cried out to prevent a killing. A television news team stopped him, asked him stupid questions, captured him on tape, and went off after more important game, the hero of the day, the man who'd deflected the shot.

Harry went home, roused Alice from her nap and made love to her in the hungry manner of soldiers who have survived battle.

They watched Harry on the news at five o'clock. Friends gathered to watch again later in the evening. Walter Peewit arrived with his wife Janet and a brown sack full of beer. A funny kid named Bondi who'd attached himself to Harry sat in the living room staring at him with something close to hero worship. Hush, the lesbian who lived across the court, and her girlfriend Evelynn came over. They made a party.

Michael recorded the newscast on video tape. After Sheri went to bed he played it over and over again. He saw the President walking loose and easy, himself walking alongside. He remembered, with a touch of vanity, that he'd heard his name whispered among the crowd as often as he'd heard the "Man's." When the camera zoomed in at the moment of the President's plunge into the crowd, it lingered for a moment on Michael's face. He saw his eyes shift alertly. He looked the way secret agents look when they're played by high-priced movie stars in high-priced movies, only the reality seemed heightened. His eyes had the look of a plainsman—pale, intent, filled with the determination to protect the nation. The camera recorded the smile given him when the President was herded back under protection, and the smile he gave back—the casual, humorous understanding exchanged between two strong men.

He saw the sudden awareness on the President's face when someone had shouted, "No!"—the quick turn of his head, the draining of blood from his face when he saw the gun, and the automatic crouch he took even as the gun was smashed into the air. Michael watched the President's instinctive search for safety among the men sworn to protect him with their own lives.

But most of all he was fascinated by his own image on the television screen. He saw the way he seemed to move forward to place himself between the President and the gun and knew that it was a trick of the camera angle, for he was actually preparing himself to run. He remembered the weakness that had touched him at the knees, the instant drying of the spit in his mouth, the fear that his sphincter muscles might give way when he saw the gun and heard the shout. He'd been afraid and grateful that he was netted along with the President and shepherded safely into the limousine.

Once inside the cool interior, they'd smiled nervously at each other. "Son of a bitch," the President had said.

"Son of a bitch," Michael had answered, and then they'd both laughed like hell out of sheer relief.

Michael played the tape over and over. Sheri came into the room.

"Film really does lie," Michael murmured as she sat beside him.

"You mean you ain't really Gary Cooper in *High Noon*?" she teased.

"I was scared half to death," he said. There was a stirring in the back of his mind, an image of a dark bundle on a worn carpet, another of a mouth filling with blood.

He knew he was going to have a bad night.

Law enforcement officers looked at the film, examined tape recordings and read written depositions of eyewitnesses. Metzler sat next to Coolidge.

"Is that joker in the school jacket yelling before, during or after the assassination attempt?" someone asked.

"During," some said. Others said, "After."

They ran the loop again. They watched Harry Smiley as he opened his mouth, a look of shocked awareness on his face, just as the President appeared beyond him.

"Before," someone said. "He saw it coming and was trying to give warning."

"Like hell," Metzler said. "I was on him the whole time. He was as mad as hell about something, but not because somebody was taking a shot at the 'Man.' "

"I know that dude from someplace," Coolidge said in a flat New England voice.

"What do you mean?"

17

"Just that I've seen the fella somewhere before. Don't know where, but I reckon it was in a crowd."

"Think about it, Coolidge."

The film clips and tapes were shown again and again for a long time.

"I saw him in some still pictures," Coolidge suddenly announced.

"You remember where?"

"Public event."

"Check it out."

"Do I get any help?"

"Lieutenant Jill?"

Metzler's superior glanced over at him, took his nod. "You want to assist the FBI?"

"If he'll promise to stop exploding in my ear."

"Son of a gun," Coolidge muttered in a friendly fashion.

Saturday morning Harry woke up in bed with a hangover of considerable dimensions. He still had his trousers and socks on but was without his shirt and shoes. Alice was on one side of him, under the covers, one shoulder and arm exposed, the bra strap cutting into her flesh.

Janet Peewit was on the other. She'd removed her bra to free the weight of her heavy breasts. They lay exposed to his look, flattened out somewhat against her ribcage. The nipples were standing up in the morning chill. The sight of them aroused little lust in Harry. Even without the hangover, he wouldn't have been much interested. He didn't much like Janet Peewit, tolerated her more or less because of his friendship with her husband, Walter. He thought her a useless bitch.

There was more than that to the woman who'd

once been known as Janet Bojack back in Wheeling, West Virginia.

She and her mother had moved there after her father had died of black lung disease contracted in the coal mines. She'd been seven at the time, already beautiful in a ripe way older than her years. There was a certain knowingness in her large eyes. Her hair was very thick in a womanly way. Her mother sometimes laughed and wondered aloud if her second husband hadn't been more attracted to her small daughter than to herself. He laughed too, but it had a hollow sound. His jolly ways with Janet had been excuses to touch her and receive her wet, maturely sensuous kisses. Certainly by the time she was a full-breasted fourteen-year-old there wasn't much doubt that Ralph lusted after his stepdaughter. When she was sixteen Janet won a local bathing beauty contest, and the next day her mother, hard-nosed and prudent, asked her to leave the house and go it alone.

Janet went to Hollywood, drawn by the persistent legend that beauty is the touchstone to film success. Her back got sore waiting for the big break. She grew bitter-mouthed and dull-eyed, until she met and married Walter Peewit, who adored her. She married the ex-fighter not so much for the security it might afford her as for the chance to see herself forever reflected in his eyes as the most beautiful girl in the world. After a while she decided that the dullness of marriage with Peewit wasn't really worth the adulation, but she was too indolent—or afraid—to go through with divorce. Instead she became demanding and petulant, using him until his look of worship was sometimes replaced by that of an old horse that's been haltered too long in the stable.

She had a pained and searching look about her, craving excitement but not knowing how to find it, waiting for someone to show her the way to it. In vain. The good years, if any, were coming to a close-out.

So far as good years were concerned, Walter Peewit had them in hand right now. There never had been any in the past, though he had a foolish boaster's belief that there had been.

Right from the beginning, Walter Peewit was reckoned to be a second-rater among the boys in the know. He was strong and willing, but he didn't have it upstairs. He knew his left from his right, but anything much more complicated than that was beyond him. No matter how hard his trainers and managers tried, they could never teach him how to pace himself; how to hold on when he was hurt and rest on the other fighter's arms. All he knew how to do was lower his head between his shoulders and wade in, punching away flat-footed, every punch he took in return jarring right down the bones of his head and spine, wearing him out. He'd fight hard, and if he could take his opponent out in the first three, he'd make his win; any more and he tired fast, until by the fifth he was blown out and ready for the slaughter.

Bringing him along slow and easy at the beginning of his career, his manager matched him against good club fighters who fell under his powerhouse punches often enough to give him a nice little reputation; but when he stepped up in class and was matched with better, smarter men, he began to fall. He never got ring-wise, and it wasn't too long before he was handed into the ring to make some comer look good. He was half punchy by then, certain that he was climbing to the championship.

He was signed for a fight at the Olympic Auditorium in Los Angeles. A California fighter was being groomed for an assault on the eastern fight establishment, and they needed a fighter with a reputation for toughness and heart to fall under his gloves. Walter Peewit was the man. His last manager saw a way to wring a final purse out of the failing boxer; for an extra three bills he guaranteed the opposition a flashy win, figuring Peewit wouldn't last ten with the help of a tank against the younger man. But he forgot to mention to Peewit that he was expected to lose without doing much damage to his opponent.

Peewit lost but showed well, knocking the younger fighter down three times before being KO'd himself; chopping the hell out of the kid's face, breaking his nose and making him gun-shy forever. The owners of the ruined fighter were underworld connected. They couldn't find Peewit's manager, so they took their pound of flesh out of Peewit just for spite, busting his ribs with an iron bar and breaking the fingers on one of his hands.

Peewit was lucky; he'd made some friends and found work in the studios, where he learned the propman's trade.

He got luckier and met Janet Bojack, who was calling herself Beau. She was, he thought, about the most beautiful woman he'd ever met. He still thought so—sometimes—but the knowledge gave him less pleasure than it had at the beginning.

Coolidge wasn't a talkative man. He spoke only to deliver bits of information or ask terse questions.

"Peace marches. Violence. Student protests. Notable trials," he said as he and Metzler searched through hundreds of grainy photographs. He was getting downright chatty.

By four o'clock Saturday afternoon Metzler had developed a headache and suggested a break. They sat sipping coffee and resting their eyes on the view of the building across the way, a block of glass and steel throwing back the reflection of the sky.

"Courthouse," Coolidge said. "A crowd around a courthouse."

Two hours later they found Harry's ugly face circled in red on a photo taken at the Sirhan Sirhan trial. The coded back directed them to a file where they discovered the incident of the desecration of the mock grave.

Coolidge returned to his chair, leaned back, patted his gut and smiled. "We've named and numbered the villain. Now we can go eat."

"Don't we follow this up?"

"We give the crazy dude's name to the Secret Service, then we eat."

"That's all?"

"He belongs to them now. We did our duty. We get a gold star."

"That's all?" Metzler asked again.

"We could pick up this Harry Smiley and wonder into his ear why a guy pisses on a paper grave. We could ask him how come he hangs around courthouses with a couple hundred other people and goggles at fellas who shoot other people. We could ask him what the hell's he doin' hanging around Century City with a couple of thousand gawking at the President on a sunny afternoon. And he can tell us to stuff it."

"The Service must have more on him if he's on their sentinel list."

"Maybe so; and if so, they'll know what to do about it." Coolidge unfolded his rack of bones from the chair. "Let's eat."

Harry wasn't tired anymore, felt almost good again, the edge of his hangover blunted by a new alcohol glow.

Peewit and Janet were still there, Bondi out getting a new supply of liquor. A friend of Alice's, a hooker called Assy by her friends and Miss Marvel by cops and customers because of the red satin working duds she wore, was out in the kitchen helping Alice dish out potato salad from plastic cartons and line up cold cuts on a platter. Evelynn and Hush banged in and out as they pleased. Harry sprawled out in his easy chair and cursed them all under his breath in a friendly way. He stared at the tube, dumbly waiting for the CBS special on "A History of Assassination" announced on the late news the night before. Harry hoped that his part in yesterday's incident would be part of it. Maybe he'd have the opportunity of tasting celebrity one more time, his moment surrounded by a documentary that wouldn't disappear altogether. A commercial came to an end. There was a long moment of silence and a blank screen, solemn preparation for a "public service."

The coats of arms of kings and princes, the seals of heads of state and governments appeared as background for the title "The Killing of Kings" written in convoluted script.

Bondi came in through the back door, slamming the screen behind him, arms laden with jugs of wine, six-packs of beer, bags of potato chips and other junk.

"Shut the hell up!" Harry shouted from the living room.

Bondi grinned at Alice and hunched his shoulders, a likable kid without a hell of a lot of brains, shy even for his years, peeking at Assy out of the corners of his eyes. He colored when Alice whispered her friend's name by way of introduction. He never used rough language around women.

In the living room Harry leaned forward in his chair; Peewit and Janet perked up a bit. A face appeared on the television screen.

"It's Jack Lemmon," Janet said.

"I worked with him one time," Peewit said.

"What flick?"

"I forget."

"Shut up," Harry said.

Jack Lemmon's head began to talk. "It's no new thing for political extremists and malcontents to attempt to kill kings, queens and princes. It's not uncommon in the histories of nations for chancellors, prime ministers, premiers and presidents to be the victims of assassination plots. But no era has witnessed a greater wave of such terrorist tactics than the twentieth century; no decade has offered a greater variety of weapons to the political murderer than our own."

Assy walked into the room with a tray of food. "Hey," she asked brightly, "isn't that Jack Lemmon?"

"Yeah," Janet said. "Getting old, isn't he?"

"I loved him in *Some Like it Hot*," Assy informed everyone as though they'd really like to know.

"Shut the hell up!" Harry shouted.

"Excuse me," a voice said from beyond the hall and the screen door at the front of the house. "I didn't mean to disturb anybody."

"Who the hell is that?" Harry asked, rising from his chair, ready to have at somebody. He peered through the dust-laden mesh of the screen.

"It's me. It's Marco Epstein. I saw you on the news last night, Harry, and I thought I'd come congratulate

24

you in person. I didn't think you'd be down at the benches today."

"Come in," Harry said. "Come in and grab a seat. This is Marco, everybody. We argue politics down in Venice sometimes. Say hello later. Now shut up, everybody."

Harry flung himself back into the overstuffed chair and fixed his eyes on the television again. Marco came into the house with elaborate care, closing the screen door behind him without a whisper of sound, mouse-footing it across the floor and wincing when the sofa creaked as he sat down between Janet and Assy.

He was a small man, immaculately clean, collar starched, frayed ends clipped from the cuffs, shoes well shined, socks held up by old-fashioned garters, precise, shy, apologetic in his manner. He smiled all around and mouthed "hellos," received silent greetings from the others sitting like so many mourners at a funeral.

"Now shut up and watch this," Harry said. "It's history."

Marco burped nervously behind his hand and Assy giggled.

5

Michael sat on one half of a love seat upholstered in a wheat-toned hand-loomed fabric that retailed out at one hundred dollars a yard. Sheri sat on the other half, her hand on his thigh.

On the television set Jack Lemmon spoke of the assassination of kings and emperors, prime ministers and presidents. His words were accompanied by illustrations and newsreel footage. Finally the program focused in on the events of the previous day. Stop-action photography and isolated frames showed baldly the gut-fear on the face of the President in that split second when his eyes fell on the gun in the hand of Mary Margaret Masters, the latest would-be assassin. In the background Michael loomed, flint-eyed, seemingly imperturbable, rocking forward on the balls of his feet like a guard dog about to go to the defense of its master. There were two or three isolated frames of Michael's face, blown up, grainy and heroic.

Sheri moved closer to Michael, seeking the shelter of his arms.

On the screen he was being interviewed by an efficient-looking lady.

"I don't know what I felt when I spotted the gun," he said to her with a small, modest smile. "I guess I was getting ready to run like hell." The interviewer laughed in charmed disbelief.

"Your biography tells us you were a war hero," she said.

On the screen Michael smiled and said nothing.

"Isn't that true?" she persisted.

Michael wished he'd had the courage to tell the reporter that that was a damned lie.

The pictured Michael waved a hand in the air, dismissing any further discussion. The real Michael drew Sheri closer to him.

"I've got to tell you," Michael said.

There was something in the abrupt urgency in his voice that made Sheri stiffen.

"I'm no hero," he said.

Sheri relaxed.

"That's perfectly all right with me. You'll keep safer that way," she murmured.

"No, I mean I never was a hero. Not today. Not during the Korean War."

"I don't understand, Michael. You have all those medals. Are you trying to tell me that . . ."

She hesitated.

"Oh, they were awarded to me all right," Michael said. "But I didn't earn them."

Sheri remained silent still clearly in the dark, knowing that he was about to release some long pent up distress and pain.

"I was sent to Fort Meade in Maryland for basic training. The instructors talked a lot about the buddy system—how you had to know you could depend on the guy by your side. This character Carter Nordland—that's where I got my last name," he said at Sheri's look of inquiry. "—this guy walks up to me and says, 'Foley, you better be good to me. You better buy me beers, let me cadge cigarettes, lend me a tenner when I'm broke, and share your most private nookie with me, because one day I'm going to save your ass. I'm your buddy.'

"He was, and I was his buddy as well, all through basic, right into combat. We became closer than brothers. It really does happen that way. Only once, when he tried to drag me into some damn fool fight with some English soldiers in a bar in Pusan, did one of us let the other down. I'd just about gotten fed up with some of his screwy games and reckoned I'd let those Limeys teach him a little lesson.

"We didn't make it up during that R and R. Before we could talk it out, we found ourselves at the foot of some goddamn hill. It didn't even have a name, just a number."

Michael's face was in a fury. Sheri spoke his name very softly. He shook himself like a dog.

"Was that the hill where you won the Silver Star?" she asked.

"I don't remember charging up that hill. I remember seeing blood pouring from Carter Nordland's mouth. I remember seeing my buddy start to fall, and that's all I remember, until I was standing over a bunch of dead gooks at the top of the hill."

He started to shake, and Sheri took him in her arms.

"Don't try to remember," she said. "Don't try to remember."

"That's just it," Michael cried out against her neck. "I can't remember. No matter how hard I try. I can't remember what Carter was trying to say to me before he died."

Harry's eyes were fixed on the screen with a terrible intensity. He worked hard at waiting for his moment of glory. He watched Nordland's head leave the screen, a man beheaded, to be replaced by Roger Berkley, the hero who'd deflected the shot. He seemed genuinely modest, bewildered by the fuss created by his instinctive act of defense.

"I felt somebody pushing at my arm," he said to the efficient interviewer. "Like they was trying to push ahead of me in the crowd." He looked very indignant for a moment. "I started to turn to see who the hell—sorry—who the wise guy was and I looks down at what's pokin' me in the ribs and I see this goddamn—sorry—this gun in some dame's hand."

"How did you know it was a female hand?" the interviewer asked rather testily.

"What? Hell, I don't know," Berkley said. "Just knew. Was small, I guess. The fingernails was painted red, but I guess that don't tell much anymore." He laughed at his clever social comment. "That's it. I saw the goddamn—sorry—I saw the gun and knocked it up in the air so nobody would get hit in case it went off."

"Did you realize that the President was in danger?"

"You're fuckin' 'A.' "

It wasn't bleeped out, had already become words for Americans to live by, like "Damn the torpedoes, full speed ahead," "Remember the Alamo," and "The buck stops here."

The special ended. There'd been no film clip or interview with Harry Smiley.

It was dead quiet in Harry's living room as the screen faded to black. Bondi began to choke on a half-swallowed mouthful of beer, held his mouth closed against the offending sound, and then sprayed it out through his nose in panic. It sounded like a strangled laugh. The others looked at him as though they'd been offended.

"Somebody see something funny?" Harry asked.

"Bondi choked on some beer," Alice said.

"I thought Jack Lemmon was very good," Assy commented brightly.

Harry got up from his chair then, turned around and stared at her. His hands went to his hips, and he cocked his head as though examining a bug in his soup.

"I don't believe it." His eyes flickered toward Marco, who saw clearly that Harry meant to attack the girl because he'd been hurt to the core and had to have somebody's bones to chew on. Marco smiled a coward's encouragement and hated himself for it.

"They just gave us an expensive history lesson. Something to teach us a little bit, exercise the old brain."

"Who wants pizza? I'd really like to have some pizza," Alice said, hoping to deflect Harry and spare her friend.

"They spent thousands, hundreds of thousands, on that program," Harry said, building his effect, "just so this stupid whore, this bitch, can say she thought Lemmon was great."

Bondi flushed at the language, started to stand up, looked into Harry's eyes, and sat down again in a hurry.

Harry turned his eyes back to Assy, who sat with her mouth open, looking at the crazy man. Harry laughed in an ugly way, inviting the others to join him in abusing, humiliating the girl. Assy wouldn't cringe. She fixed her eyes on the wall in order to think better.

"Actors are very important people," she said. "More people know Jack Lemmon than that woman who tried to kill the President. In fact, more people probably know Michael Nordland than know the President."

Bondi nodded his head, wanting to help Assy. Everybody else was quiet and motionless. Harry stared at Assy and smiled pleasantly.

"You're not so dumb after all, are you?"

Alice frowned, wondering what he was setting her friend up for.

"You're right. Everybody in this country— everybody in this whole world—probably knows Nordland or Wayne better than they know the President of the United States."

Assy nodded her head brightly. Marco relaxed and leaned forward a bit, giving Harry his attention.

"And if anything happened to some movie star— some actor on television—some rock-and-roller shot full of dope, they'd cry one hell of a lot longer."

Marco raised a finger—as if Harry were posing a question in a debate—to dispute the point, but Harry flicked his glance at him, and Marco subsided at once.

"Actors, singers, athletes are the real royalty of America. They're the ones we love, hate, and envy."

He felt good. He flashed back on the days when fellow students had sat around listening to him give them the word. It was like that. Even that haughty dyke Hush was looking at him with something like respect.

"Kill a politician and another one steps right up to take his place. Kill one of the beautiful people and you murder a piece of everybody's dream. Scare the hell out of them. Rattle their cages."

Oh, he had them. Bondi's mouth was open. Janet had a hand to her throat as though his words were stirring something in her. Even Peewit with his punchy dull eyes was sitting poised like a hound dog ready for the hunt.

"Anybody wants to do something to shake this country up, all they've got to do is kill off a couple of movie stars. Everybody would listen then. They'd listen to somebody who'd tell them what was fair. What was just."

He felt eloquent. He couldn't go too far, too fancy. He sorted out some phrases, ready to carry on. Loving the feeling of power it gave him to hold an audience this way. Just with words and the fire in his belly.

"And wouldn't they just remember the vigilante that chopped them down, Harry?" Hush said in her cool, sardonic voice.

Harry blinked at her, startled, as though just now realizing that actions could be the result of such words.

"Yes, they would," he said in a soft, stunned voice.

He suddenly recalled that passage by Conrad read so many years ago when the character of the embassy secretary ordered Mr. Verloc to commit an "act of destructive ferocity so absurd as to be incomprehensible, inexplicable, almost unthinkable: in fact, mad."

6

Two o'clock Sunday morning, everyone else having gone, Alice off to work the night shift, Harry found himself alone with Marco. The old man, eager for the conversation and company, seemed to have more stamina than Harry, who lay back into the corner of the couch, eyes half closed, scarcely listening.

"You're right, of course, Harry," Marco said. "Not having any hereditary royalty, America manufactured its own, changing their attributes with the times."

"What the hell are you rattling on about?" Harry asked with sharp disdain.

"I mean to say that we first idolized men who made fortunes in furs or land or cattle out on the frontiers," Marco stammered.

"No kidding?" Harry taunted.

Marco had tasted the knife-edge of Harry's sarcasm and irony before. He never knew how to disengage himself from the punishment to his spirit and always went headlong into the grave he dug for himself.

"After the industrial revolution we lavishly honored men like Carnegie and Vanderbilt who made their millions by the exploitation of the working class," Marco floundered desperately.

"Going to quote me a little of the *Manifesto*?" Harry sneered.

"I'm agreeing with you, Harry." Marco was nearly shouting in his struggle. "Now we adore these instant millionaires of football fields and rock concerts and the television screen."

"Yeah, yeah, yeah," Harry said, looking at the old man with hooded eyes, like a snake sizing up a rabbit for a meal. "You think we should do something about it?"

"What?" Marco said in some puzzlement.

"Think we ought to write up a protest to the *Times* or something?"

"You're teasing me, Harry."

Harry bolted upright. "Maybe we should machine-gun a bunch of people in a movie house or at a basketball game."

"Please, Harry."

"Why not?" Harry demanded, awake and agitated now. "It's been done before. Plenty of times. There's historical precedent all over the place. The airport at Lod."

"Modern madness," Marco protested.

"Want a little history, do you? O.K. How about Emile Henry?"

"Who?"

"He was the young French anarchist who walked into the Café Terminus one fine day in 1894 and threw a bomb at the orchestra in the middle of the room, killing one customer and wounding twenty others."

"He murdered innocent victims," Marco said, appalled.

Harry grinned. "That's just what one of the judges said at the trial. Do you know what Henry said?"

Marco shook his head.

"He said, 'There are no innocent victims.' " Harry

laughed as though that were a great joke. He stopped abruptly. "You better get going," he said.

"Are the buses still running?" Marco asked.

"Don't you know when the buses run? Didn't you get here on a bus?"

"Three. It takes three buses to get from Venice to here."

"Why don't you get a car?"

"You know I don't drive," Marco said, getting up, staggering and nearly falling from the lack of circulation in his old legs.

"I didn't know that at all," Harry said. "The only time I ever see you, you've got a bench stuck to your foot or your ass."

"Well, I don't drive. My reflexes aren't so good anymore. Besides, all those years I lived in New York I didn't need a car."

"Now you need a car. You really need a car. The buses don't run all night, you know."

"Maybe I could use your phone to call a cab?"

"Use it. Go ahead, call a cab. You got twenty bucks to throw away, go ahead."

Marco felt unbidden tears crowding his eyes. He knew that Harry was exacting some kind of payment from him, turning him into a fly on the end of a pin.

"I don't know what else to do, Harry."

"You got twenty bucks? Go ahead, look in your pocket. See if you got twenty bucks."

Marco counted the few bills he had held together by a large paper clip.

"Twelve dollars. It's not enough?"

Harry shook his head dolefully, a strange smile on his mouth. How was one to read the grins, grimaces, sneers, smiles, leers and quirks that played about

35

this man's lips? Marco wondered. He made his own rueful face.

"I'm sorry, Harry. I don't know these things. When a man grows old and is alone so much, he can't remember such things, can't take proper care of himself."

Tears came then, and he lowered his head, feeling the age in his bones. Harry made a sound of sympathy.

"You just lay down on the couch and rest. You think I'd let you spend a twenty on a cab even if you had it? You just get yourself a good night's sleep and I'll run you home first thing in the morning."

"You've got a good heart, Harry," Marco said, knowing, somehow, that the ritual of abasement was over.

Harry patted him on the arm, stood up, yawned and went off to bed himself.

He awakened in the weak light of morning, instantly aware that someone was sitting on the bed. He was angry because he thought it was Marco looking for his ride home. He squinted through the hair falling into his eyes and saw Alice staring at the floor as though coming to some decision about her shoes.

" 'Morning," Harry mumbled.

"Yeah," Alice replied.

"Anybody asleep on the couch?"

"No. Who'd you expect?"

"The old man. He kept me up gabbing until two this morning."

"Two o'clock this morning," Alice said, "a couple of guys got into a fight over the mustard. One nearly gutted the other with a steak knife."

"Drunk?"

"Drunk, stoned or crazy. What's the difference?" She shuddered.

Harry sat up and leaned back against the headboard. It made an irritating sound, high and cutting. Both Harry and Alice winced. He rubbed his eyes and rolled the bits of gummy grit mined from their corners between thumb and finger.

"Hey, you look tired," Harry said.

"I am."

"Well, get undressed. Take off your clothes."

Alice lifted one foot and rested it on her ankle in order to remove her white nurse's shoe. She did the same with the other, reversing the movement like an automaton. She peeled back the topcoat and struggled her arms free from the sleeves. The pink uniform was stained from food, and there were dark wet circles beneath the arms. She stood up and unzipped the dress down the front and stepped out of it.

"Good Christ, I'm so tired," she said and sat down again.

Harry watched her but made no move to push the coat off the bed or do anything else that would tell her that he felt sorry for her weariness. She began to reach behind her for the hooks of the brassiere. She cried out softly.

"Oh, my God, my arms ache like hell."

"Gettin' old, are we, honey?"

"Why the hell do you have to remind me of that?" she said with sudden heat. But her anger didn't last. She didn't have enough energy even for that.

"Help me, dammit. Don't just lay there making wise remarks about me getting old," she said.

"I'm getting old too, hon," Harry said soothingly as he leaned forward and undid the snap of the bra, freeing her breasts.

She raised herself from the bed and slipped the panties down her legs.

"I don't think I've got the strength to shower," she said.

"Who needs it? I like the way you smell," Harry said, tapping her on the back. When she didn't turn he grabbed her shoulder and pulled her to him, then spun her around with his other hand and crushed her to his chest.

"Christ, Harry, I hope you're not feeling horny. I really hope to hell you're not feeling that way so early in the morning."

Harry maneuvered her around like a load of wet wash, molding her this way and that, managing to get her legs under the sheet and blanket. He cuddled her head against his shoulder with surprising gentleness.

"Wonder where that Marco is," he said in sudden annoyance.

"Is he still here?"

"I think so."

"Then you should take him home. It wasn't a good idea for me to come here from work, Harry. I should have gone straight to my place."

"Well, there you are," Harry said. "Why the hell should you be running back and forth from here to there? Why should we have separate houses?"

"I got an apartment, Harry," she said.

He laughed, and she laughed back, pleased that she was able to make him laugh, her own spirits brightening at a hope that was growing in her.

"I know that. You're so damned literal, you know?"

"I just say things like that to make you laugh."

He obliged and then went on about how much they'd save by doubling up on rent, phone, gas and electric. Similar arguments from her in the past had always met with the stoniest of silences.

"I think you ought to move in here," Harry concluded.

"Live together?"

"Yes, live together. Half the country's living together."

"Half the country's married."

He turned his head away sharply. "Let's take it a step at a time."

It would have to be enough, Alice thought. At least it was better than being alone so much.

"I'll bet I know what the first step is," she said, putting her tongue in his ear.

He ran his hands over her breasts and thighs, turned her over again and mounted her heavily.

The toilet flushed.

"That's where the old bastard is," Harry said.

7

"Lou's" was a ramshackle tavern established half a century earlier in a tiny derelict concrete shed. Its two plate-glass windows were crowded with fly-specked neon beer signs. It drew its custom from the farmhands who worked the slopes of the Santa Monica hills, some small ranchers around Calabasas, Okies homesick for the red dirt of Texas and Oklahoma, movie stuntmen, and horse wranglers.

It was the place where Bondi had first latched onto Harry almost two years before. Harry'd gotten himself backed into a hard place because of his filthy, jeering mouth. A couple of regulars were going to stomp his bones and bust his teeth. Harry had cursed them out, daring them to come at him. They did, one on either side, and tore him loose from the wall. They were taking turns knuckling him in the short ribs when Bondi, big as an outhouse, came out of a corner and asked them to stop. They laughed at him, so he busted one man's arm and closed the eye of the other.

Now Harry and Bondi were regulars, glaring at other newcomers who wanted to play tough.

After Harry took old man Marco home to Venice, he whipped out into the Valley across the freeway and up to Lou's, where he found Bondi sucking on a beer and fooling with a radio.

"You drink too much," Harry told the kid after he'd ordered his own brew.

"Not as much as you, Harry."

"You're not being a smart-ass with me, are you?" Harry glared, pretending to be stern.

Bondi colored like a girl. "Hell, no, Harry. I wouldn't do that."

"You're so dumb you don't even know when I'm kidding."

Bondi laughed. "Yeah, I know."

The radio let out a screech.

"What the hell you doing with that?" Harry asked.

"Fixing it."

"Don't sound like it."

Bondi fiddled with a long, slender screwdriver at the back. The radio clicked and music blared. Bondi set the volume, leaned back and grinned at the owner, whose name was Patsy.

"One I owe you, kid," he called from behind the bar.

"That what he gives you for fixing his crummy radio? A beer?"

Bondi shrugged, lay back in his chair like a contented fat old cat.

"How come you're so stupid but still you can fix radios and automobiles?" Harry asked, trying to get the youngster on the prod.

"I don't know. Just lucky, I guess," Bondi said, refusing to rise to the bait.

"You look too happy. You got anything to tell me?"

"Well."

"Well what? Well, what the hell, what?"

"You know that girl?"

"What girl?"

"You know, the one with the pretty red hair."

"You mean Assy?"

"Jesus, I wish I knew her real name," Bondi said and colored slightly. "Assy doesn't sound polite."

"I don't believe you sometimes. So what about her?"

"Well, I took her for a sandwich after we left your place."

"Yeah?"

"She invited me up to her place after."

"Yeah?"

"And I screwed her," Bondi crowed. He got up, did a little jig, then sat down, sprawling like a rag doll.

"Wore you out, did she?"

"Just about," Bondi agreed happily.

"She should know how."

"What do you mean?"

"She's a pro. A whore."

Bondi's fair skin flushed, his face completely red except for angry white half-moons at the corners of his mouth.

"You shouldn't say that about her."

"Are you kidding me? Are you putting me on? I'm telling you she peddles her ass for a living. Be thankful. I'll bet she gets a hundred bucks for what she gave you for free."

Bondi leaned toward Harry. "I don't like you to talk that way about her. Not even you, Harry."

"What are you planning to do about it, you little mother?" Harry grinned his killer's grin.

Bondi stared at him a long time. Finally he stood up and went over to the bar to get his free beer and to pout.

Harry shook his head in bald wonder. He never could figure it every time he backed the overgrown kid down. He knew that Bondi could break him in half, and Bondi must know it too, but the kid would take all kinds of crap from Harry and never raise a hand to him.

Bondi was an only child, and even that one was too many as far as his old man had been concerned. His father liked to get drunk and fight. He didn't like responsibilities and blamed Bondi's mother for getting herself knocked up. After she got pregnant she kept his house, serviced him when he didn't have the price of a whore, and was his punching bag after his Saturday night drunks. Bondi had every reason to hate the old man, but even abused creatures have to have something to love. There was nothing in his mother to admire, so Bondi looked up to his father. When he started growing, a certain rough camaraderie developed between them.

One night his father beat his wife more viciously than usual, broke a chair across her back, then took the leg of it and slugged her repeatedly across the neck and shoulders. Bondi was twelve, already as tall as his father and nearly as strong. He wrestled the chair leg from the drunk and smashed him across the head with it three times, shattering his temples like eggshells, killing him on the spot.

He was acquitted of murder because he'd only been coming to the defense of his mother. She died soon after, and Bondi was left alone.

He liked Harry. He looked up to him.

Lou's started filling up after dark with men and women heavy with a weekend of drinking. Bondi still sulked at the end of the bar. Harry was sullen and stayed where he was. Somebody spit on the sawdust floor, and half a dozen people glared at him, ready to kill.

It was a long time since Michael had visited the

tavern. He'd stopped coming just a couple of years after making the rodeo film, had lost touch with the friends he'd made. Maybe he wanted that feeling of rough camaraderie again.

He came in dressed in jeans and work shirt. He was wearing dark glasses. No one paid him any mind at first—none of his old buddies were in the place. The sentimental journey was already sour. He stepped up to the bar and ordered a beer, knocked half of it back and turned to go. He accidentally bumped the girl sitting on the stool next to him.

He apologized.

"Watch yourself," the hard type talking her up said. He had "Tex" picked out in studs on his leather jacket.

"Sorry," Michael said again, smiling.

"Hey," the girl said, "you know me?"

"I don't think so."

"Well, I'm sure I know you from somewhere." She plucked off his glasses. "Oh, my God, its Michael Nordland!" she shrieked.

"Don't," Michael snapped automatically, snatching for his glasses.

"Who you yellin' at, fella?" Tex said, trying to make points with the girl, coming on tough. He blocked Michael's path away from the bar.

"Will you excuse me?" Michael said.

"I ought to knock you right on your ass," Tex said and pushed Michael. He fell against Bondi, who turned instinctively, lashing out and knocking Michael to the floor. Harry started over. Bondi bent to help Michael to his feet and got a boot in his face from Tex.

It started then, a Texas duster, a gut-stomper. Even the ladies got a piece of the action. Bondi chopped

Tex alongside the ear and nearly tore it off. Tex's buddy smashed a beer mug on the bar and went for Bondi, but Harry was on his back before he could finish the swing. The fight boiled along down the bar like a bowling ball in an alley filled with tenpins. Tables went over; bottles got thrown.

Some dude got kicked in the stomach and sat against the wall, vomiting all over Michael's leg. Michael scrambled to his feet, skirted the battle, paused at the door to look back. Harry caught the look, knew that the big hero was scared and on the run. It gave him a great deal of satisfaction.

"Would you like a cup of coffee?" the assistant DA asked the prisoner.

She shook her rather ridiculous Shirley Temple curls and smiled. Mary Margaret Masters was deceptively mild, about forty-three years old. She looked like a lonely woman who'd lived an isolated life. She was a political activist in the manner of those who hover about on the fringe of campaigns, avid-eyed, willing to be used in small tasks. Her affiliations had been very nearly as temporary and erratic as Harry Smiley's.

Watching her as she softly answered questions put to her by an assistant prosecutor, Metzler was struck by a certain charming quality and, seeking a word to describe it, hit upon that old-fashioned word "winsome." She was winsome and had been hot to do murder.

As she answered the young attorney's questions, she glanced frequently at Metzler, who stood modestly to one side. The glance was coquettish and childishly curious.

"Who are you?" she finally asked.

Metzler looked at the attorney to see if he could answer within his promise to remain a silent observer. The lawyer nodded.

"I'm a detective with the Los Angeles Police Department," he said.

"Oh? And what are you doing here? Were you at Century City?"

"Yes, ma'am, I was on duty that day."

"I nearly killed him, didn't I?" she said with a proud smile. "I nearly killed the President of the United States."

"Yes, you nearly did," Metzler agreed softly, and then took a shot in the dark: "When your aim was deflected, why didn't your co-conspirator fire his gun?"

She blinked her eyes several times. She looked at the prosecutor as though questioning Metzler's competence.

"I was alone," she said with that simplicity of manner which marks the perfect truth or the perfect lie. "What are you talking about?"

"I was watching very carefully, ma'am."

"Watching what?"

"The President, you and the man who was in the front of the crowd opposite you."

She paused a moment, then smiled impishly. "You must have exceptionally fast eyes to watch so much."

Metzler refused to smile. "We're trained for it, ma'am. Do you remember the man opposite you in the crowd?"

"Oh, yes," she said. "A red-faced fellow wearing some sort of outlandish schoolboy's jacket. I remember."

"You seemed to know him."

"Oh, I did."

Metzler felt a surge of triumph.

"Not well," she went on. "In fact, I rather doubt that he would remember me. At the time I thought it a marvelous coincidence, a strange quirk of fate. This man had once debated me; treated my ideas with contempt. He'd advocated violent confrontation with authority."

"Preached sedition?" Metzler asked.

"Debated," she said patiently. "It was all theory. I defended the rule of law. And there we were, playing turnabout in a way; me daring to act and he only a face in the crowd."

"Do you remember his name?"

She shrugged. "Smiley. A suitable name for a man who smiled all the time."

"Where did you have this debate with him?"

"In some political study group to which I belonged."

"Where did this group meet?"

She smiled pleasantly again. "In the Adult School in Santa Monica Community College."

"Can you remember any of the other students?"

She regarded Metzler with shrewd, appraising eyes. "You really are breaking your asses to manufacture a conspiracy," she said with startling harshness. It was as though a mask had slipped for a moment and was immediately replaced. "Well, let me see if I can dredge up a few names for you," she said sweetly. "They'll have had nothing to do with my act of protest, of course, but perhaps they'll serve to give me a good character reference. A lady by the name of Jenny Upgood was a special friend. Ninety-two and bright as a button. There was Marco Epstein, very small and frightened of nearly everything, and a Mr. Costigan who had a wooden leg and a glass eye."

She twinkled at Metzler in mock innocence.

"Thank you," he said and left the room.

She hadn't given him much, but Metzler suspected that if he was ever to pin anything on Smiley it would be something gathered up in little bits and pieces. Cops are junk collectors.

8

On the way to 20th, Harry stopped at a drugstore and bought half a dozen movie magazines, something he'd rarely done even as a teen-ager. Suddenly he had an appetite to learn more about the people he knew as fifty-foot heads on a movie screen, seven-inch bodies on a television set. Everywhere he looked—on billboards, magazines, the front pages of newspapers, a thousand products from breakfast cereal to toilet paper—the faces of the beautiful people stared at him, trying to seduce him with their eyes and teeth.

There was Robert Redford, lying face up on the car seat beside Harry, eyes squinted up against the expensive sun of some fancy ski resort, cheeks all rosy, smile demanding that you like him because he was such an easygoing, everyday sort of fellow.

"Good ol' Bob schussin' down the mountain!" Harry shouted as he waited for the traffic light. "'Ol' shoe' Rob ready for a fight or a frolic with other good ol' boys who make a million bucks a year. Just good ol' fuckin', funnin' ol' shoe, son of a bitchin' Bob-Eee Red-Ford." The driver on his left was looking at him, laughing and nodding his head as though urging Harry on to greater rage against the traffic, city, boss, wife, weather or world. Harry stared at the man without any answering smile, and the motorist

49

turned his attention back to the road, as though sensing that Harry was a real danger.

Harry looked at the next magazine cover and saw the face of Michael Nordland. A flash of nearly uncontrollable rage swept through him.

"King asshole himself," he muttered.

The photograph was as grainy as the blowup on the television show Saturday night. Grainy and mysterious. Nordland seemed to be looking off to far places, dignified by the photographer's art, the actor's features distilled into a symbol of all that was best in American men. Harry suffered the comparison.

Accident had juxtaposed the two men in an unlikely design. Witnesses and participants of a moment of history. Made rivals by chance, at least in Harry's mind and heart. In the moment he solidified a specific hatred for Michael Nordland without attempting to analyze the reasons behind it.

Charlie Clabber was senior man on the gate, fifteen years a guard, a staunch union man and a fellow who was rumored to know where a couple of skeletons were hidden. All this served to make him arrogant, sarcastic and surly. However, he seemed to like Harry in an offhand way. When Harry stepped into the gatehouse, Charlie grunted.

"Ah, go to hell," Harry said. "Am I going to be caged up with a grizzly all day again?"

"You can draw your pay and turn in your badge if you want."

"Before I go turning in my badge, I'll shove it up your ass."

"Make sure you let go quick or I'll fart and blow your hand off."

They were in good spirits.

Harry dropped the small pile of magazines on the counter, reached into his pocket and put on a pair of wraparound sunglasses, placed a whistle on a lanyard around his neck.

A shiny red Porsche pulled up to the black-and-yellow-striped traffic arm. The girl in it was fresh, beautiful and red-haired.

"Pussy, pussy, pussy," Harry said under his breath. He paused a moment to let the girl know that he was in charge, not about to go running to her like a dog in heat; then he stepped up close to the car so she was forced to stick her head partway out the open window and tilt it up toward him. He touched the center of his goggles with his middle finger, the way he remembered Marlon Brando doing in the old cycle flick.

"Ma'am?" he said.

"Sleepy this morning, Harry? Don't you know me?"

"Ma'am?"

"Open the gate, Harry," she said, smelling a put-on.

"Do you have an appointment?"

"I'm going in to see Sy Salkowitz. He's head of prime-time television." She wasn't smiling. "My name is Carteret. Marion Carteret. Look it up on your schedule."

Harry went to the pass rack. "Sorry, nothing here," he called out.

"Call his office. Tell Sy that Marion's here."

Harry turned back to the counter, started to lift the phone, pretended to see the pass he hadn't seen before, plucked it out, stamped it and hurried over to the car with it as though he'd just come to realize that he was dealing with the Princess of Razz-Matazz.

"I'm sorry, Miss Carteret; someone must have misfiled it. 'Course I should have recognized you right off, but—"

He hesitated, pushing his hat back and scratching his head in the best Gary Cooper tradition. She took the chance to make it up between them.

"I colored my hair a little differently, Harry. Maybe that's it."

"Sure, that's it."

"It's a little redder than I usually do it."

"That's what fooled me, Miss Carteret."

"Marion. Call me Marion," the girl said and drove onto the lot. Harry softly tooted his whistle after her.

"You are a mean, lowdown son of a bitch, Smiley. Love it. Love it," Charlie cock-a-doodle-dooed.

At eleven o'clock Michael Nordland drove up. Harry sent the gate up without hesitation; no pretending he didn't recognize the star. Nordland didn't go on ahead but waved Harry over instead. Harry stepped lively and quick, hating himself, but made up for it by flashing as insolent a grin as he dared. Nordland glanced up at him from behind the same sort of wraparound sunglasses as Harry wore, but his were nearly black.

"I've got some voice-over to do. Where?"

Harry went to look at the roster and came back. "Dubbing stage four." He laid his hand on the car door. "I saw you on television when that broad took a shot at the President."

Nordland smiled and waved a modest disclaimer.

"I was there, too," Harry said. "I was in the crowd."

Nordland nodded and looked at Harry's hand. Harry pulled it away.

"I saw you at Lou's last night, too," Harry said and

met Nordland's stare, eyeball to eyeball, behind the double barrier of lenses. "Studio four," Harry repeated.

"I heard you. Where the hell's studio four?" Nordland asked with sudden heat. "I'm just a day laborer around here."

Harry gave directions, and Nordland roared off, burning rubber.

"What the hell was that all about?" Charlie asked.

"Yellow son of a bitch," Harry said.

"What're you ravin' about?"

Harry wouldn't answer. Fifteen minutes later the phone rang and he picked it up to identify the gate. He recognized Nordland's voice right off.

"Are you the idiot who directed me to studio four?"

"Yes, sir. I mean I'm not an idiot, but I—"

"Yes, you're an idiot," Nordland insisted. "This is the wrong stage. Get on the ball."

"Studio four is the dubbing stage listed on the sheet."

Charlie reached over with a pen and changed the four to an eight.

"Sorry, Mr. Nordland," Harry said. "I've just been told that the schedule's been changed. The right stage is eight."

"I hope you're right," Nordland grated. "I don't want to be driving all over this damned lot."

"It's right this time," Harry whined, hating the sound of supplication in his voice, product of long habit in the face of authority when the chips were really down.

"It damn well better be," Nordland said and hung up in Harry's ear.

Harry started to shake. First his hands, then all over. He was filled with impotent rage.

Charlie laughed. "Watch out—your lid's gonna pop."

Michael fretted briefly about the guard at the gate. Had the bastard sent him off to the wrong stage deliberately? The man had looked at him with something akin to surliness pinching his mouth, something like contempt in the way he put his hand on Michael's car. The man had given off a strong aura of dislike, even hate, for Michael.

His own anger began to rise up in him. He reached for the phone and called the security chief to enter a complaint against the impudent guard on the gate.

Assistant Chief of Security Gus Benham came spinning over to the gatehouse on his electric runabout. He sat on it like a skinny chicken out for a round of golf. He raised a finger to Harry, crooked it and inspected the nail on it while Harry came as summoned.

"You the only stupid child your mother had?" Gus said.

"What's the matter?" Harry asked.

"An important personality who is very valuable to the studio at the moment has lodged a gripe against your bad manners. He speaks of a certain half-assed part-timer who don't know his ass from his elbow."

"His half-ass from his elbow, Gus," Charlie said.

"I stand corrected. The chief's just finished chewing my ass."

"This is a den of sex perverts," Charlie said.

Gus laughed. "Be that as it may, Charlie, I'm telling you to shape ass around here or I'll be kicking some." He buzzed off in his little cart, the chance to exercise power having made his day.

54

Harry was nearly choking on his rage.

"Don't get mad at old Gus, Harry. He was just doin' his thing. Everybody's got to do his thing," Charlie crowed.

"Yeah, you're right. Someday I'm going to do my thing," Harry said.

He saw Bondi standing out on the sidewalk then. Bondi saw him looking and raised his hand.

"Lunch break?" Harry said and walked off before Charlie could say yes or no. Charlie didn't call him back.

"You mad, Harry?" Bondi asked when Harry walked up to him.

"Goddamn mad."

"Not mad at me for coming here, are you?"

"Hell, no. Why'd I be mad at you?"

"I got some delicatessen here," Bondi said, lifting the brown paper bag he held.

Harry smiled. "Great. We'll have a regular picnic."

They drove out to the back lot, walked through the streets of false fronts and climbed a hill topped by a leafy shade tree. Harry was quiet most of the way, and that bothered Bondi.

After they'd eaten the sandwiches and drunk the beer, Bondi said, "Who made you mad?"

"Everybody makes me mad. All these bastards tossing their big houses and expensive cars and beautiful broads in your face. Everybody hitting on you. Hitting, hitting, hitting."

"If anybody's hitting on you—I mean if there's one person in particular—just tell me his name and I'll punch him out for you if you want."

Harry punched the big kid lightly on the arm. "Would you do that for me?"

"Sure."

"You really mean you'd work over anybody I said?"

"Yes."

"Just on my say-so? Without even knowing what the guy did to hurt me or even if he'd hurt me at all? Just because I was pissed off at him?"

"I would, Harry. I really would."

A movement down along the deserted back-lot road caught Harry's eye. What the hell was Gus Benham doing cruising around the back lot? Up to no good, I'll bet—the dirty little bastard, Harry thought. The electric cart approached the hill. Harry was sure Gus hadn't seen them yet. He put his hand on Bondi's powerful arm.

"You really mean it?"

"You're damned right," Bondi insisted.

"That guy there." He pointed to Gus, who'd stopped the cart and was taking a leak against a signpost.

Bondi looked startled, almost laughed. "You mean it?"

"Yes, I mean it. Question is, did you mean it, or were you just bullshitting me?"

Bondi brushed his hands together. Harry ducked back behind the shelter of the tree as the kid walked down the slope toward Gus, who was just putting himself back into his pants. He looked worried at the approach of the giant. Harry heard him say "Hi" in a distant, doubtful way just before Bondi punched him in the mouth. The older man went down, feet and legs kicking like a wounded bird. Bondi reached down and lifted Gus to his feet.

Harry couldn't believe it. The kid had offered to beat up somebody for Harry. Anybody. All Harry had to do was point and the kid actually was doing it. Bondi hit Gus in the gut. Gus started vomiting and fell to his knees. Bondi looked back up the hill toward Harry, who'd moved out from the shadow of the tree. Harry nodded his head. Bondi picked Gus up again. The old man was crying. There was blood running out of his nose and mouth. He was trying to say something but couldn't get the words out around the puke and the tears. Bondi hit him in the ribs. It made a hollow sound in the warm, still air, like an ax chopping a melon. Gus sagged and would have fallen if Bondi hadn't held him up by his grip on the front of the guard's uniform. One word managed to get past Gus's smashed lips. "Why?" It trembled in the air. Harry started to run down the hill.

"That's enough," he shouted. "You'll kill him."

Bondi stopped punching and loosened his hold on Gus. The old man fell to the ground unconscious. Harry looked into the kid's face and saw the thrill of violence there. Felt it in his own blood and bones. He felt twelve feet tall.

Harry put a gentling hand on Bondi's chest. Bondi stood there, breathing hard, smiling strangely, poised like a killer dog waiting for the fatal command.

Harry had given an order and Bondi had followed it without question. He understood all at once that this was the essence of power, the anatomy of terror. An irrational act, like lightning, was totally unpredictable. Madness couldn't be bribed or persuaded or placated in any other way. There was a certain purity about it that couldn't be threatened or avenged.

"Back off. You better get the hell out of here," Harry said.

He pointed the way out over an unguarded stretch of fence concealed by bushes.

"Hey, kid," he called as Bondi walked away, "better get some salve to put on those hands."

9

The next day when Harry arrived at the gatehouse, Charlie wasn't there. About half an hour later he came buzzing up on Gus's runabout, parked it and slouched over to Harry like the local sheriff in a B western.

"What the hell you doin' on Benham's baby carriage?" Harry asked.

"You ain't heard?"

"Heard what?"

"Gus is in the hospital."

"Jesus Christ. Heart attack?"

"Somebody beat the shit out of him. Nearly killed him."

"No kidding. Where'd it happen?"

"At the end of the main street on the back lot, right by that hill with the old tree on it."

"Who the hell'd want to do that to an old man like Gus?" Harry said.

"Yeah, who. Yesterday you were in the mood to kill the old man."

"Hell, I was just blowin' off steam." Harry put his hands up on the window ledge. He knew that Charlie would glance at them, and he did.

"Well, you'll have to work the gate alone this morning until I get another guy in."

"You the acting assistant chief, Charlie?"

"Yeah," Charlie said suspiciously.

"Lucky."

"What the hell do you mean by that?" Charlie nearly shouted, immediately hot under the collar.

"I just mean whoever beat up on old Gus did you a favor in a way."

Charlie stared for a minute, then relaxed. "You ain't pullin' my string, Smiley." He looked into the gatehouse at the pile of movie magazines. "You find out what color shorts Al Pacino wears?"

"I found out what color pants Raquel Welch wears."

"What the hell would you do if you ever got around that girl's pants? Probably piss yours." Charlie laughed.

Harry didn't. "You're not pulling my string either, Charlie."

Charlie's face closed up tight and took on a sullen redness.

"Put those magazines away, Smiley. You're workin' the gate. You're workin' for me, and I don't want any goofin' off."

Harry had a flash that somehow, someday, he might need ol' Charlie Clabber. He did a little knuckling. "All your talk of underwear got me going, Charlie."

"Whose underwear?" Charlie asked, ready to accept the disengagement. "Raquel's?"

"Hell, no," Harry said, right on cue. "Al Pacino's."

Charlie let a split second go by, then started to laugh. Harry joined him.

Michael Nordland barreled up to the gate about the same time as he had the day before. Harry kept his back turned, feeling himself beginning to tremble again. He heard his name called and finally turned to see Nordland smiling at him. The actor held a package out to him.

"Take it from where it came, will you?" Nordland said as Harry went to the car. "I had a bad night. No sleep. I was on the prod."

Harry didn't lift his hands to the bottle in the brown paper bag.

"That business at Century City shook me up worse than I thought it did—you know what I mean?"

Harry felt tears of anger damming up behind his eyes.

"You a veteran?" Michael asked.

"Yeah."

"Korea?"

"Yeah."

"Me too. Well, you know how it is, then. After the fight's over, that's when you get the shakes, you know?"

"Hell, yes," Harry heard himself say in a hearty voice that made him sick. He took the peace offering and felt bought.

"You say you were in that crowd at Century City?"

"I'm the guy who shouted the warning," Harry said.

"Well, well," Michael said appreciatively, smiled, waved and went on through the gate, apology over.

Harry still felt the anger in him. He looked at the bottle. "Maybe that was enough for you, Nordland, but it's not enough for me."

It was announced on the portable radio in the gatehouse that Hiram Evers, a producer currently at 20th, had been named for the Academy Awards Presentation spectacular. Harry had no particular brief against Evers, but when a big chauffeured limousine arrived to take a dinner-jacketed Evers straight from work to some formal function, Harry was still angry enough to include him in his rage against anyone rich or famous.

"Have a nice evening, Mr. Evers." He smiled and imagined the man dead in a smashed-up limousine. He formed the image of Evers's smiling, condescending face breaking apart, the mouth opening to scream, blood forming a lacework across his talcumed cheeks, brought to his death by Harry Smiley. He saw all of them—Wayne, Newman, MacLaine, Dunaway, Bancroft, Poitier, Nordland—brought down to death. It shook him. He knew that he wanted to pin the smiles on their faces with bullets, chop off their arms as they patted one another on the back, bloody their goddamned mouths even as they flashed their million-dollar teeth.

Suddenly he was clear in his purpose. He'd kill them during their gaudiest celebration, most outrageous ego trip. He'd kill them at the Oscar Awards.

10

Harry called in sick the next day because he wanted to keep on with his fantasies and figure ways to make them realities. He lay in bed with a full belly, Alice having made him a breakfast before going off to pack more of her things and buy some new curtains for the kitchen. The bed was scattered with movie magazines. There was Jane Fonda on the cover of one, hair falling over her face like a shaggy dog. The common man's movie star. There was a spread of pictures about her on the inside. The caption under one of them read, "I've always been an actress. I am an actress. I will always be an actress."

"Christ, I'm glad to hear that," Harry said to the picture. "I was losing sleep nights, worrying about your giving up the silver screen, that you were going to quit making a bundle every time you spit."

Still, looking at the black and white photos, stripped of the sweet colors on the cover, he thought that it wouldn't be bad to have a gutsy broad like her with him when he put his plan to work. He turned the page and found an old picture of Jane in some crazy costume from a science-fiction flick called *Barbarella*. The bottom of the costume was cut so high that the lines below the cheeks of her ass were evident, the buttocks half exposed in a teasing way, as though they were breasts. Her belly was naked under an insert of clear plastic, her tits sheathed in some shiny material that looked like patent leather.

"Motherfucker," Harry said and closed his eyes, suddenly imagining his lesbian neighbor Hush in the same costume. It suited her, made her seem one hundred percent the woman he'd like her to be and one hundred percent the man she'd like to be. He became aware that her preference for women made her all the more attractive to him. Plenty of broads liked to work both sides of the street, he thought, and started to get a hard-on. He put her lover Evelynn in another sexy, crazy getup. She just stood there, beautiful, silent, unmoving. Even in a fantasy she was languid and nearly inert.

When the two women had first moved into the court of cottages, Harry had struck up a conversation with Evelynn when she was alone. She had been sunning herself on the little grass plot outside her front door in a scrap of bathing suit that made Harry's breath come short. Harry went over and stooped down beside her, squatting on his heels like an old wrangler. She smiled up at him without comment after he'd introduced himself.

"You an actress?" he asked.

"No."

"You're pretty enough."

"Thanks." She raised herself up on one elbow.

"I mean usually when a pretty girl comes to Hollywood, it's because she's hoping to become a movie star."

"I was born in Ohio," she said, as though that were an explanation.

"What do you do?" Harry asked.

"Nothing."

"How about your friend?"

"She does nothing too, most of the time. Some-times she models."

"It must be nice to be independently wealthy," Harry joked.

Evelynn didn't smile. "Oh, we're not rich. I mean I'm not. Maybe Hush is, come to think of it."

Harry got the feeling that the girl was putting him on, but she looked into his eyes with a bland lack of expression that made him unsure. He felt his legs growing tired, tried to move to a more comfortable position and fell against her.

"Sorry."

"That's all right. You couldn't help it," she said and smiled briefly.

He felt the weight of her breasts on his arm. He couldn't move, wanted to stay there.

"Feel good?" she asked.

"Jesus, I'm sorry," he said, scrambling away.

"That's all right."

He looked at her closely, puzzled by her impassive ways.

"You got something?" she asked.

"What do you mean?"

"You know."

"You mean a drink? You mean booze?"

She made a small face. "Got any dope?"

"Hell, no," Harry said.

"No pills? Li'l grass? Coke?"

"None of those damned things."

"You want to party?"

"Party?"

"Do I have to explain that to you, too?"

"I get you." His balls cringed with expectation. "Yeah, I'd like to have a party."

"You get some dope and we'll have a party," she

said, springing the trap. "Otherwise, it's fifty bucks a trick."

She laughed at him lazily.

He went back to his own place, cursing her under his breath. "Goddamn whores," he muttered, wishing to hell he had the price.

As it turned out, the pair didn't screw around where they lived, pay or no pay. They were lazy hookers, working only when the need arose. Part-timers. Amateurs.

Seeing them in his daydreams, half-naked in trick getups, gave Harry an erection that tented the light sheet he'd thrown over himself. He added Alice to his fantasy. Blond the way she was, he put her in the middle of the dark copper-haired Hush and the brunette Evelynn. He gave her a costume with the tits exposed because that was the best part of Alice. She had terrific legs, but her tits were the greatest, small and gently mounded with no sag to them.

The erection was getting urgent in its desire of a place to go. If something didn't happen, it would end up finding a haven in his hand.

He added Janet to the vision. She was getting a bit heavy in the thighs and breasts, but it was a warm and comfortable heaviness, like an overripe peach about to burst.

There they stood all in a row—his soldiers. He'd have them for his purposes. He'd have them for the killing that was no more than a glimmer in the back of his mind. He'd have them other ways in the process. He was the leader. He was the goddamn leader. Act like a leader and everybody would follow you. Hitler knew that.

"Sieg Heil!" Harry said, and threw his arm out straight into the air. "Sieg Heil! Sieg Heil!"

"What did you say, Harry? You call me?" Alice cried out from the kitchen. He hadn't heard her come in.

"Get your ass in here!" Harry shouted back.

She came into the bedroom and stood just within the doorway, smiling a small quizzical smile, as though trying to read his mood.

"Get out of your clothes and hop into this bed," Harry demanded.

"I was going to make some lunch," she said. "You want some lunch, don't you?"

"A box lunch," Harry leered.

"No, Harry, it's the middle of the afternoon."

Harry whipped off the sheet, scattering some of the magazines to the floor as he exposed his shaft.

"I know it. Look what I got for your lunch. You want to brown-bag it, or do you want to eat it here?"

In the gloom of the bedroom, with the shades drawn against the day, Alice lay with Harry and drowsed. She was tired from moving all her things into his place with little help from him or anybody else.

Harry was speaking softly. It was hypnotic, compelling. She could scarcely understand the words, but a terrible fright was growing in her. He reeled off curses and condemnations for anybody who'd made himself a rich life, who enjoyed fame. He laughed bitterly at the rags-to-riches stories that were supposed to prove that everybody had a clear shot at the brass ring.

Elvis Presley drove a truck for seventy-five bucks a week. Steve McQueen lived in a cold-water flat and drove a hack. Jack Lord had been a used car salesman. Barbara Eden had worked in a bank. Nordland had worked the docks. They'd all made it the American way.

"And everybody starts out sucking tit," Harry said.

Alice was aware that Harry was trying something out on her, shaping a speech of some sort, a statement of some purpose. It was all murky, but she knew that whatever Harry had on his mind was going to be bad for somebody.

She was half scared to death, half lulled by Harry's soothing voice talking about murder. She shivered. She slept and didn't hear him anymore.

He described the gory deaths that were waiting for the rock stars, the professional jocks, the television stars and the movie "greats." He knew Alice slept and didn't care, because he'd fucked her mind enough. Now the excitement of his obsession was just for himself. He saved the goriest death for Michael Nordland and rocked his mind.

He imagined the effect such a stunning act would have on the world. If safely escaped, he saw himself reading the newspaper accounts, the speculations as to the identity of the bold leader of the terrorists. If captured, he saw himself condemning a brutalizing society, unjust and cruel, in open court. He would be the center of the world's attention. When and if convicted, he saw himself writing the book in his imprisonment that would make his name stand with the great political and social martyrs of history.

He counted the money he would earn from such a best seller. He would hire the best attorneys, seek a retrial, and win acquittal. He'd be a national hero, and the nation would reevaluate its priorities, regretting the deaths of the sequined butterflies but understanding the necessity for them.

He fell asleep to visions of bloody murder.

11

The beach at Venice, California, might well be compared to other, more celebrated ones along the Mediterranean coast. It is not so grand as some, but the sands are very wide along most of its length, almost white beneath the sun. There are benches here and there topped with wooden canopies, coffee shops, and small cafés. Unfortunately, parts of it are not safe after dark. Hoodlums often prey on the elderly and weak. Winos, thieves, dopers and the occasional slasher wander about.

Marco Epstein had a small room in a small residence hotel called the Cadillac, once a place of summer swank, now a rest stop for old Jews on the way between Brooklyn and the grave. He pretended not to be afraid, but he was—of nearly everything, not the least of which was his own death. He fought the fear by staying out late and, during the day, talking to his peers at the benches, arguing old political differences, recalling old dreams of the past and speaking occasionally of the present but never of the uncertain future.

Harry found him standing with one foot up on a bench, repeating some of Harry's own remarks about the "manufactured royalty" of America. The old people stared past Marco at Harry. The old man turned to see what was distracting his friends and nearly stumbled. Harry grabbed his elbow to steady him and called him "old-timer" in a joking way that meant that Marco wasn't really very old at all. Everyone smiled up at Harry in his comparative youth.

"Hello, Harry. Meet my friends?"

Harry reached a hand all around. "I think I know most of them. Hello, Mrs. Samuels. Joe. Phil. Miss Isaaks."

"What are you doing down here?" the little old woman simpered. "Coming to get a noseful of good clean air?"

"Came down to see my friend," Harry said.

"Well," Marco said, pleased as could be. "Well."

"Thought I'd buy you a cold beer for a warm day."

"Well," Marco repeated.

"Will you excuse us?" Harry said to the others.

They nodded like a row of puppets.

"Don't get him drunk now, young man," Miss Isaaks said. "Marco's a devil when he gets a few in him."

Harry and Marco walked away with the happy sounds of the old people cackling behind them. After several steps Harry put his arm about the shoulders of the older man. He knew in the most calculating way just how proud that would make Marco feel, strolling along like father and son.

It was cool inside the tavern. Harry ordered two steins and carried them to a small table.

"Heard you talking about some of our ideas," Harry said.

"Yours, Harry—yours."

"Don't be modest. I've been thinking about what you said at my house the other night," Harry said thoughtfully, sucking Marco in with a show of seriousness.

"Oh?" Marco said.

"You know. That business about an act of terrorism being more effective if it's random and crazy."

Marco didn't remember saying anything of the kind. Was he getting forgetful? Senile?

"What you said about these super-stars acting like royalty gave me plenty to chew on. Isn't that what you said?"

Marco shrugged modestly, feeling somehow pleased at the sound of praise in Harry's voice.

"They go on television interviews and hand down the word on art, politics, philosophy, and how things should be run, don't they? Get the younger generation to thinking that a pretty face, a pair of tits, fucking the right people, knifing other people in the back is the way to make it big. They say it and, goddamn it, they seem to prove it. You told it like it is."

Marco was sure he hadn't said any of those things, but at his age every shred of respect was a feast, and the compliment was too flattering to give up. He nodded his head like a wise old rabbi.

Harry leaned forward confidentially. "What did you do when you came here from the old country?"

"What do you mean?"

"You got a job—right? Worked hard—right?"

"Twelve hours a day, six days a week."

"You piss your money away at the racetrack? You spend your money on satin-assed cunt? You get yourself a Stutz Bearcat?"

"No, Harry. I saved every penny. I slept in my clothes so I wouldn't have to put coal in the stove. I lived on potatoes—sometimes only the peelings. I saved."

"What did it get you?"

"My shop. It got me my tailoring shop and a wife and five children. I sent them all to school. I gave them all a wonderful start in life. It gave me enough savings to come here after my Sada died and live in the sun."

"Did it, Marco? Did it? I know you're living on the butt's end. I wouldn't be surprised if you told me you were eating cat food."

"No, Harry, no," Marco protested.

"You've got too much pride to say so, but things aren't as good as you'd like them to be after all those years of hard work."

Marco fought back his tears.

"You can't make ends meet and you know it. Want to know why?" Harry demanded.

"Why, Harry? Tell me why."

"Because everybody's gone nuts for a buck. Cheat, steal, lie, fuck, murder, but get that buck. Be somebody. Be a million-dollar idiot with a guitar you can't play. Be a billion-dollar stud with a cock that gets hard for boys. Be a whore with all your brains in your cunt. Make it, make it. Money, money, money. Do it the easy way. Fuck hard work. Fuck saving your pennies. Do it on the arm. Get there on the flash. Kids see these assholes on top of the jelly bean mountain and they take the same route. Anybody can be bought if the price is high enough. And most can be bought for a counterfeit three-dollar bill."

Marco was shaken by Harry's intensity.

"What can we do about it?" he asked with no real expectation of an answer.

"Make a protest."

"A march?"

"Something bigger."

"A new social manifesto."

"Shit. We're going to engineer an act of protest that will make the whole world pay attention."

"In what cause, Harry?" Marco floundered. "There has to be a cause."

Harry leaned back and grinned challengingly.

"What would you like, Marco? How about an independent Quebec, or a united Ireland, or a homeland for the Palestinians? Who the hell cares? There's plenty of things wrong."

Harry began to laugh softly, watching the old man's eyes, his own filled with bright, callous amusement. Marco tittered as though seeing the joke Harry was playing on him. Then he composed himself as though for serious debate, one of two political philosophers discussing an abstraction of human conduct.

"Of course," he said, "even the most fanatic of terrorists find or manufacture a cause that appears to make even the most irrational crime seem purposeful."

"Why don't you just write up a warrant of grievances against the aristocrats," Harry challenged, "before I give 'em the knife?"

Marco didn't know how seriously he was intended to take Harry, who seemed mightily amused at his confusion and laughed louder and louder.

12

It was dark when Harry got home. He opened the door and stepped into the hallway. No lights were on anywhere in the house. As he took a step into the living room, there was a sound that made his heart leap.

"Who the fuck's there?" he blurted out.

A lamp clicked on. Hush sat curled up in the easy chair, a kitten cuddled in her lap.

She smiled. "Like my pussy?"

The little creature mewed and looked up at her, its eyes very large in its small face. Hush's eyes looked catlike as well, muzzy, as though her mind were not yet awake. She unfolded her long legs, stretched them out and, pointing her bare toes, threw her arms wide. She yawned, curling her tongue in her mouth.

"Alice here?" Harry asked.

Hush stood up, cradling the kitten against her breasts. "No."

"Where is she?"

"Went to work early."

"Why?"

"How do I know? You ought to tell her to quit."

"That's just what I'm thinking of doing."

He sat down on the couch and watched Hush stride around the room, jiggling the kitten against her. She was wearing blue jeans torn off high on her legs and a sweat shirt small enough to emphasize her nipples. Harry knew she was giving a performance and wondered if maybe she wanted to turn a quick trick for a bargain price.

"Alice asked me to wait for you," she said.

"She think I'm afraid of the dark?"

"She's the one who's afraid, Harry."

"Of what?"

"The things you've been saying to her in bed."

Harry grinned. "Those stories get you worked up? That how you get off?"

Hush sat down on the other end of the couch. "Fuck it, Harry. What kind of game you playing?"

"You tell me."

"What's all this crap about killing? Murdering famous people? She tells me you've been talking about offing every star in Hollywood, Nashville and New York."

Harry laughed out loud.

"You just spitting in the wind?" she demanded.

He looked at her and wouldn't answer, enjoying the irritation that showed on her face, the excited flush on her neck.

"Goddamn it, do you mean it, Harry?"

He grinned. "Mean what?"

"Just who do you intend gunning down?"

"The whole crowd," Harry said, not smiling anymore.

She cocked an eyebrow.

"That's right," Harry said vehemently. "The whole fucking crowd of them. The night of the Oscars— right there on the stage of the Music Center, when they're all in one bunch—I'm going to chop them down. Right on television. Right in front of the whole world," he said, emphasizing every single word.

74

The kitten cried out as Hush's hand closed convulsively about its neck.

"You're just going to kill them where they stand?" Hush said.

"That's it."

"What about after?"

"What about it?"

"You'll be dead, Harry."

Harry was silent for a long moment. He shrugged his shoulders. "Yeah, I guess that's the way it'll be. But I'll have had my say. I'll have made my point."

"Sure, you'll be another corpse in the history books."

"That's what I want," Harry said in such a voice that Hush knew he was caught up in the vision of himself as martyr.

"That's not all a man as smart and bold as you should want, Harry."

Harry peered at her eyes, somewhat obscured in the shadows. She leaned forward so that he could see the sincerity in them.

"You don't have to be dead," Hush said. "You could walk out of there just as famous but a hell of a lot richer."

Harry's eyes fell to her lips. He seemed fascinated by their mobility.

"We could lift a couple of super-stars, maybe the winners of the Oscars for best actor and actress, and take them with us for ransom."

Harry started shaking his head a little, a somewhat pitying smile forming on his lips.

"We could hold them for millions and safe passage out of the country," Hush went on.

Harry's eyes glittered with amusement.

"You don't get it at all," he said. "Nobody does something like this just for money."

"All right," she said before he could go on, "we'll do it for any reason you like."

He looked at her intently.

"You're going to need help," she said, turning to face him on her knees, lithe as a weasel. "I can help you."

Harry pretended to think about it. "I don't think so," he finally said.

"Why not?"

"You'll get to talking to your girlfriend in bed, husband to wife, and you'll let something slip. Next thing I know, the cops'll be on me."

"I expect to bring her in this with me. She'll have a gun in her hand, too."

"How do I know you can make her do that?"

"I'm telling you."

"But how can I trust you?"

She was trembling like a bitch in heat, a funny smile touching her lips.

"Sex, Harry, sex."

"What do you mean?"

"You're a big reader, Harry. You read about the Mau-Mau pledges where they took it up the ass, binding themselves to the leader with shameful acts? Manson used sex, along with drugs, to hold his family together. Jim Jones used it too. It's a ritual as old as man.

"We'll swear loyalty to you, Harry—Evelynn and me. We'll get into your bed one at a time and both together. Alice, too. All of us, Harry, in one big fuck. We'll take that oath."

She watched him carefully as he thought it over; could practically see him imagining his cock in passive Evelynn, turning Hush around with his manhood.

"I've had men in my time, Harry," she tempted

and promised. She leaned forward from her knees, put her mouth on his and offered her tongue. The kitten mewed in protest. Hush leaned back, figuring she'd won her case.

"It's not enough. It's not nearly enough," Harry said. "I'm talking about killing, not fucking."

Her eyes went to the kitten crawling about her lap. Harry looked at it. They looked at each other. She placed her hands, palms flat, on either side of the kitten's tiny head and began to squeeze. The little creature screamed out in pain, but Hush didn't let up. There was a fragile sound like the snapping of a glass. The kitten didn't scream again. Harry looked down at Hush's hands. They were covered with gore.

"I'd better clean up this mess before it ruins the couch," Hush said in an everyday voice.

13

Hush sat in the bedroom of the tacky little court cottage, staring at her hands. The way the shadows cast by the moonlight coming through the curtains fell upon them, she could almost imagine they were still stained with the kitten's blood. She shivered, oddly aroused.

Evelynn lay in the big double bed on her back, one arm flung out in a child's gesture, the other doubled so that her hand was against her cheek. The sight of her, so helpless and trusting in her sleep, brought memories to Hush, squeezed her heart.

Hush's birth into a family of the merchant class, prosperous and conservative, was greeted with considerable pleasure and—because she was the second of two daughters—the prudent decision that she would be the last.

Her upbringing was loving and solicitous, but her father gave nearly all of his attention to business; and her mother, uncomplaining, took the affection he no longer asked for in full measure and gave it lavishly to the two little girls.

The first one, Cecily, was older by only a year and a half. She'd been somewhat sickly from her infancy, and by the time young Hazel Bostock was twelve she was not only taller than her sister but had taken on the role of Cecily's protector. She treated her in every way as the younger one, fussing over her at mealtimes, scolding her gently when Cecily got her dresses soiled and generally doting on her in a way that should have been clearly seen as excessive.

In the winter of 1965 Cecily took ill with a flu. Her weak constitution couldn't fight it off, and she died before her sixteenth birthday.

Hazel was inconsolable. She grieved deeply and silently for more than a year. When she roused herself from the orgy of mourning, it seemed that she'd lost much of her loving nature. Her treatment of kittens, puppies, or anyone who appeared weak and helpless seemed based on anger, not sympathy. She was often needlessly rough and cruel with such creatures.

Her mother and father determined that she needed a change of environment. The monies the father had been saving for the higher education of two now had to serve only one, and Hazel was enrolled in one of the better schools for girls.

She was fifteen, tall for her age, willowy and graceful one moment, angular and awkward the next.

She was sexually initiated within three months by an older girl who'd been riding to the hounds with her parents since she was six and was very handy with a short whip.

The game of trade—pleasure for pain, satisfaction for subservience—went on for some time, until Hazel tore the quirt from the girl's hand, assuming the dominant role, giving blow for blow, tit for tat. Their activities came to the attention of the games mistress, who was all too ready to fulfill the obligations of the stereotype placed on her profession by custom and popular literature. She taught Hazel the fine points of field hockey, bowls and sadomasochism. They were caught at it with their pants down. The mistress was dismissed and Hazel packed off to home.

Her father wouldn't confront the issue; her mother clearly had no idea how to do so. Both acted wary toward her because she'd destroyed their fondest dreams of propriety and was no longer an example of their love, industry and sacrifice.

She completed her secondary school education in a school close to their London flat. She had no trouble with the academics; she was, in fact, exceptionally intelligent. But her conduct was sullen and vicious, her control over other girls and even some of the boys suspect, and her attendance random. In less permissive times she would never have been allowed to graduate. As it was, her teachers were happy to get rid of her, even if a diploma was the cost of it.

During her last schooldays and after, Hazel began running with a gang of girl toughs who were then introducing to the streets of the Soho district the unusual spectacle of muggings, robberies and beatings perpetrated by young women. They were, as a rule, smartly dressed. Some, like Hazel, were very pretty, finding it easy to lure unsuspecting men into dark nooks and alleys. Hazel, with her public school manners and soft voice, was exceptionally good at such entrapment. She became known as well for the expert use of a nylon cord which she habitually wore as a belt. One night she employed too much pressure on a man who fought back desperately and killed him. She left that life abruptly and completely, taking the professional name "Hush," and immediately found work as a model. Her beauty was a bit too lush for the highest echelons of that profession, and when the proper offer came along from the proper older man, she became his well-paid mistress. He was pleased to know that she gave her favors to no other man, was less pleased to discover that she was actively lesbian, and attempted to get rid of her without a fuss. That proved to be expensive. Hush accepted nothing less for her discretion than passage to the United States and sufficient funds to last her at least a year.

She made her way over the course of years from New York to California, never with any visible means of support, nursing some soul-sickness and hoping for that something that would give her a reason for living. Until that came along she dreamed of the fabulous score that would make her famous or financially independent, and she looked for someone to love. She wasn't aware of it, but that someone was the dead sister she had so cherished. When Evelynn came into her life, she finally found the centerpiece of her own otherwise disordered life, a weak creature she could protect and own, while preying on every other weak creature that came her way.

Evelynn was admirably suited to the role.

She was orphaned when she was ten. An aging bachelor uncle took her in, cared for her and loved her in a tentative, frightened way. They lived alone like two nuns in a decaying cloister.

At sixteen she was a beautiful sight, sitting in the parlor with the sunlight pouring through the lace curtains, making patterns on her hands as she worked at needlepoint.

One night she appeared at a neighbor's front door to say that her uncle was dead. They hurried over to see what must be done, and by the time they looked for her, Evelynn was gone. A search was made locally. She was listed as a missing person, but she was never found, and people forgot about her.

She'd found her way to the highway and hitchhiked west. The man who picked her up gave her a taste of marijuana and kept her with him all the way to Los Angeles. She walked off on him and took up with a street dealer who did pot and cocaine in a small way. When he got busted, she took her things to his friend's apartment. She passed around and got passed around that way.

She was the more or less passive member of a lot of heavy scenes, some of them sadomasochistic. Hush was the principal punisher at one of them. As she was being beaten, Evelynn made no protest but simply lay there crying softly. Hush's attitude changed instantly, became softly maternal. They left together, and Hush never tried to abuse her again. Her feelings toward Evelynn were sometimes confused, but she was certain of one thing. She would never let her go.

They were meant to be together. Hush knew that. Their separate souls had been fashioned in such a way that they had to be together if they were to be of any use to themselves at all.

The curtain blew aside in a sudden flourish of the wind. The moon spotlighted Evelynn's face. Hush started to cry very softly.

14

Harry got up the next morning with a feeling of power in his belly. He went into the kitchen where Alice was standing at the stove making breakfast, raised the skirt of her housecoat and took her for the feeling of dominance it gave him.

"Christ, Harry, if this is what it means living with you, I'm not sure I'll be able to take it."

"You love it," he said and burrowed his bearded jaw into the softness at the back of her neck.

She giggled, but she didn't really love it at all.

Harry went to sit at the kitchen table. The sun poured through the window, warming his naked thighs and belly.

Alice served up the bacon and eggs. "You going to sit there with nothing on?" she asked in a mildly disapproving tone.

Harry grinned. "Don't you like it?"

"Suppose somebody should walk in without knocking?"

"What rude bastard would do that?" Harry kidded.

"Well, Evelynn—or Hush."

"One of them walks in, I'll just wave my dingdong at her by way of greeting," Harry said in a mock Irish brogue.

"Oh, Harry." Alice sipped her orange juice and

looked over the top of the glass like a child. "Hush talk to you last night?"

"What were you trying to do, Alice?" Harry demanded, not smiling anymore.

"What do you mean?"

"Were you trying to tempt me with her?"

"No."

"Were you testing me?"

"I wouldn't do anything like that. I just wanted her to talk to you. She doesn't do things with men, anyhow." She hesitated. The girls next door were still something of a mystery to her. She had no idea how they survived. "Does she?" she added.

"What if she did?"

Alice became flustered. "Well, it'd be a good thing. I'd be happy for her. I don't think it's really right for girls to fool around with girls."

"Would you like to see me fuck her? Set her on the straight and narrow?"

"What's the matter with you, Harry?"

"What if she wanted to fuck me? Would you have any objections?"

"I don't know."

"Yes, you know. Yes, you goddamn well know," Harry said viciously. "Everybody knows how they'd feel about something like that. Jealous, that's how."

"Well, I wouldn't want you to like her better than me, or have you go and leave me in the lurch."

"You want to own me—that it?" Harry's voice started up the scale. He was grinning again, but it was painful even to look at. "You see now, don't you?"

"See what?" Alice asked, becoming really afraid.

"Why I held off living together all that time. You want to own me. If I wanted to be owned, I'd get married."

"I didn't say you didn't have the right to have her or anybody else you wanted to," she said.

He leaned back and scratched his balls absently. "You mean that?"

"I'd be hurt, though. That's all I'm saying; I wouldn't be too happy about it. I mean, I love you," she said and immediately wondered if she really loved him at all.

"So if you love me, wouldn't you want me to have the pleasure? I mean, after all, you wouldn't give a damn if I took her out for a meal, so what's a fuck between friends?"

"Where would you take her to eat?" Alice asked, making Harry laugh, as she meant to do.

"Fucking isn't loving—remember that." He reached out and patted her hand. "You're my girl and don't you forget it."

"Did you do it to her?" she asked after a bit.

"No, Alice," he said, "but maybe I will. In fact, I'm pretty sure I will, and if that bothers you, maybe you'd better leave now."

There was a silence again. Finally Alice nodded her head. She wasn't entirely surprised that she didn't much care.

"More coffee?"

"I'll get it," Harry said. He got up from the chair to get the pot. The flesh of his ass made a hissing sound as the plastic pad released him.

"Well, did you?" Alice said.

Harry turned around ready to shout.

"I mean did you talk to her," she added quickly.

"Yes. She told me what was worrying you."

"What does it mean, Harry? Are you just making up ideas about what could be? Are you just mad at things the way they are and making speeches? You don't really want to kill anybody, do you?"

When he didn't answer, she finally lifted her eyes from the coffee cup. He was standing there holding the pot. He'd drawn himself up and pulled in his belly so he looked taller and somehow younger.

"We won't talk about it now, Alice," he said. "Not all of it; but I will say this much. We're not getting any younger, honey. The world has passed us by. Nothing much good has ever happened to you, and nothing much but shit has ever happened to me."

Tears sprang unbidden to Alice's eyes.

"We've got nobody. No family. No chance for kids. That's passed us by too. We're just two more little nothings, honey. We're so small a mouse would refuse us for his lunch.

"Are you going to be a famous model, a movie star or even the assistant manager in that lousy restaurant you slave for? Am I going to become a professor or a councilman or even the assistant chief of the studio security force? No, Alice. We go on the way we're going, and one day you'll sigh and be gone and I'll pop like a dead balloon, and nobody will even know. Nobody will even cry because we busted."

Alice was in full flood now, feeling sorry for Harry and herself and all the lost years, for every pain in her legs and every line that traced the corners of her eyes, for every scrap of hope blowing in the wind. Her head went down on the table. Harry came up behind her and stroked her hair.

"I'm not going to let that happen to us, Alice. We're going to be remembered. We're going to make those bastards sit up and take notice of us. Even if we have to kill a few of them."

Her tears crested but the sobs went on.

"You understand? You understand?" he asked softly.

After a moment she nodded.

"You know I'm right. We got to do this thing. You can see that, can't you?"

She nodded again.

"Hey, love, stop your crying. Have another cup of coffee," Harry soothed, and grinned above her head where she couldn't see.

15

Sometimes you can wake up in the morning with a tune running through your head and it won't go away all day until you think you might go crazy. Detective Metzler woke up with a face before him more toothy grin that anything else: Harry Smiley's face. He decided to look into Smiley's past a little bit. Nothing official; just a quick frisk.

He called Coolidge at the FBI field office and asked for the name of some Secret Service operative in Washington who might cooperate with him unofficially. Coolidge offered the name of Sergeant Paul Vogt.

Vogt took the recommendation of Agent Coolidge right off the bat and asked Metzler what he could do for him.

"Did your office get that identification on one Harry Smiley spotted at the scene of the assassination attempt on the President?"

"Yes."

"Was he on the sentinel list?"

"No."

Metzler felt let down.

"But he had been on the list and was taken off," Vogt added.

"So he was checked out and given a clean bill?"

"No. He's now on the list of those persons taken off the sentinel list."

"Was that incident with the fake grave the only item on his sheet?"

"You want a copy?"

"I've got nothing to make it official. I'm just fishing a little."

"Wait a minute," Vogt said. He came back in a couple of minutes. "O.K., here's the readout. Veteran of Korea. Served two years stateside. No overseas duty. No combat. Discharged honorably. In '53 he was in school at Berkeley. Roused a little rabble against the late Senator McCarthy, then switched sides and made a little more fuss. It didn't mean much one way or the other. In '57 Smiley surfaced in Little Rock when the schools were being integrated. Smiley picked up for defying the law. Twice. Seems he got it coming and going."

"Smiley picks lousy causes," Metzler remarked.

"He does. In '60 he came to the attention of the California state cops for hanging around outside 'Q' when Chessman took his deep breath. He worked for Kennedy's election that year and wrote crazy letters to him the next. You got the rest."

"Not a hell of a lot, is it?"

"It never is until one of them blows somebody's head off," Vogt said. "Now I've told you some things, you got anything to tell me?"

"No. There's just something about the guy's face, the way he grinned and shouted, won't get out of my head."

"That's all?"

"That's all, believe me."

"I do. I know just what you mean. I was assigned to watch Governor Wallace in '72. I spotted this character with a pale face at the Pfister Hotel in Milwaukee. In April I saw him at a victory party, popped up again at a rally in Cadillac, Michigan, and again in Kalamazoo. I thought he was one of the regulars, a campaign worker or a reporter. He seemed to know people. Still, it bothered the hell out of me—there was something very odd about the bastard. I didn't act on my hunch. How the hell could I? So Arthur Hermann Bremer shot Wallace. I know just what you mean."

Roger Berkley, the hero of Century City, was being questioned by LAPD Intelligence detectives for the third time since the assassination attempt. Metzler was present for the first time.

"We don't like to bother you with this constant repetition, Mr. Berkley," Lieutenant Jill said, "but we find that very often some new fact emerges when a witness thinks he's really told us all of it."

"I don't mind," Berkley said pleasantly, clearly enjoying every bit of attention he could get. "I'll try to remember something new."

"Now that's just it, Mr. Berkley; we don't want you to try to remember anything new. If it comes—well, that's just fine, but please don't try," Jill said.

"How long had you been there before the President made his appearance?" a detective named Striet asked.

"Oh, about an hour. I got there early. I didn't have anything to do."

"You say you got there early. How did you know what time the President would show up outside the building in the mall?" Jill said.

Berkley looked blank for a moment. "Oh, yeah," he said, "I heard it on my portable radio that the President and 'notables' had gone in to eat. I figured that'd take about an hour. I mean you can't take much more than that just for lunch."

"That's right, you can't."

"Does that mean anything?" Berkley asked.

"No. We're just trying to lead you slowly through the events leading up to the time when Miss Masters—"

"Ms.," Striet broke in.

"What?" Jill said.

"Ms. Masters wants to be called Ms."

"Oh, sure. Up to the time Ms. Masters pointed the gun at the President."

"Right," Berkley said and frowned in concentration.

"So the President came down right on time?"

"Almost on the button. I moved to a spot where I figured he'd pass by."

"Then what?"

"I saw a Secret Service man open the glass doors. Some cops—officers in uniform—came out next, then the President with this actor walking alongside."

"Which side was the actor—Mr. Nordland—on in relation to the President?"

Berkley thought a moment. "On his left."

"Go on."

"The President jumped into the crowd once, reaching out to shake people's hands. A couple of his men got between him and the crowd and sort of shooed him back away from them. I don't mean they actually shooed him—"

"We understand."

"He smiled at Mr. Nordland and then came on toward me."

"Your eyes were on him?" Metzler asked.

"On who?" Berkley asked.

"The President."

"Oh, sure."

"Every second?"

"Sure."

"Even when you felt something poking you in the ribs?"

"Well, no; then I looked to see what it was."

"But your eyes were on the President every second up to then?"

"I might have looked at the actor."

"Nowhere else?"

"I looked at the people on the other side of the clear lane where the celebrities were walking."

"See anything unusual?"

Berkley half closed his eyes. "I saw a guy in a blue and gold school jacket."

Metzler leaned away from the wall where he'd been slouching. "Why did you notice him?"

"He was red in the face, grinning in a funny way like a snarling dog, you know?"

"Did you notice anything else about him?"

"I don't think so."

"Could you see his hands?"

"No, they were in his pockets. Wait a minute— only the right hand was in his pocket."

"You're sure?"

"Positive."

"Why would you be positive about such a little thing?"

"Because he was trying to drag something out of the pocket. Something black and shiny."

"Like a gun?" Metzler urged.

"Yes, it was a gun," Berkley said, like a man who'd just had his mind made up for him.

"O.K., Mr. Berkley," Lieutenant Jill said loudly.

Metzler took the warning.

"Then you felt the poking in your ribs?" Metzler prompted.

"Yeah, and I looked back and saw this *other* gun in this lady's hand. I knew it was a lady because the nails were painted red—though you can't always tell these days—and I heard somebody shout." He looked at Metzler. "I heard on television it was the guy with the blue and gold jacket who shouted."

"Did it sound like a warning?" Metzler asked.

"What did you do then, Mr. Berkley?" Jill asked.

"I smashed her arm up in the air and the gun went off."

"Now, that's just fine, Mr. Berkley. You can go now. If we need you, we'll call on you again," Jill said.

"Anytime," Berkley said and stood up to go. At the door he turned and looked at Metzler. "I think the guy had a gun in his pocket," he said and then went out of the room.

Metzler turned to Jill. "Why did you step in there, Lieutenant?"

"Because you were practically drawing a picture for Berkley of this guy Smiley with a gun in his pocket, shouting his head off because he was pissed off at Masters for jumping his shot."

"Well, it could be."

"If you've got a hard-on against this Smiley, it's O.K. with me, but I'm not going to let you manufacture evidence."

"Can I at least bring him in for questioning?"

"Sure. He might enjoy the attention. Berkley does."

16

There's a special section of the entertainment crowd that attends about every sporting event of any importance. Some make sure they have private boxes for football, baseball, hockey and the racetracks. Mickey Rooney is one of these. So is Walter Matthau. Michael Nordland can be expected to attend every home game of the Los Angeles Kings in season.

On Saturday night he sat in celebrity row, with Sheri beside him wearing a sweater and ski pants that complemented his own. Jim Truman, Michael's personal manager, was with them, looking businesslike and uncomfortable in topcoat and felt hat. The boxes were half empty, the crowd still coming in. The skaters out on the ice were running drills. The excitement that runs around sporting arenas was building up, a promise of violence, injury, even death.

Harry and Bondi came up the ramp into the grandstands at the loge level. Their seats were back up high in the colonnades, but Harry liked to walk along the oval close above the ice and then climb the steps to the cheaper reserved seats. Bondi had his hands stuffed into his pockets as they walked along. Harry stopped and watched the players slamming the puck around.

"Your hands hurt you from the other day?" he asked.

"They're O.K."

"Let me see."

Bondi hesitated, looked around cautiously.

"Come on, let me. What's the matter with you? For Christ's sake, you are stupid. Nobody here knows about Gus."

"Jesus, don't talk so loud, Harry."

"All right. Let me see."

Bondi took his big hands out of his pockets. The knuckles, decorated with scabs, were still puffy.

"Nothing busted?" Harry asked.

"No. They're fine. How's the old man?"

Harry looked at the kid sharply, searching for any sign of sympathy. "It bother you?"

"I was just wondering."

"You nearly killed him."

"Yeah," Bondi said casually, "I hit him a couple of good ones."

"He'll live."

"Who's your money on?" Bondi asked.

"What?"

Bondi indicated the ice with a gesture of his head. "Who do you think's gonna win?"

"I don't know. I don't care."

"Ain't you a fan?"

"I just like the action."

"Me too," Bondi said.

"I'd like to give that bastard a little action," Harry said.

"Who?"

"That faggot actor sitting right down there."

Bondi followed Harry's stare and saw Nordland leaning close to Sheri, sharing some little joke with her. She kissed him lightly on the mouth. Bondi felt a tightening in his groin. He made fists of his swollen hands.

"You want me to beat him like I did the other guy, Harry?" he asked doubtfully.

"No. Not now." The veins that had popped out in his neck in anger subsided. "Maybe some other time. Yeah, some other time," he said.

"Maybe we better go to our seats," Bondi said, noticing that the crowd was getting thicker around them. The fans jostled Harry and Bondi as they hurried to get to their seats before the face-off.

Harry kept staring at Nordland. He cupped his hands around his mouth. "Hey, Nordland!" he yelled.

Michael turned his head and looked questioningly into the stands for a moment. Seeing no one he recognized, he gave his attention back to the ice.

"Son of a bitch," Harry said.

The whistle blew for the start of the game, and the teams arranged themselves for the face-off. The referee dropped the puck between the centers and got out of the way as the sticks flew.

Harry and Bondi hurried up the long flight of steps and found their seats.

The Kings took the puck, and their forward raced down the ice toward the opposing goal, the hiss of the blades sounding like knife slashes through silk. The forward passed the puck off to his center, who raced to set up a play, eluding defenders as they rushed as a power unit down the ice. The crowd began to shout raggedly, not yet in full voice, warming up to the promise of blood. A defender moved in to check the center, who passed off to the right wing. The player raised his stick until it was parallel to the ice and brought it down, the slap shot traveling ninety miles an hour to the goal, where it was stopped by a thrust-out mitt.

The game roared on back and forth, the players spurred to great speed and effort by the adrenalin pumping through their veins and the screams of the mob. Every ninety seconds or so, forwards were substituted without pause. Defensemen, not required to make rink-length rushes at speed, stayed on the ice somewhat longer.

The Kings' center retrieved the puck after a failed shot, lost it almost at once when checked by two opposing players, then went after one of them, stick held in both hands above his shoulders, slamming into his opponent with crushing force and knocking him to the ice.

The crowd roared, and Bondi was on his feet and shouting madly with the rest. Harry sat there, staring down into the arena, unmoved by the drama and violence of the game.

Bondi sat down. "Hey, Harry, what's the matter?" he asked.

"The son of a bitch didn't give me a nod. Didn't want to let on he knew me."

"Maybe he didn't see you, Harry."

"Oh, he saw me all right. Couldn't you tell he was looking right at me?"

"Well, I mean, how good do you know him?"

"He knows me all right. He gave me a bottle of booze just the other day. Sure, it's O.K. to know me at the studio, but it's different when he's out in public with his friends."

"How can you be sure he saw you?" Bondi persisted. "I mean, he's wearing dark glasses. How could you know he was looking at you?"

Harry flashed at Bondi like a striking snake. "Because I say so."

"O.K., Harry," Bondi said and went back to watching the game. He focused on the goalie standing with his gigantic padded legs spread wide like some monster from a horror film and imagined himself standing that way there in front of the cage, daring any son of a bitch to make a score against him.

Harry saw himself as the center, the leader, the shot maker and spoiler. His attention was now split between the game and the back of Nordland's head, which he saw crushed in a dozen different ways. Nordland dead, and his woman unprotected and available to Harry for whatever use came into his head.

Michael identified with the swiftest player on the ice—clever, elusive, snugly protected by pads at shoulder, kidney, knee and thigh. But when player slammed into player he winced, wanting to be away from the violence, yet fascinated by it.

The game blasted on, with penalties and fouls, fights and some blood. It was won in the last two minutes by a backender past the Kings' goalie: Bruins, 3; Kings, 2.

A restaurant called—with no great imagination—The Puck was a favorite hangout of the after-game crowd.

Harry scarcely ever stopped in, but he had an idea that Nordland and his bunch would be going there, so he drove over, telling Bondi he'd buy him a beer. Michael was already at the far end of the bar when they arrived. They took seats closer to the door.

The bartender made something of a fuss over serving Michael, Sheri and Truman. He repeated the order twice, calling Nordland "Mike," which nobody, least of all a friend, would ever do.

Teasingly, Sheri batted her eyes at Michael and cooed, "Are you a celebrity, mister?"

"Indeed I am, little girl, and you'd know that in an instant if I hadn't left my mustache at home."

"Oh, shoo, I recognize you now," Sheri said, slapping his sleeve lightly. "You're Steve McQueen."

Her voice carried a little more than she had intended. She looked around to see if anyone had overheard, reluctant to draw attention to them. Her glance met that of a big man with the careful grooming of a traveling salesman and the massive hands of a stevedore. Right away he flashed a smile as though he considered her remark to be directed to him.

Trapped by her own good manners, she smiled back briefly, hoping that would be the end of it, but the stranger wouldn't let it go.

"Your boy friend does look a little bit like McQueen," he said.

"Not so good looking." Sheri laughed and turned away. He left his stool and stepped over behind her.

"My name's Fritchie. Wally Fritchie. Hey, you're Michael Nordland, aren't you? I mean you really are a celebrity." He stuck out his huge hand to be shaken.

Sheri drank half her Dubonnet in one swallow and looked off toward the dining room as though anxious to be fed. She started to slide off the stool, taking up her small purse, clutching Michael's arm with her other hand. He moved to stand up and accidentally knocked his own drink all over Fritchie.

In a moment of awkwardness Michael reached for Fritchie's hand, but the man snatched it away in order to support Sheri's elbow. She jerked away, and the whole thing became a flurry of false moves.

"Just a minute there, mister," the bartender protested, knowing nothing about what was really going on.

"It's all right," Michael said.

"What the hell you trying to do?" Fritchie asked fiercely, his words slurring all of a sudden. "Trying to make me out a masher or something?"

His face was suffused with angry blood; his mouth twisted in warning.

"No one's accusing anyone of anything," Michael said.

Truman stood up and handed Fritchie one of his business cards. "Have the jacket cleaned and send the bill to me," he said.

"Who the hell are you?" Fritchie demanded.

"Mr. Nordland's business representative."

"I'm sorry about the drink," Michael said quickly.

"Fuck the drink. And I can afford to have my own jacket cleaned. I don't need your ass-kisser to hand me his card."

"Easy, mister," Michael said.

"Fritchie, goddamn it, the name's Fritchie. That's who I am. If I can remember your fucking name, you can damn well remember mine."

"Cut it out, fella," the bartender said, "or you'll get tossed out on your ass. Begging your pardon, miss."

Fritchie turned a look of bland innocence on the bartender. "Now why the hell would you want to do that? My friend and me can settle this."

"There's nothing to settle," Truman said. "You're not getting any fight here."

Fritchie looked at Truman and narrowed his eyes. "What's the matter—no men here?"

"No damn fools. Nothing to prove."

"Afraid of getting your face messed up?" Fritchie said to Michael.

"It's a consideration," Michael said evenly. He hoped that no one noticed that he was trembling and that anyone who did would assume he was trying to control his rage. He was gut scared, as he'd always been at such confrontations. "We're leaving now," he said, staring at Fritchie.

"No need to run on my account," Fritchie said.

"You've made me lose my appetite," Michael said.

"Look here, I don't want to do that. I'm just a stranger passin' through. I don't know too much about you Hollywood people." Suddenly he had a pronounced drawl, was a "good ol' boy."

"We're just friendly folk like yourself," Michael drawled right back.

"It's not like I was some saddle tramp," Fritchie said. "I'm a pretty big heap back where I come from."

"You'd be a pretty big heap anywhere," Michael said.

Fritchie stared at Michael for a moment, ready to take up the argument again, then began to laugh. He started to raise his hand to slap Michael on the back but thought better of it.

"Buy you folks a drink?" he asked.

"I want to go home, Michael," Sheri said. They made their way to the door, passing Harry and Bondi on the way.

"I was right here with my friend, ready to pitch in if that character got rough, Mr. Nordland," Harry said with mock solicitude. Michael glanced at him but made no comment, seeming scarcely to recognize him.

As they left they could hear Harry's rude, insulting laughter.

17

There always comes a time when a dream becomes action or dies altogether. Harry was absolutely certain of his intentions the day after the hockey game.

He made a barbecue in the tiny backyard and invited Hush and Evelynn, Peewit and Janet, Bondi and Marco. Harry hadn't thought to tell Alice not to do any inviting on her own, so she asked Assy to come over.

They ate plenty of Italian sausages and potato salad, drank a lot of wine and beer and smoked a little dope.

Harry went to sit with Peewit in the corner of the yard. "Had enough, old buddy?" he asked.

Peewit belched. A moment later he farted, and they both laughed.

"I guess you've had your fill," Harry said. "How's it going on the job, Walter?"

"Shitty, like always."

"You get that series?"

"No, I wasn't kissing the right asses."

"You don't go around kissing asses, do you?"

"Hell, no. That's what I mean. I wouldn't brown-nose the production manager, so he looked the other way. I don't like the bastard anyway. He's a second-rater, and I don't like working with second-raters."

"You never did step into the ring with any bums, did you, Peewit?"

Peewit smiled broadly, showing a rather fine set of false teeth. "Oh, hell, I guess I went a few rounds with my share of bums," he said modestly.

"No real bums. I wouldn't believe that. I wouldn't believe you'd fight any setups even if it would've got you the crown."

"I could have been champion if I'd wanted to play the rotten game," Peewit said.

"I know you could," Harry said, allowing a tinge of disbelief to show through.

"I could have, goddamn it," Peewit said, aroused to anger.

Harry backed up, throwing up his hands in mock fear. "Hold it. Hold it. Don't get mad at me."

"I ain't mad at you, Harry. I'm mad at them. At what they done to me. They kept me away from being champ because I wouldn't play footsie and take dives and fight a bunch of bums."

"I know, I know," soothed Harry. "They wouldn't let you have a crack at the champion because they knew you were too damn good," he said.

"Those bastards. I could have been champion," Peewit shouted, loudly enough to draw everyone's attention.

"You could have." Harry agreed with him enthusiastically, watching him get his temper up, pleased and sure of the ease with which he could manipulate the punchy has-been.

"Look what they done to me," Peewit demanded, holding up his hand, broken knuckles forward. "They busted me up."

"Busted you up and tossed you on the scrap heap," Harry added.

"I could have had a shot at the title, those bastards hadn't done the dirty on me," Peewit raged. He started to stutter. A light froth appeared at the corners of his mouth.

Janet called out Harry's name. She saw what he was doing and wanted to tell him to stop. He flashed one of his deadly grins at her, and she shut her mouth but started toward them.

"That ain't all," Peewit said, jumping on to other grievances without pause. "I was on this fight picture, see? There was some questions about how it goes. I know more about fights than anybody on the set, but did they ask me to set the fight up for them? I tried to tell them I knew how to do it right, but this bastard director tells me to mind my own goddamn business. I tell him fighting is my goddamn business, and he tells me he means I should do what I was getting paid for, seeing that the buckets and sponges and water bottles was in the right places."

Janet ran to her husband and put her arms around his chest. His arms continued to wave above her head as she made soothing sounds.

"I'll get back at all them bastards someday!" Peewit screamed out.

"Yes, you will, and I'm going to help you do it!" Harry shouted back.

Harry and Janet helped Peewit back into the house and put him on the bed. Janet lay down beside him and Harry left them there. He had started back to the yard when the front doorbell rang. A man was standing there peering through the screen door.

"It's about time you got around to me," Harry said.

"After something as serious as an attempt on the President's life," Metzler said, "there are so many witnesses to be questioned that it takes a while to see them all."

"Yeah, but I'm the guy who yelled out a warning."

"Is that what it was, Mr. Smiley?"

"What the hell do you mean by that?"

"I had my eyes on you just at the time you yelled out in rage."

"In what?"

"I mean that's what it looked like to me—like you were angry as hell."

"Well, I was. I mean this broad was taking a shot at the President. Naturally I was angry."

"Of course. You cried out a warning, then?"

"Yes."

"But you didn't direct it toward the President, Mr. Smiley. You shouted 'No' at the assassin."

"Attempted assassin," Harry said.

"That's right," Metzler agreed blandly. "Why didn't you shout your warning to the President? Isn't that what you'd expect someone to do?"

"I don't know what I'd expect. You're telling me what I did. I don't remember exactly what I did."

"But you do know what you did."

"What do you mean?"

"Didn't you watch yourself on television?"

"Sure. That's right. I know I shouted at the attempted assassin, but I didn't know I was doing it, or why I was doing it, at the time."

"Then you do know that you shouted at the woman?"

"I'm saying so."

"You shouted when you saw the gun?"

"Yes."

"Do you have a gun?"

"What the hell's this all about?"

"I'm simply asking you if you have a gun in your possession," Metzler said mildly.

"I've got a gun."

"Registered?"

Harry stood up. "I don't know what all these questions are about, but it seems pretty funny to me that you'd be interrogating me as though I was under suspicion."

Metzler looked up at Harry innocently.

"Where the safety of the President is concerned, everybody is under suspicion."

"Fair enough, but I'm not answering any more of your questions. It's Saturday afternoon, and I've got some friends over for a barbecue and a good time. You're spoiling my day off."

Metzler stood up. "If you don't wish to cooperate," he said. "I simply asked about seeing your gun."

"I'm not saying I won't cooperate. I just said I won't answer any more of your wise-ass questions on a Saturday afternoon. You want to look for a gun, you get a warrant."

Metzler went to the door. Harry walked him part of the way like a homeowner shooing a dangerous dog from the house, not wanting to get too close.

It grew chilly before it grew dark. They all went inside. Alice passed out more drinks. Hush rolled some dope. Harry turned on the television to catch the evening news. An item said that the producer of the Academy Awards Presentation Show, Hiram Evers, had made his first staff appointment: Eddie Barnes, the choreographer who had practically been a contemporary of Busby Berkeley. The theme was going to be the roaring twenties. Evers announced it as though he'd invented the decade.

Alice squealed when the camera pulled back to

catch Eddie Barnes, late sixtyish, small, sparrowlike and chirpy, waving to the crowd.

"Must be a slow news night," Harry said.

"I know him," Alice said.

"Here's the noted choreographer Eddie Barnes," the newsman said.

"Not choreographer, son—dance director. Never call an old-time hoofer a choreographer. Dance director."

The two heads chatted for a while about movie productions in general and the upcoming Academy Awards show in particular, and the little man left the stage, cutting figures with his feet, flapping his elbows, shrugging his shoulders and nodding his head with an excess of energy.

"I worked three pictures with him," Alice said.

"You hear that?" Harry said, sounding amazed. "Alice worked three pictures with that little character."

The rest of them made a fuss. Alice smiled and tried a little time step as the old memories came flooding back. She kicked her legs up one after the other.

Bondi pushed the coffee table out of her way. Hush and Evelynn started clapping their hands when they weren't toking on the joint that was passing around. Janet hurried over and put a record on the turntable. She fiddled the knobs, and the music came up loud and brassy. Harry reached over and killed the television set. Peewit, laughing and red in the face, watched Alice as though he'd never seen her before, looking up her dress each time she kicked a leg into the air, turning on the floor lamp next to him and tilting the shade so that the light fell on her like a spot. Alice kicked higher.

Her legs were white and still quite beautiful. They

flashed in the light. Their rhythm was hypnotic. Alice felt the sweet vigor of youth. Her eyes glazed a bit as she fell into a spell of the past.

"I'll just bet you could put on your old dancing shoes and show those kids a thing or two right now," Janet shouted in a kind of hopeful joy. She really meant that if Alice could kick up her heels and show her pants, then *nobody* was really getting old.

"You could do it," Janet screamed again and looked up Alice's dress toward her crotch. Alice smiled in the glow of rose-colored spotlights, kicked her legs and shook her curls.

"I'm too old," she protested, perspiration glistening on her chest. She drew her shirt off over her head, revealing a white brassiere paneled with transparent insets. Her nipples shone through, pink like a young girl's.

Marco sat in the corner of the couch, looking at her with joyous pain. Remembering. But the flesh that had been exposed to him was never flesh such as this. He clenched his fists with shocked pleasure as he felt the rising of the slightest of erections.

"You could do it, Alice. You could get a job," Harry said. "Couldn't she?"

They all shouted their agreement.

"You could do it," Bondi yelled, smiling broadly, sweating, his hand on Assy's knee. She gripped the hand and drew it up the inside of her thigh, outside her jeans, toward her crotch.

Alice's face was flushed, the tendrils of hair at the temples damp and tender looking.

"Take it off! Take it off!" Peewit shouted. He stomped and clapped, half-looking at Janet, but his eyes never completely leaving Alice's legs.

"Take it off," Hush sang out in her deep voice.

"You can do it, Alice. You can show those young cunts," Janet yelled. "Take it off!"

The atmosphere was suddenly steamy, like the musty guts of struggling strip joints, the topless bars where men bought the raw products of nightly masturbations for the price of a beer, the backstages of theaters where the dancers' tights could be seen to be sweat-stained and torn. It was glittery with the illusions of glamour that live in those same unlikely environments.

Harry clapped and stomped with the others. He looked at Hush and found her looking at him.

"Take it off!" she said to him. "Now, now, now."

He knew what it was she sensed. This was the moment to bind them all together. This was the occasion to so mark their souls and minds with intimate guilts that they'd be lost to his commands, hoping to expiate their sins—or wanting more of them.

"You can get the job, Alice. Take it off!" Harry yelled. Hearing his approval and wanting to take off her clothes to show them that they were right, that her flesh was firm and ripe and desirable, Alice dropped her skirt and kicked off her slippers. She felt a momentary sense of exposure, of shyness.

"Come on, Janet, you too," she said laughingly, seeking support.

"I can't dance," Janet said.

"You can too," Alice insisted.

"You dance at home," Peewit leered. "In less than that."

Hush tapped Evelynn on the back between her shoulder blades. The usually placid Evelynn jumped as though touched by a knife. She stared into Hush's eyes for a moment, and Hush nodded a bit. Evelynn got to her feet and danced, her flesh quivering.

The others stared at her as though she were a statue miraculously come to life. The eroticism she displayed in her every gesture, coming as it did from the usually perfect and placid girl, seemed to bless as legitimate any outrage of manners that might follow.

Janet began then to dance too. But first she removed her slacks and blouse and, going Alice one better, her brassiere as well, in order to display her breasts, as rich and heavy as melons. She held them from beneath, containing their weight, as she kicked her legs high.

The record stopped, but the driving tempo of clapping hands went on. Assy squirmed beneath Bondi's hand. He took his eyes away from the three women dancing in their various states of undress and saw that Assy was removing her jeans. She wore nothing underneath. She remained balanced for a moment on her heels, her pelvis thrust up toward him. He shifted his glance to her eyes. She smiled, the tip of her tongue between her teeth.

"Go on, do it, do it," she whispered.

"Right here?" Bondi protested with the modesty of the young.

"You're among friends," Hush said at his back. "Go on and eat her."

Bondi got down on his knees between Assy's legs. Hush grabbed the erection that bulged in his crotch. She worked the zipper of his fly, loosened his belt and, with a little awkward cooperation from him, stripped his ass as he put his mouth on Assy's cunt.

Harry watched them all, nodding, clapping and grinning as though he were the great god Pan. Then he stood up, removed his shirt, kicked off his shoes, pulled down trousers and shorts and posed, cock erect, a Priapus worthy of worship.

Janet was the first to attend Harry's cock, which

had somehow become, because of his position and bearing, the symbol of a new freedom grown among them. She stopped dancing and went down on her knees before him. She hesitated a moment, turned her head over her naked shoulder and looked at her husband.

Peewit was staring at them both with a kind of dumb wonder. He'd been known to beat a man senseless in a bar for passing some innocent remark to Janet, but now his look was one of fascination. He looked up at Harry, who returned his gaze with dignified gravity. This was not an act of sex, his look suggested, but one of the most exalted ritual. Peewit looked at his wife and smiled.

Janet took Harry's cock in her mouth, ran her lips along the shaft and tongued his balls.

After she'd worshipped at his cock for a while, Harry pulled away from her mouth, wanting to orchestrate matters to a fitting climax.

Janet rolled away and tore off her panties, then lay on her back, knees spread wide, welcoming him. Welcoming anyone. When Harry made no move between her legs, she cast her eyes around the room. She saw Alice, naked now as she was.

Alice shook her head, as though trying to shake off some spell or examine some thought that would not reveal itself. Her tongue reached out and wet her lips. She gave up her will to the group and joined Janet on the floor. They embraced each other, explored each other's breasts. Janet excited one of Alice's nipples with her tongue, ran it under the crease of the small breast, explored the cup of her navel. She moved further to Alice's thighs. Alice spread them, and Janet placed her mouth between them gently, ever so gently.

Peewit was there with them all at once, naked, his

limbs all knotted and fierce. He rolled Alice over onto her knees after urging his wife's head away from her and mounted her from behind.

Janet placed herself in such a way that she might kiss the place where Peewit and Alice joined.

Alice stared up into the violet shadows, feeling the sensations flaming through her but thinking of other things. Old thoughts of childhood when she was safely kept, when no decisions were ever required of her.

They drank at times. And cursed. Laughed and touched one another everywhere. The men groped one another's cocks with nervous restraint, but this, more than any other evidence of their abandonment, was the truest test of the compact that was being born among them.

Even the old man found himself naked, ashamed at first of his powdery, sagging flesh but laughing soon as Alice called him dear and kissed his cheek, gasping as Janet kissed his mouth, crying out as Hush took his cock into her mouth.

Finally, showing how knowledgeable she was, Assy aroused a mighty erection, mounted him gently and drew a climax from him that might have killed a less happy man of his age.

They lay in a tangle of naked flesh, drunker with fucking than with booze or dope. They heard Harry's voice lifting them above moral considerations, making them crusaders in a cause, holy saints.

"What has come to pass this night is a wonder and an obligation. The spirit that entered into us, charging us to share our bodies most intimately and freely, was a bonding. We are sisters and brothers to a purpose. The arrogant must be punished."

"What?" Bondi said stupidly, nearly ruining the effect.

"Must be punished," Harry repeated and went on without pause. "Who is there to beat them; to take their sins from them? The churches? Will the wealthy churches demand that these monsters of greed place their fellowmen before more and more personal gain? Is there anyone who will do that? I see no one. No one but us."

"Who we talking about?" Bondi asked. Assy giggled.

"The greedy! The vain! The corrupt royalty of America. I tell you these cannibals, these flesh-eaters, are out to destroy us, but we're going to kill them first."

"We'll kill them first," Bondi said, awed and obedient. Some of the others echoed him. Harry couldn't tell whether they all agreed, but it didn't matter; they were all in it now.

He told them of his intention to forge them into a holy weapon against the symbols of American decadence and injustice, the overrewarded, overloved, overconsumed stars of motion pictures and television.

His voice was low and vibrant, rising to ringing, brazen notes that thrilled when he chose to employ it. He was never in better form. He felt in him the power to sway them.

He talked to Assy with his eyes, assuring her that through the means of murder she would regain the dignity that had been taken from her by a corrupt and corrupting system. He demanded loyalty of Bondi. He joined himself to Peewit, made them brothers in adversity, unappreciated and abused. He wept with Janet for the lost beauty that had been ignored.

113

He played no games with Hush; her eyes were too wise and cynical. He left the control and manipulation of Evelynn to her.

He saw the fear in Marco's face and thought of driving him away, discarding him. But he was pleased by the terror he saw in the old man's eyes, wanted those mirrors before his own eyes, wanted that intelligence to silently comment on his success.

Alice was afraid too, in a dull, animal-like way. Harry knew she would close out what she didn't want to remember and alter that which she did recall. It was the way she survived.

He stood before them silently for a long while. Their attention was still dumbly riveted on him.

Harry placed his hand on his cock. He massaged it deliberately to emphasize the intimacy that existed among them all.

"There won't be any turning back," he said.

Hush rose from the floor where she'd been lying across Bondi's thighs.

"If anyone breaks the covenant between us, they'll be executed," she said.

She went to Harry and took his erection in her hand, rising up on her toes. He placed his hands at her waist and lifted her. She embraced his shoulders with her other arm and led his cock into her. The high priest and priestess fucked in the name of murder.

Only the two of them really understood that murder was where it was all to lead, was meant to lead. The others watched the capstone of the ceremony like children stoned on drugs and dreams.

18

There was a shyness among them the following morning. They acted uneasy, as though just admitted to adulthood. How long the orgy had continued not one of them could have said for certain. They'd fucked, rolled over to sleep, awakened to drink, smoke and fuck again, changed positions, changed partners, crawled about here and there in various pairs and triplets.

When they were all asleep at last, Alice and Janet warmed Marco's old bones between them in Harry's bed. Bondi jealously managed to isolate Assy for himself, and they lay twined together on the floor, mouths half open, breathing like children. Peewit sat propped against the couch, his old fighter's legs, hairy and roped with veins, flung wide. Evelynn's head was on his thigh, her mouth an inch away from his flaccid manhood.

Hush lay on her back, a pillow beneath her hips, close enough to touch Evelynn. Harry lay nearly on top of her, fast asleep. She regarded him—all of them—appraisingly. With them asleep and herself awake she felt she had power over them. The exercise of power was her most urgent dream, most powerful wish.

Later, from time to time one or another would rise,

relieve and wash themselves to return in robe, skirt and blouse, or trousers or still naked, to find some place of greater comfort away from last night's lovers. In the morning they all got up and started to put together the scattered pieces of their common experience. As they sipped coffee and complained of hangovers, not one talked about what had happened the night before, everyone pretending they had been too drunk to remember clearly.

Marco, dressed in his crumpled old suit, fumbled with the watch fob given him by his long-dead wife and sat alone in the living room as though waiting for a commuter train. When Harry came into the room, the old man stood up on trembling legs.

"Well, Harry, I should be going. I want to thank you for the barbecue and for letting me stay the night." He laughed hollowly. "I'm afraid I had a bit more to drink than I'm used to. I never was much of a drinking man."

"Were you drunk, Marco?" Harry asked flatly.

"I think I may have been. I find it hard to remember everything that happened—when I fell asleep, when . . ."

"Do you, Marco? Do you really forget? I'd think you'd want to remember."

Marco's face suddenly collapsed, screwed up like an infant's about to wail. "I don't want to remember, Harry."

"But you've got to. We made a solemn bargain with one another last night."

"Not me, Harry, not me," Marco cried out.

Assy entered the room with a cup of coffee in her hands. Her face was very white, the lipstick on her mouth as red as blood. She sat on the arm of Harry's

116

chair. There was something threatening in her casual manner, in her silence.

"Yes, you, Marco, along with all the rest of us. We swore an oath," Harry said.

"I swore nothing. I couldn't; it would be against my faith," Marco argued, clutching at ridiculous straws.

Harry laughed. "Don't come on the pious old Jew with me. I saw you in action last night. You should be proud of yourself. You used the girls like a man half your age."

Marco heard himself say "Thank you," and feared that he might be going insane. Alice entered the room with Janet and Peewit, and he looked to her for some support. She kept her eyes averted and sat on the couch, cradling her coffee cup in her two hands.

"Well, I have to go home, Harry. I thank you once again. I don't think you'll be seeing me for a while. The trip up from Venice is a little too much for me. I should stay at home with my own people," he said desperately.

"We're your people, Marco," Harry said.

"I mean people my own age."

Bondi came in and stood beside Assy, his hand on her shoulder. Hush and Evelynn came softly into the room. They looked at Marco with innocent eyes, half smiling. They all waited for Harry to name what had happened between them.

"You're one of us, Marco. You joined in the ritual," Harry said reasonably. The others nodded.

"I swore to nothing," Marco protested weakly.

"You got fucked, Marco. That was the ritual. That was the oath. The fucking was the oath," Harry said.

"Well, I want no part of it," Marco said. "There's no reason to any of it."

117

Janet was looking at him as though she'd been dropped back into the terrible magic of the night.

"There's not to be any turning back, dear. Didn't you hear Harry say that last night?"

"Turning back from what?" Marco demanded. "Harry says he means to kill. Who shouldn't turn back from that?"

They all looked at one another in the vague way of people listening to the ravings of a madman. But no one challenged what he said.

"Anyone who breaks the oath will be put out of the way," Hush said in an odd voice. She might have been speaking of some mild punishment, a spanking.

"You're going to be our theorist, Marco," Harry said. "You're going to explain what we're going to do to the world."

Marco knew, with horror, that he was alone for certain and felt something crumple within him as though consumed by a heatless flame.

"Bondi'll drive you home, Marco," Harry said cheerfully. "I wouldn't dream of letting you take a bus."

Finally everyone was gone, leaving Harry and Alice alone in the kitchen. Alice was beginning to feel sick on too much coffee.

"I want you to see this Eddie Barnes tomorrow, Alice."

"Why?"

"To ask him for a job."

"There'll be a hundred young girls there. I wouldn't have a chance," Alice said.

"You've had a lot of experience, Alice. That has to count for something."

"Dancing jobs aren't all that easy to come by. The

competition'll knock me out in the first cut. I'm over the hill."

"Experience has to count for something," Harry repeated patiently. "When you danced for Eddie Barnes in those pictures, didn't you have some 'experiences' with him?"

"What do you mean?"

"Didn't you fuck him to get the jobs, Alice?"

She gasped as though he'd struck her.

"How do you know I did that with Eddie—Mr. Barnes?"

"Everybody knows that. Everybody would know that if anybody really cared."

"I didn't go to bed with him for the jobs. It was after. I liked him, and I went to bed with him after. I got the jobs on my own."

"So get another job on your own."

"It'd be embarrassing to beg Eddie for a job."

"Eddie? I'm glad to hear you're friends again. I want you to go down to the tryouts and ask him for a job, Alice."

"Don't ask me to humiliate myself in front of Eddie and all those young girls."

"I'm not asking you; I'm telling you. I don't want to get mad at you. I don't want to have to punch you out."

His violence was finally out in the open. Alice was afraid.

Down the street, under the concealment of a shade tree, Metzler roused himself from an uneasy sleep. He straightened up, plucking at the clothes that clung to him at armpit and crotch, feeling sweaty and filthy. In the light of morning he couldn't understand what craziness had led him to come back to Smiley's house after questioning him about the gun and parking himself across the street for this ridiculous stake-out.

For what? Was he expecting Smiley to shoot off a pistol at two A.M. or expose himself to some old lady walking her dog? He laughed at himself, but it didn't still the deep suspicion in his heart about Smiley. Was it the strange, threatening grin that wouldn't let Metzler forget about him?

He'd listened to the sounds of the party bursting out of the cottage from time to time and waited for a citizen's complaint to come in over the police radio so he'd have a legal reason for getting back inside, but none came. For a moment he'd even considered crawling beneath the windows and spying on them, but prudence won out.

In the morning he saw an old man leave with a young one and get into a '73 Ford wagon with banged-up light tan bodywork. A red-haired girl came out moments after and drove off in a red Bug. He took down the license numbers. Later two attractive young women crossed the small patch of court-yard and entered a cottage across the way. Finally he noted down the license number of a car belonging to a battered-looking man and another woman.

He drove off, feeling all kinds of a damn fool. That crowd was probably a bunch of friends, blowing dope and maybe whacking off a little kinky sex. Shit! Maybe they were a self-improvement group studying old madrigals.

19

Alice went to the tryouts reluctantly, but she went. She strode along feeling the flexibility of her thighs against the stretch material of her practice tights and began to feel better about it. After the action of last night, the frightening but strangely wonderful activities that had welded them all together in some remarkable family of lovers, she felt submerged but oddly rejuvenated.

She caught a glimpse of herself as she passed through the plate-glass doors of the rehearsal studio. Her reflection was wiped clean of the lines of age about her eyes and mouth; her hair was as bright as honey butter, and her mouth smiled pinkly. It'd be good to see old Eddie again, she thought. He hadn't been a serious lover; there were few serious lovers in those young years. His energies in bed had been those of a windup toy—erratic, swift and brief—but there'd been a certain good-natured fun in it; kids playing in a sandbox. She'd been fond of him and not much more, yet she climbed the stairs with some expectation, as though hurrying to the arms of her own true love.

There must have been two hundred dancers there ready to show what they could do, not really wanting the dead-end gig, but desperate for it all the same, because the pay would handle the rent.

Alice pulled up short when she saw them, not one of them as old as she. Fresh faces, clean limbs, proud tits, solid asses. Eyes flicking over to see what new threat had walked in the door. Smiles when they saw it was just some old broad kidding herself. She was about to retreat, go home and tell Harry that she'd been dropped in the first cut, when she heard her name called. She looked around to see Eddie Barnes, small as a bantam rooster, face wrinkled like a midget's, prancing toward her, hands out to grab hers. The faces of the young girls tightened with the fear that there'd be one job fewer, that the old bag would cop a job because she clearly knew the old director from the old, old days. She'd be given the spot on the end where she might not even be seen from one side of the auditorium, kicking away and picking up a check all the same.

"Alice Belmont! Where you been? How you been?"

"Around," Alice said in the old formula. "Been fine, Eddie. I don't have to ask how you are. I can see."

"Go ahead and ask me anyway," he said, tucking her hand into the crook of his arm and drawing her off to one side.

"How you been?" Alice laughed.

"This is the first legitimate job I've had in two years. It's a bitch, but what the hell. It don't pay much, but 'looka me, Ma, I'm dancin'.'" He held her hands and did a little time step all around her. At the end of it she joined in right on the beat, and it looked and sounded good. There was a little rainfall of applause.

"For the old folks," Eddie whispered. "What are you doing here, my darling girl?"

"It's crazy."

"What the hell, it's a crazy world."

"I thought I might try getting in the chorus on this show."

"You mean it? Need the money bad?"

"No, it's not that, Eddie. I can't exactly explain it. I was sitting home last night watching the news on the television—"

"You married, Alice?" Eddie interrupted.

"No."

"Got a fella?"

"Sure. I live with this guy. You know how it is. Modern times."

Eddie nodded. "Yeah, the only modern times I ever liked was the picture with Chaplin."

"Well, I was watching the TV, and all of a sudden there you were. Those days came back so fast and heavy I thought I'd drown, you know?"

"I know, I know."

"Then this crazy thought came into my head that I'd come down and look you up."

"Gee, I'm glad you did."

"You mean it, Eddie?" When he nodded and patted her hand, she felt bold enough to go on.

"Then I thought, why not try out for the line? I keep in good shape, Eddie. I work out every week, and I can pick up the steps again like that," she said, snapping her fingers.

"A regular Ruby Keeler, you are."

"Don't say that, Eddie—who'd remember?"

Eddie pulled his lower lip between thumb and finger. His assistant came over and asked him if they should begin the auditions.

"Ten at a time. Get them doing a simple time step. See who don't know left from right," Eddie said.

"Well, I better be going, Eddie. It was good seeing you again."

"Yeah, then what are you running away for?"

"You're busy. You've got things to do."

"I've got to pick out my line for this show. You're a dancer looking for a job, ain'tcha?"

"It's a crazy idea I had, that's all."

"You've got a job, Alice, but we still got to make it look legitimate. We don't want these people thinking you're sleeping with me, do we?"

He looked at her with the eyes of a beagle. There was a small, begging question there but not a bargain.

"No, we wouldn't want them to think that," Alice said and wondered why, after last night, going to bed with this old friend would seem wrong to her. Maybe she just wanted to know that wasn't the price of the job.

Metzler checked with Motor Vehicles. The wagon was registered to Arnold Bondi, male Caucasian, eighteen, six feet two, one hundred ninety pounds, hair blond, eyes brown, residing at 17439 Westhaven Drive, apartment six, Hollywood.

The second car belonged to Mara Courtney, twenty-four, five feet six, one hundred twenty pounds, hair red, eyes blue, residing at 3737 Windemere Avenue, Hollywood.

The third was owned by Janet Peewit, thirty-four, five feet four, one hundred and twenty pounds, hair brown, eyes brown. Must wear corrective lenses while driving. Residing at 1379 Martin Lane, Pacific Palisades.

Metzler checked with the phone company and found out that the telephone in the cottage across the court from Smiley's on Broom Street was listed in the name of Hazel Bostock.

The name Mara Courtney, out of all of them, rang a

bell. He checked around and found out that she was on the books as a convicted prostitute who worked under the sobriquet Miss Marvel.

Then he sat back and wondered why he was doing all of it. No matter what his hunch told him, did it make any sense to try to plug the dike before it sprang a leak? If all it took to be sure a killing was on the way was to see a man grinning savagely, half the people in the city would be behind bars. Yet he knew he'd go on with this Smiley until the pressure of other cases made him stop.

Alice returned home feeling full of herself. She didn't even seem to mind that her beautiful neighbor Hush was at home goofing off with Harry while she'd been out looking for a job.

"You were right, Harry," she said. "I can still beat those young things when it comes to flat-out hoofing."

"You got the job?"

"Sure. You want to know the best part of it?"

"What?" Hush asked helpfully and opened a beer for Alice.

"Eddie said he'd have picked me even if he'd never seen me before. He said I was that good. 'No favors asked, none given.'"

She smiled proudly and lifted her good tits to let Hush know that old Alice still had plenty left.

"So when he said that, you know what I said?" she went on.

She waited for Harry to prove he was interested.

"What?" he finally did say.

"I said, 'If there's no favors done and none owed, I got this friend Janet who needs a job.' 'Christ, Alice,' Eddie says to me, 'you want me to load the line with your friends? Evers will figure I'm setting up a bank

125

account of ass for the future and kick me out on mine.' 'No, Harry,' I said. 'This girl's very good with a needle'—Janet *is* very good with a needle, you know?—'and I thought maybe you could ace her into wardrobe before they hired everybody they needed.' "

Alice drank the whole can of beer in one go, then, as though she wished to cap off one grand performance with another. "He'll see what he can do for her."

Harry was regarding Alice strangely, as though he'd been accosted by a fire hydrant and engaged in a philosophical conversation.

"What made you think of asking the favor, Alice?"

"I'm not stupid, Harry," Alice said. "If you wanted me to get a job in the line, it seemed pretty clear you'd want somebody on the inside to tell you what's going on. And two ears are better than one." She laughed. "I mean four are better than two."

"You are a wonder, Alice, no question," Harry said and reached over to kiss her on the mouth. It made Alice feel very good. When he petted her she didn't have to think about what Harry might have in mind that had anything to do with the Academy Awards presentation.

20

Harry bought tickets to a symphony concert at the Chandler Pavilion in the Music Center. Marco was to go because Harry considered the visit a reconnaissance, the beginning of the operation, and he wanted it all down in an authorized document that would one day be made public. Hush went along because she was his second in command, Bondi because he'd lost his job at the radio shop where he'd worked and had moved in with Harry and Alice to save expenses. Alice and Assy went along to complete pairs—three couples out on the town for a cultural evening. They made an interesting group of music lovers.

When they arrived in the Grand Hall its opulence thrilled them all. Bondi gawked openly at the three great crystal chandeliers that dominated the room. The sense of limitless space was enhanced by the reflections in the mirrored wall that faced the sweeping staircase, doubling the images of the chandeliers, the arriving audience and the small band of terrorists.

They settled into the luxury of the plush seats. As the others read the program notes, Harry looked over the physical layout of the theater. The first balcony of eight or nine rows, with two small wings to right and left, had four doors. On either wall was a large crystal sconce. The second balcony was cantilevered out above the first and had five doors. There were no overhead chandeliers or wall sconces. Just below the first-row railing was an inset row of about thirty-five spotlights. Above that was the largest balcony, split nearly in half by a broad aisle with two doors at the top. The main auditorium was entered by eight doors on each side.

Harry squirmed about, taking it all in, trying to commit the details to memory. Hush leaned across Alice and whispered, "Don't worry about the layout, Harry. There are books that have very detailed plans of public buildings."

She smiled sweetly, making him feel foolish. He frowned and continued his appraisal of the theater. There were six additional crystal sconces fixed to the walls, three to a wall, down near the stage. A large number of spotlights and wall washers were set into the ceiling.

The musicians began to tune up. When the curtain rose, the orchestra crashed into the swelling martial air of the *Eroica*.

Harry was charged up by the powerful sound. He suddenly felt that he was a man of destiny no less forceful than Napoleon. He was certain that he was a man born out of his time, a master tactician and strategist. He began to form plans.

They must have guns. They must have explosives.

At the conclusion of the performance, applause shattered his fantasies of carnage. The audience stirred and rose to their feet, moving to the opened doors along the sides.

Harry pushed his way through them, impatient, angry, wanting to get away from the crush of the mob. Hating their touch. People stilled their protests at the sight of the fury of his grin. His party trailed in his wake, afraid to slow his progress. Harry's fantasies had placed him in a dark mood.

All the way home on the freeways, driving Bondi's station wagon, Harry poured forth a nonstop condemnation of wealth, fame and privilege. A filth-spattered litany of hatred for the bright, the beautiful and the blessed. More than once his rage seemed to find focus in the person of Michael Nordland.

Alice made herself small between Harry and Hush in the front seat, the torrent of evil spoiling the night for her beyond repair, destroying her attempt to forget what the evening at the theater was really all about—an examination of Harry's intended killing ground.

Hush looked out the car window, watching the rushing landscape, sensitive to Harry's fixation on one man, the actor Michael Nordland. She wondered briefly if Harry's determination to make what he termed a terrible social protest was no more than a schoolboy's spite. If that was the case, was it simply that Harry had fixed on Nordland as the celebrity who had stolen Harry's thunder during the reportage of the presidential assassination attempt? That would be so trivial as to be madness. But, then, she recognized in Harry the knife-edge of insanity, sharp and bright.

Harry went on and on until the words lost their meaning. Assy and Bondi were dozing, nearly asleep, resting against each other before they reached home. Marco was wide awake in a world of fresh terror.

Once at home, Alice excused herself and hurried off to bed, no longer able to deceive herself that they were ordinary people of cultured tastes.

Marco stood about like a stranger at a funeral, mournful and unfocused, appealing in a subtly helpless way. Harry told Bondi to drive the old man back to his hotel room in Venice. Hush extended her hand.

"Mr. Epstein," she said, "there could have been a time when we might have traveled the world together. I enjoyed your company this evening."

"My dear," Marco said, much moved by the compliment. Bondi and Assy followed him to the car. They drove off, leaving Hush and Harry alone.

"Seeing as how we're being so formal tonight," Harry said mockingly, "will I see you to the door?"

"I know the way, Harry, and I'm not afraid of the dark," she said sharply.

He reached out for her, but she eluded his grasp. Harry took two steps with startling speed, grabbed her wrist and spun her around.

"Aoooooo," she said, a tight smile on her lips.

"Don't play with me," he said.

"I'm not playing, Harry. We've got to be careful around the others. We can't be caught having any stand-up fucking at the door."

"I was thinking of more than that," Harry leered.

She placed her hands on his chest and leaned back slightly, a very feminine gesture that held a man off while flattering him with the recognition of his superior strength.

"So am I. I want time to enjoy that and a long talk as well."

Harry tried to pull her close.

"Listen to me," she said. "We've nailed them down with the power. We don't want to shake up our soldiers with any private screwing around. We've got to keep it public. We've got to keep it holy."

She kissed him lightly on the mouth. It was a promise.

"Bedtime," she said. "Sweet dreams of me, Harry."

21

Alice felt good, like old times. The dancers no longer looked at her as though she'd copped the job on juice. They sought her out to ask her advice and thought of her as "that friendly old hoofer."

What Alice lacked in stamina she made up in savvy, like an old fighter who knows how to pace himself and outlast the younger, perkier fighter; she knew how to take the weight off her feet every chance she got and leave the knee-bending and high-kicking to pole vaulters. She felt bright-eyed, alive and young.

Eddie was running around stepping high, wide and handsome, loving the chaos of putting a show together; trying out ideas, yet still finding time to look Alice's way and smile encouragement.

He wasn't much pleased with Evers's choice of the twenties as the show's theme; nostalgia had been throttled till it no longer laid golden eggs, and "twenty-three skiddoo" was practically a mod phrase. But he was also acutely aware of the fact that without the twenties he'd be without the job. He was a bit satin and old lace himself, an old valentine being dusted off for a final kiss.

He decided to put Alice right up there in the center of the line to show everyone that the years weren't always killers.

He clapped his hands and twinkle-toed across the stage, down the steps and into the third-row seat.

"Let's have 'em, kiddies," he cried out happily. "It's time to pay the rent."

And break your hearts, you little darlings. Dance, you dolls. Pay your goddamn dues just like I did. Just like old Alice up there did. Eddie smiled at the tippy-tippy-tapping of sixteen pairs of feet laid down at one time.

"This is not Agnes De Mille!" Eddie shouted. "This is not Martha Graham! This is that old-time religion! Pick 'em up and lay 'em down. Hoofin' is the name of the game and Fred Astaire is the fame."

Alice picked 'em up and laid 'em down. She gave Eddie the stomp and the clear, loud smack of the tap on wood. The youngsters watched the old girl go, the last of the red-hot mammas. The sweat gathered at her breasts and at her crotch. Bam, bam, bam! Pick 'em up and lay 'em down.

"Give that little lady in the blue blouse a cigar," Eddie said. Alice laughed, and the rest of the dancers laughed, and suddenly she felt so good she wanted to cry.

Eddie went up the steps two at a time and pranced across the stage. He threw his arm around Alice's shoulders, nearly having to reach up to do so.

"Now all you youngsters figured that old Eddie Barnes was going to throw away one of *your* jobs on an old girlfriend of his—right? Now you see for yourself how a trouper hoofs it. Anybody think I give her the job on a freebie?"

Alice half-turned toward Eddie to hide her face, thinking that the salad days might not be all gone, even if they were wilted a bit around the edges.

132

Eddie asked Alice to lunch and made it special by driving all the way up the Strip to Cyrano's instead of dumping into some hamburger joint close to the rehearsal hall. Cyrano's felt like show business.

A couple of people knew Eddie, and it made Alice feel important to be with someone who was known. They ordered salads and coffee, which came right away.

"I must drink twenty-two gallons of this a day," Eddie said. "My pee comes out with cream and sugar in it."

Alice laughed and Eddie placed his hand over hers. "We always could have a couple of laughs, couldn't we? Sometimes, when the nights get rough or hard times kick me in the teeth, I remember all those good times we had."

Alice wanted to remind him that they'd been playmates for only a few nights—nothing special—but she didn't want to hurt his pitch.

"You all alone, Eddie?"

"Alone as any man can be."

"Jesus, Eddie."

"He won't have anything to do with me either," Eddie joked.

Alice laughed again but wasn't certain if she was expected to.

"I wonder if maybe we could have a night on the town," Eddie said.

"I'm living with this guy."

"I'm not talking about anything hot and heavy. Not even warm. Just walkin' around for old times' sake," he pleaded.

Alice looked at his little monkey's face and wanted to cry for him, but even though Eddie was playing the tune on that string, he'd get mad if she did.

"What do you say?" he insisted.

"I don't know, Eddie. It's not like we were ever any hot number—"

"Who's in love at twenty-three or -four? I mean who's not in love with every goddamn body you meet? And that's the same as not. All I want is a date, Alice. A little conversation. Maybe even a good-night kiss." He leered humorously. "No more."

"O.K. Eddie, we'll work something out," Alice said, sorry that she would have to pay off for the job after all.

The salads came and they started to eat and talk about the show, the big number designed around the twenties. A couple of big old touring cars. Wasp-waisted, striped suits for the men. Light grey fedoras, worn down on one side like the memorable Capone. Shoulder holsters and Tommy guns. Molls with garters above their knees, fringed dresses, and tits bound tight to make them look like sexy boys. Hair cut like helmets; cloches of felt. Showgirls— long-legged, bit-titted, half-dressed. Broads all feathers and powdered flesh.

"It's a pain in the ass. It's been done to death. It's old hat," Eddie complained cheerfully. "But I'll make it an eye-popper."

"Hey, Eddie," Alice said, "how does an old hat get to be an old hat?"

She giggled at her silliness; he laughed excessively and squeezed her knee under the table. If Eddie had been possessed of a shrewder eye, he would have seen that a moment was at hand if he would grab it; if he had taken Alice to a handy motel, he would have had a young and eager fuck for sure.

But old Eddie had lost that touch; his nose was worn out. He made do with another squeeze.

"Let's set up a date for soon, Alice. Hell, we can

have a lot of laughs. Oh, yeah," he said, cutting his eyes toward her, "it wasn't easy what with the unions, but I got your friend a job as a gofer. Send her down to Western Costume first thing Monday morning. It's the best I could do."

"That's plenty. More than we hoped for," Alice said, knowing the ante had just gone up.

"I'm glad it is, Alice," Eddie said. "I'm really glad it is."

She went away feeling sad. What if Eddie was a different sort, a guy who'd sweep her up and keep her safe? What if he'd ask her to come live with him, throw Harry over? Would she be safe then?

She shuddered, feeling death in her bones, knowing that if she left with any man, Harry would kill to get her back. If she left on her own, this Harry who was coming out of the old Harry's skin—who had always lurked there, she was certain—was capable of murdering her just to teach her a lesson.

She closed out what she feared and went back to the rehearsal, changed into her patent leather shoes with the taps. She picked 'em up and laid 'em down.

22

They sat in the living room as solemn as an under-takers' convention. Harry knew that was all to the good. They were taking him and the conspiracy seri-ously. He knew that joking around and laughter, un-less bitter and acid, could be the death of action and revolution.

He called on Alice to give a report on what was going on down at the Academy Awards rehearsals. She stood up like a schoolgirl and told about her job, Janet's job and, after some prompting from Harry, the idea behind the big production number. When she was through, everyone but Marco applauded, and nobody thought it was a crazy thing to do.

Harry grinned all around.

"That's going to be the cover we use to get every-body within killing distance. That's going to be the place where we bring in the hidden guns," he said.

They looked attentive, but he simply winked and wouldn't say any more about the details.

"You're doing good, Alice. Now I want you to do a little more and go out with this Eddie."

"What for?" Alice asked.

"So you'll be close to his mouth in case he drops anything we can use."

"You mean you want me to fuck him?" Alice asked shrilly, in sudden anger.

"I didn't say that now, did I?" Harry snapped back. "You telling me you can't go out with this turkey a couple of times without laying down on your back? Play him a little, Alice. You haven't forgotten how, have you?"

He stared at her, daring her to come back at him, proving his power over her in front of the others.

Alice buckled under the pressure, dropped her eyes and shook her head.

"Damn right," Harry said. "You still got it, honey. That's why I'm always so hot for you."

Everybody laughed and he went over and hugged her. The stick and the carrot.

"I want you to get next to that midget," Harry said, "and ask for a couple of favors."

Alice reared back and started to protest, but Harry closed his teeth on her neck, and Alice knew it wasn't a playful gesture but a threat.

"What favors, Harry?" she asked after he released her.

"Eddie Barnes needs showgirls for that big production number, don't he? Well, we've got showgirls." Harry gestured toward Hush and Evelynn. "Two beautiful broads with long legs and big tits."

"What about me?" Assy said. "I ain't chopped liver."

Harry glanced at her as though he didn't trust her.

"You're somebody I don't know too well," Harry said. "I figure the rest of these people made a pledge to me and the cause last Saturday."

"What the hell, I was part of the ritual fuck—or whatever the hell that was supposed to be. A fuckin' booze and dope orgy is what it felt like."

"That's just what I'm saying. It was an everyday thing to you. No big deal. It meant something different to the rest of us."

"What the hell would you like me to do," Assy yelled, "to prove I'm in on this with you?"

"Would you kill?" Harry asked.

"Isn't that what this whole damn thing's all about? Ain't we going to knock off all those snotty bastards with their dirty secrets? I could tell you things. I could tell you about some of them. You wouldn't have to wonder if I've got reasons enough to knock off some of those cock-suckers!"

Her voice kept pace with her words, mounting higher and higher. "Who do you want me to kill?" she finally shouted at the top of her rage. Everyone but Harry recoiled from the power of it.

He stood there safe behind his vicious mask, then went into the hall and returned with the gun he hadn't used against the President. He cocked the weapon and handed it to Assy.

"You know how to fire it?" he asked softly.

"I know how to pull a trigger," she said, holding the automatic purposefully, without the slightest fear or awkwardness, straight out in front of her, finger curled around the trigger.

Harry's eyes flashed across the faces of everyone sitting so silently. He'd trapped himself into the moment and couldn't step away from it. Assy's response could affirm his leadership, his power, once and for all, but if he chose a target that she might refuse, he could end up on the wrong end of the play.

He stepped up close to Assy, placed his fingers around her wrist and, guiding her hand, passed over Bondi very slowly, tracked the room past Evelynn and Peewit, Hush and Janet, paused half a moment with the gun aiming at Alice's breast. She let out a laugh like a nervous hiccup, and the gun traveled on till the muzzle of it was pointed straight at Marco's heart. The old man tried to rise, but his knees were suddenly too weak to bear his weight. He floundered about on the sofa like an old grey fish, his mouth twisted in a grimace of terror. He gasped for breath that wouldn't come. Having no strength, he used the tricks of the weak and appeared weaker, hoping to elicit pity.

"Go ahead," Harry whispered. "Pull the trigger."

Assy's slender finger tightened as she stared into Marco's terrified face, hypnotized by something she saw there. Marco made a strangled sound and she laughed.

The hammer fell on emptiness with a dry snap like the breaking of a twig. Everyone exploded. They howled until tears rolled down their faces. Assy hugged Marco and swore that she'd known Harry would never have given her a loaded gun to kill one of their own. Marco lied that he'd known as much as well, hoping that no one would remark that his trousers were wet with urine.

The terror in his mouth was as rich as sour cream. He knew, without doubt or hope, that Harry Smiley and these other monsters meant to do exactly what they'd sworn they would do. He started to make frantic plans about an escape, listening with only a small part of his attention as Harry laid out the rough outline of his plan.

He leaned forward when he heard his name.

"When you write all this down, Marco," Harry said, "I suggest that you set it up in the form of dispatches and military orders. You know how to do that?"

"I'll go to the library and look up the proper forms," he heard himself saying, even as he thought that they were all evil, insane children playing at vicious games.

In the early hours of the morning, during the long

hours of drunkenness, coupling and new oaths, Harry and Marco remained somewhat aloof. Harry sat in his big chair, one leg outstretched, the other bent at the knee, an arm along the arm of the chair, the other raised in such a fashion that his fingertips were fanned out on his brow. It was a romantic pose, a thoughtful and judicious pose. He watched them all in their copulations with the eye of one who looked upon dogs and bitches.

Marco didn't join the others. He was naked because he sensed that there was safety in nakedness among this mad company. He drank nothing. He refused to smoke the marijuana or sniff the cocaine supplied by Hush. He sat with his hands folded on his groin and sorrowed after the human race and himself.

Once, in the near dark, Assy had come to him, her eyes bright and begging. She whispered to him that she'd truly known that the gun was not loaded. Marco was certain she lied, that she hadn't known the chamber was empty and in her rage hadn't cared. She placed her hand on his shriveled manhood and seemed to know and regret the soul-destroying fright she'd caused him. She offered to arouse him with her mouth. He wanted to say to her that such an act would soil him beyond cleansing, but he was afraid to speak. He was saved from the horror of the succubus by Bondi's renewed demands upon her.

Marco was still awake when dawn broke outside the window. He rose, feeling the cold and age seep through him. He dressed himself as Harry watched and then went to the door.

"Be careful, old man," Harry said.

Marco nodded and left to find his own way home.

140

23

At one time, assassins were forced to close with their victims with knife or garrote, to meet the death they traded in face to face. Today's terrorist most often kills at a distance with a long rifle, plastic dynamite, the explosive letter and the radio-triggered bomb, killing impersonally, sometimes indiscriminately. The handgun, grenade and cyanide spray may shorten the killing distance but are no more intimate.

Harry had his "war souvenir," Peewit a small collection of hunting rifles, Hush a Baretta she kept in her purse and another in the nightstand beside her bed. Bondi liked guns but couldn't afford them, Alice feared them, Evelynn avoided them, Janet was curious about them, Marco abhorred them, and Assy was eager to become expert in their use.

Willard Geneva loved them, repaired them, collected them, spent most of his earnings on them, and if it were possible would have had intercourse with them. He worked in the Frontier Gun Emporium on Ventura Boulevard in Tarzana.

The shop sold everything—rifles, automatics, semiautomatics, breech and muzzle loaders, lever-, bolt- and pump-action long guns. They had blue-steeled ranks of handguns in every known make and caliber; pistols, derringers, palm guns, revolvers;

old, new and historic. They had cannon from both world wars, Korea and Nam stored in a shed at the back. They had bazookas, rocket launchers, mortars, machine guns—air and water cooled. They had a supply of ammunition large enough to kill off the population of Detroit.

And they had twenty-two vintage Thompson machine guns, the infamous Tommy guns of the gangster era, plugged with lead according to the law, but exact twins of the replicas that would be used in the Oscar show.

Willard showed off his expertise. "Hell, all you got to do is heat up the barrels and melt out the lead. Ream 'em out, rebore, regroove, mill 'em for the ammo you want to use and *breek!* they fire just as good as when Dillinger and Capone shot up the pea patch. How many you want to buy, Harry?"

"Eight, maybe," Harry said.

"Shee-it! You kiddin' me? What would you do with eight of them things?"

Harry grinned one of his "don't-fuck-with-me" smiles. "How much, Willard?"

"They're collector's items."

"Don't sell me—tell me."

"Eight hundred apiece."

"I'm negotiating for eight of them."

"Well, I suppose Jack would discount 'em ten percent."

"Say fifty-seven and a half."

Willard smiled. "Shall I wrap 'em up?"

"Sheee-it!" Harry said, waved jauntily and went on out.

"Money? I haven't got any money," Hush said.

"There's nine of us. I'm talking about maybe six hundred and fifty bucks apiece."

"Evelynn and I haven't got anything like thirteen hundred dollars."

"I don't believe it. You said you wanted a piece of the action. Was that just a fart in the wind?"

"Bondi hasn't got it. He's living on the arm with you right now. The old man hasn't got it, for sure. That Assy's got a sockful, but she wouldn't part with six hundred dollars to witness the resurrection of Valentino's pecker."

"What the hell are we talking about here?" Harry shouted. "What has the money got to do with it? We're talking about an act of violent protest. We're talking about glory."

"You sure you're not talking about a way out, Harry?" Hush said in her coolest voice.

"What the hell is that supposed to mean?"

"You're talking about mass murder on the one hand and buying the guns to do it on the other."

"We don't want to paint signs with arrows pointing to us."

"Guns are stolen every day, Harry. We're not the only ones in town with a use for guns."

Harry stared at her, not liking the confidence she displayed in her opinion.

Hush brushed her hair back in a very feminine gesture. "Are you thinking about it, Harry?"

"Yeah."

"I'll bet you're thinking that stealing the guns would be a chance to prove some things. We don't know who's really ready for blood, even with that little charade between Assy and Marco; no killer and no victim. Training a dog to go for the throat isn't much good unless you really give it a throat to go for."

"We're going to steal those guns," Harry said.

"That seems much the best idea," Hush said.

Metzler sat on a bench in Venice, shoulder to shoulder with Marco, watching the front of the Cadillac Hotel getting a many-colored new paint job.

"What do you think?" Metzler asked.

Marco didn't reply but smiled to let the young man know that he was giving his question sociable consideration. He glanced up at the name of the hotel painted in red letters on a yellow background surrounded by a green border.

"One shouldn't eat much before looking at it," he finally said.

Metzler laughed.

"But the painter seems happy, and that's the most important thing," Marco added.

"You see much of it?"

"I live in the hotel."

"You're lucky, living right by the ocean. I live up in town, West Hollywood."

Marco felt a slight warning along his spine.

"You know it?" Metzler asked.

"I have a friend there."

"No kidding," Metzler said as though that were the most marvelous coincidence. "Whereabouts?"

"Broom Street," Marco said, feeling that the answer had been forced out of him somehow.

"You're kidding me."

"Why do you say that?"

"I live on Broom Street. What's your friend's address?"

"Forty-eight, I believe," Marco said, standing up, anxious to be on his way.

"That's something. I live at ninety-six. Just a hop, skip and a jump. Come to think of it, I think I might have seen you a couple of Saturdays ago when I was out walking my dog."

144

"It's been nice talking to you, mister," Marco said, "but I really have to go."

"Metzler. The name's Metzler." He stood up. "Why don't you tell your friend that? He might know me."

Metzler wanted to rattle Harry Smiley's cage. He was hoping something—anything—would shake out. There wasn't a damn thing else he could do.

24

The Frontier Gun Emporium was well lit and exposed to view along a well-traveled boulevard, but it had been robbed twice during the previous year by simple smash and grab and so was protected by an alarm system of considerable complexity. An alley ran along the back of the shop, with a beauty salon on one side and a pet store on the other. A late special customer in the one and alert animals in the other would have to be considered. Signs on both announced a daily closing time of six o'clock. The heavy wooden back door was covered with sheet iron, its single window barred.

Willard Geneva showed Hush several handguns, nearly tipping over on his nose trying to look down her blouse, as Harry noted that the back door was deadlocked and heavily braced with a length of heavy strap iron slotted into sturdy hasps.

He could see no electric eyes but knew there might be some concealed in such a way that only a much closer inspection would show them up. There were acoustical detectors spotted along the coving, ready to pick up the slightest sound. Harry was struck by the difficulties revealed in even this preliminary and minor invasion.

How the hell were they going to get in? What would he tell the others in order to impress them with his planning abilities? He didn't know how to deal with the wired alarms or the sonic detectors and couldn't be sure that there weren't other, more sophisticated devices around the place. All of a sudden he had to pee.

"I got to wring out my sock," he said to Willard.

"In the back. Don't waste too much time. The boss doesn't like customers using it," Willard advised.

Harry found his way to the toilet; stood pissing away some of his tension. He looked above his head and saw a window too small to put a monkey through. There were two similar ones in the back workroom. Nothing doing. He went back to the main store. Hush looked up and winked at him. Suddenly Harry felt reassured.

"Anything you like?" he asked her.

"I'm really afraid of guns, Harry. Maybe I shouldn't get one at all. I'd end up shooting myself instead of a prowler."

"I don't like to think of you alone in that canyon house without a gun," Harry said, playing along with her.

"You wouldn't be afraid of it once you learned to use it," Willard said judiciously.

"But I don't know how," she said.

Harry knew she did. Very well.

Willard shifted from one foot to the other. "Harry's a pretty fair shot."

"Hell, I couldn't teach her. Besides, I got no time," Harry said.

"I got plenty of time," Willard said eagerly.

Hush bent over the counter, looked into his eyes and said, with her buttery English accent, "Would you really be so kind as to teach me to shoot?"

Willard stared down her blouse.

Harry grinned. "Watch yourself or you'll be falling

into her blouse and getting smothered between her tits."

Willard snapped up straight as a post.

"Stop teasing Willard," Hush purred. "You're making him blush."

"It's O.K., Willard. Hush doesn't mind a little kidding. She's one of the boys."

"Hardly that," Hush flirted.

They all laughed. Willard was still laughing, his hand in his pocket, when they left.

Harry tried to act thoughtful, because he didn't know what to say. He had no plans or ideas. But that business about gun lessons told him Hush had some idea.

"Smash and grab won't do it," she finally said. "There's no way of breaking into the place and taking out that many guns on the sneak. We'll need inside help. You agree?"

"I cased it all over, front and back. I couldn't see any way in. Bondi might be able to disconnect the alarm."

"Is he that good with electronics?"

"He can fix damn near anything that's got a plug and a wire, but I don't know."

"It'd be taking a chance for nothing if there's a better key."

"You got one?"

Hush smiled. "Me."

She called Willard on Tuesday morning and did a number on him. By the time she was through, he had the idea that she'd practically promised to fuck him in exchange for a couple of lessons on the two-hundred-inch target range in the back of the shop.

148

She maneuvered the time and the place—after twelve on Wednesday night.

Willard never even stopped to question why a woman as beautiful as Hush was ready to lie down for a twenty-dollar lesson on pulling the trigger of a handgun.

Hush left home fifteen minutes after eleven in order to get to the shop in the Valley at twelve. Ten minutes later Harry, Assy, Bondi and Peewit followed.

They were dressed in black pants, sweaters, watch caps; carried black stocking masks in their pockets. Peewit and Bondi carried two large slings made of dark blue canvas with rope handles, Assy a suitcase. The three of them also wore sheath knives, and Hush carried a length of cord under her belt.

Hush scratched on the iron-sheathed door right on the hour. Willard opened it immediately, grinning like a fool, his lips looking parched in the harsh light of the workshop. She went around him as neat as a cat and he slammed the bolt home.

"You're pretty noisy," Hush said.

He leered. "Nobody around to hear."

She glanced up at a detector cone.

"Those things don't get turned on till the place is locked up for the night."

Willard went over to the test bench, where six guns of various designs were laid out, their butts facing the shooter. He cleared his throat, eyed Hush and waved her over.

"I figured it might be a good idea for you to get the feel of different kinds of handguns," he said.

Hush moved over to him, smiling. "Show me your favorite weapon," she said.

"Jesus Christ," Willard moaned and grabbed at her. She ducked away, laughing. A car pulled up in the alley. Willard was grinning like a man in pain. He grabbed for her again. She laughed with a sound that was deliberately tantalizing and escaped his outstretched hands, rolled along the wall and past the door, her arm raised to fend him off. Her elbow caught the bolt and slammed it back against the staples. She cried out in pain.

"Hurt yourself?" Willard asked, stepping forward. The door slammed open and caught Willard full in the face. He cried out as blood began to stream from his nose. Futilely he raised his hand to try to wipe it away.

Four black figures pushed their way into the shop, faces grotesquely distorted by the black stockings they wore over their heads.

Willard started to cry out, and Assy slapped him across the face with one hand while she held her knife to his throat with the other.

"Shut the fuck up," she said, her voice clotted with excitement.

Peewit went to the workbench and tucked a .38 Police Special into his waistband. Bondi took a heavy Luger, then looked around.

"Where're the Tommy guns, Harry?"

"For Christ's sake," Harry exploded.

"Harry? Harry, what the fuck you doing here?" Willard screamed. "What the hell kind of game is this?" He stepped toward Harry, ignoring the knife in Assy's hand.

"This a joke?" He looked at Hush with a foolish grin on his face. "You set me up for a joke?"

Hush removed the cord from around her waist. She glanced at Harry, who stood frozen by the sudden need to make a decision about Willard Geneva.

He looked like a middle-aged man ready for a can of beer in front of the television set, not a leader making life-and-death decisions.

A couple of dogs next door were setting up a clamor.

Without warning, Willard rushed at Harry, hands coming up as though he meant to push him out of the shop.

"Get the hell out of here, Harry," he yelled. "Just get the hell out of here."

Assy's knife went in just beneath his upraised arm on the right side.

"Jesus Christ, you got a big mouth, Willard," Harry complained. "Why did you have to let on you knew it was me? There's a lot of Harrys in the world."

Willard's mouth gaped open, ready to cry out in pain and alarm. Hush stepped up behind him and placed the cord around his neck. She put her knee in the small of his back and pulled with all her strength. His hands, clutching at the wound in his side, now rose to free his throat of the garrote. Assy moved in again and stabbed him in the belly. He thrashed about, a horrible clattering sound like clogged drains coming from his chest. Hush dragged on the rope harder, her eyes becoming desperate with her desire for Willard to quit struggling.

"Kill him," she grated. "Kill him."

"Why'd you open your damned mouth, Willard?" Harry said.

"Kill him," Hush said again.

Assy changed her grip on the knife, raised it overhead, and plunged it into his chest. Willard sagged.

Hush's lips touched the back of his neck as gently as a lover's kiss; then she jerked away, letting him fall to the floor. She looked at Assy. Both were breathing hard with sexual arousal.

They drove through the silent Valley streets, Hush and Peewit in one car, Harry, Assy and Bondi in the other.

Assy sat between the two men, her legs jiggling, her tongue flickering out to wet her lips, wanting to fuck. Had either of the men suggested it, she would have agreed to be taken by them in the backseat of the car, one right after the other.

Hush too was stirred by lust. As she drove, she looked down at the hard thighs of the aging fighter sitting next to her and was filled with desire for him and for his wife.

Once in the house, they couldn't rest and strode from room to room, chattering steadily. They were charged up, and when Hush touched the languid Evelynn on the shoulder, the passive girl was electrified. She rose to be taken in Hush's arms. Bondi caressed Assy's buttocks as she passed him. She took his face in her hands and brought his mouth to hers. Peewit felt young and horny. He looked for Janet but immediately considered her too familiar a partner and began to fondle Alice in a demanding way.

Of them all, Harry was the coolest, almost sleepy as he moved about like a lion that has fed too well.

In the end, as casually as though they were wild animals, he fell upon Janet, Peewit upon Alice, Bondi upon Hush, and Assy upon the old man. Evelynn was passed among them all.

Metzler arrived at the Frontier Gun Emporium representing LAPD Intelligence, which investigated all major weapons thefts.

Willard Geneva was sprawled face down in his own blood, eyes open, tongue gripped between his teeth.

"Hell of a lot of blood," Metzler said matter-of-factly to Roanoke, senior cop on the scene.

"Knife went in seven times front and side," Roanoke said.

"Defensive wounds on the hands?"

"Sliced up from the nylon cord he was choked with."

"You've got it?"

"Yeah."

"Stabbed *and* throttled?"

"Two killers. At least two," Roanoke said.

"What was stolen?"

"Haven't inventoried yet." Roanoke glanced across at a man in jeans and workshirt being questioned by two plainclothes cops. "There's the owner. You want to talk to him?"

"I'll take what you get for now."

"Good."

"How does it shape?"

Roanoke thought for a minute, squinting one eye at the corpse as though waiting for the word.

"They wanted guns. He had a hundred and twenty bucks in his wallet and a good watch on his wrist. Untouched. They wanted guns."

"They bypassed the alarms?"

Roanoke shook his head. "The deceased must have let them in. No signs of breaking and entering. Amateurs."

"Because they worked it from the inside?"

"No, because it took so many knife blows to do the job. Sign of panic."

"Or frenzy."

Roanoke nodded.

"What's that smudge on the back of his neck?" Metzler asked. He had sharp eyes. Cop's eyes.

"Lipstick."

"A woman."

"Maybe two. We found a broken fingernail with pink polish snagged in the victim's sweater."

"Why two women?" Metzler asked with a touch of rising excitement in his voice.

"I'm told by the policewoman the shades of lipstick and nail polish just don't go together."

"Two women," Metzler said with a note of speculation.

"You got a thought?" Roanoke asked, altered by Metzler's eagerness. "Got any female suspects you can give me?"

"Nothing that big. Just a hunch."

"Watch yourself."

"What do you mean?"

"You'll end up forcing facts to fit a case that won't wash."

Metzler nodded in agreement, but his sense of expectation wouldn't go away.

Michael awakened in the dawn with his body bathed in sweat. He'd had a nightmare filled with ghosts. One of them had Harry Smiley's face.

A hand gently stroked his back. He rolled over to see Sheri regarding him solemnly, her eyes bruised and weary.

"Was it very bad?" she said.

"Just nerved up," he said, slipping out of bed. "Got a location today. Way the hell out in the desert somewhere. And I have to drive all the way into the studio for the limo."

"Why didn't you have it sent here?"

"I'd just as soon not many people knew where this place was. You go back to sleep. I'm going to take a little walk on the beach before I go."

154

He walked the cold sands, looking off to sea where there was nothing, not even a wisp of smoke from a freighter's stack. He tried to recall the dream; managed the substance but not the spirit of it. He returned to the house to find Sheri fast asleep now that she was separated from his terrors of the night.

The roads were fairly empty at that hour. He enjoyed it for a while and then began to feel a mounting tension and anxiety as he approached the studio gates. By the time he arrived at the gatehouse, adrenalin was pumping into his blood, his hands were trembling, and his mouth tasted of gall. He saw the guard, mysterious behind his sunglasses, leave the shack as Michael slowed for the traffic arm. Rage exploded in him.

"G'morning, Mr. Nordland."

It wasn't Harry Smiley. Michael looked at his hands, white-knuckled on the wheel, and managed a good morning that sounded like the greeting of a frog.

"Transportation's over by the commissary, sir. Coffee wagon, too."

Michael continued to sit where he was, not trusting his ability to drive the car with the weakness in his legs caused by the rush of adrenalin with nowhere to go. The guard touched the peak of his cap and sent the arm up.

Harry drove out along the straight stretch of road that seemed to rise before the hood of his car to the curve of the horizon. The air was very clear and crisp, almost cold, the sun not yet warming the sands. He spotted a snake crossing the highway, touched the wheel and felt the slight jar as he ran it over.

He regretted having to go to work after the success of the raid, but he had to stay in tight with Charlie

Clabber, assistant chief now, and someone who was potentially useful.

Up ahead he saw the structure of the tower built of steel and cardboard and plastic, part of the set of Michael Nordland's latest film. The windows on the honey wagons, portable dressing rooms and other service vehicles left on the shooting site caught the sun and sent back blazing reflections.

The night guard came out of the trailer at the sound of Harry braking on the hardpack. They exchanged hollow morning greetings, and the man went off in his own vehicle as though escaping the silence and the loneliness.

Harry set up a folding card table beneath a canvas fly, arranged a camp chair in the shade of it and laid out a hand of solitaire. The crew had nearly all arrived by the time he'd cheated himself into winning the first game.

When the caterer pulled up in his truck, Harry was right there, first in line, waiting for the hot coffee and donuts.

"Always up front for the freebies, huh, Harry?" the caterer said, laughing.

"Go fuck yourself," Harry said.

He was stuffing himself when the limousine carrying Michael Nordland pulled up.

He got out of the cool interior into the glaring sun. His glasses threw back reflections. He seemed blind, pale, unsure of himself. He looked straight at Harry, then walked to the commissary truck as though it were a much-hated but necessary act.

He ordered a coffee and a pair of donuts. Other members of the cast and crew were suddenly milling about, crowding the counter. Michael moved aside, bumped into Harry, then looked at him when Harry wouldn't give way an inch. Michael pushed a bit harder, tight-lipped and silent. Harry's arm jerked. He spilled the hot coffee on Michael's leg. It looked almost deliberate.

Michael turned on Harry. "What the hell you up to, fella?" he demanded.

"What do you mean, Mr. Nordland?" Harry replied. He wasn't able to keep the impertinence out of his voice.

"You out to ride my ass?" Michael accused loudly.

Members of the cast and crew within earshot looked to see who was getting reamed.

"I don't know what you're talking about," Harry protested. He heard the whine in his voice and hated himself for it. "I'm not looking for any trouble with you."

"You made some smart-ass remark to me the first time I laid eyes on you."

"I just said I was at Century City—"

"About seeing me at that tavern in Calabasas," Michael interrupted.

Harry smirked, as if to say that Michael was certainly a little odd to take exception to something as innocent as that.

"You did it again at The Puck," Michael heard himself going on. He felt that Harry had taken the advantage from him.

"Jesus Christ," Harry said in exaggerated exasperation, looking at all the witnesses, asking them to mark down the ridiculous things this arrogant, quarrelsome, half-witted actor was saying.

Michael did feel like a damn fool. How could he explain that Harry had twice seen him apparently back down from a fight? How could he make rational the fear and anger he felt against Harry for invading his dreams? It was insanity to make a man an enemy because of such things. But it was real. At the same time, Michael knew he'd been maneuvered into the role of the powerful egoist stomping on some poor little bugger trying to make a living.

"I don't know what you're threatening me for, sir," Harry said loudly. "I know there's nothing I can do to defend myself if you want to get tough with me, but I'd sure like to know why you should treat me like dirt in front of everybody."

Michael turned away, frustrated and still enraged.

"I'm just a working stiff," Harry ran on, feeling his own fury rich in his mouth. He looked around for support. Some people nodded and gave him the thumb. Even some of those who disliked Harry gave him their support because they secretly disliked Nordland more for having made it big.

Harry was about to say something more, but Michael was a distance away.

Michael went to the assistant director.

"I want that son of a bitch off my picture," he said.

"What's he done?"

"I don't want to go into my reasons. I just want his ass off the set."

"I'll have to talk to the production supervisor," the AD said reasonably.

"Talk to anybody you want to, but get that bastard gone."

"The union's going to raise hell."

"For Christ's sake, don't debate with me. Either he goes, or I don't step in front of the camera."

The assistant went off to speak to the production supervisor, who listened with head lowered, disputed gently, shrugged his shoulders, and finally walked over to give Harry the word. Michael

158

watched from a distance. Harry turned red in the face, waved his hands about, grinned furiously, and glanced in Michael's direction.

With the sunglasses both wore like huge eyes, they faced each other across the sand. Two great lizards ready to fight.

25

Sheri was behind the wheel of her little Mercedes, Michael relaxing alongside her as they drove the two-lane blacktop toward Valyermo in the hour after midnight. He'd called her at noon to say that the day's shooting, if it was allowed to run into overtime, would wrap up the location. It was Sheri's suggestion that she drive out to get him for the drive home. They might stop in Wrightwood for the night and enjoy a stolen pine-mountain holiday.

Sheri glanced at Michael lying back with his head against the leather seat, his face dimly lit by the lights of the instrument panel and showing a deep weariness.

"Tired?"

"Some. Sorry I haven't got much to say."

"I understand. I don't mind if you're quiet."

"I should have been quiet earlier in the day. I should have kept my mouth shut."

"Oh?"

"I ripped into that guard Harry Smiley."

"Who?"

"That character who got smart-ass at The Puck."

"I remember him. Somehow he scares the hell out of me," Sheri said.

"I hate the son of a bitch. But I shouldn't have gotten him thrown off the set."

"Fired?"

"I doubt that. Union's too strong. But a complaint against a part-time guard can't do any good."

"I'm not sorry you rousted him, Michael."

"Well, I wish I'd handled it differently."

Lights came up behind them. Sheri reached up and flipped the mirror to night driving, getting the high-beam reflections out of her eyes.

Michael straightened up.

"Thanks for the ride, lady," he said and leaned over to kiss her just as a station wagon roared up alongside, rocketing fender to fender for a quarter of a mile before pulling away, horn blaring shatteringly. Sheri jerked hard at the wheel, nearly throwing the Mercedes into a skid as the back wheel caught the sandy shoulder.

"Jesus Christ," Michael exploded.

The distant taillights winked on and off derisively, then disappeared around a bend about a mile ahead.

Sheri drove with both hands tightly gripping the wheel as her heartbeat slowed to normal. They passed a dirt road on the right, but Michael, alert now, could see nothing lurking there. Then, suddenly, the wagon was tailgating them again, horn blaring deafeningly, headlights blazing into the Mercedes. The unseen driver gunned the motor and pushed the heavy vehicle against the bumper of the smaller car.

Sheri tramped down on the gas and the Mercedes lurched forward, the engine protesting as the RPMs went over the top. Then she slammed the stick shift into fifth, and the scream eased off. They were doing a hundred and ten along a stretch of road blowing with fine sand; a hundred and ten down a hypnotic tunnel of light created by their own headlights.

The bones of Sheri's wrists began to ache from the

tension of her hands on the wheel. Michael glanced sharply behind them, but the wagon wasn't there.

They blasted through a roadside service area—gas pumps, shack, small café—that was closed for the night. Low-wattage bulbs blurred into a smudge of light against the night sky. Something—a dog or a coyote—dashed across the road. Sheri instinctively cut the wheel, but the car shuddered at some soft impact, and there was an impression of something flung off to the side.

She touched the brakes. The high-powered machine responded, wheels locked, the steering slewed around. The Mercedes rocked on its suspension as it went into a sidelong skid across the film of sand. Sheri hit the gas to pull the car out of the uncontrolled skid, and when they were straightened out, they were facing back the way they'd come. She'd accelerated to seventy before she was aware of it. The station wagon was approaching at equal speed or better. The lights of the Mercedes shone on the windshield of the wagon, illuminating the inside of it for a flash before the driver turned away and swept past them, fender touching fender.

Sheri touched the brakes again, this time deliberately putting the car into a controlled skid, turning it around a full one hundred and eighty degrees.

"Pull into the station," Michael said tightly.

The Mercedes bucked forward, and there was the station wagon bearing down on them again, out to kill. Sheri swung the wheel hard, running the powerful car off the road onto the tarmac service area, braking, skidding and finally slamming into the corner of the café.

Michael instinctively threw up his arm as he hit the padded dash. Sheri screamed out in pain. There was a moment of silence following the impact; then the station wagon went by a last time, its horn hooting at them in the desert night.

Sheri grasped a wrist with the other hand as a light went on in the small house behind the café. A dog came running toward them, barking furiously.

Michael told Mr. August and his wife Emma that he'd rather they didn't call the police, but it was already too late for that. While Mr. August had gotten into his clothes, Emma had called the law first thing.

They arrived, two men in a sheriff's car, respectful and concerned when they saw whom they were dealing with.

"You say you were coming back from location out near Hi Vista?"

"That's right."

"Pretty late."

"They didn't have any sleeping facilities on the location. It was just as easy going toward home than away from it."

"You stop anywhere?"

"Stop?"

"You know, like for a sandwich or a cup of coffee at some diner?"

"No, we didn't. Why?"

The deputy shrugged and smiled pleasantly. "Thought maybe some jealous damn fool got a look at a famous person with a beautiful girl, driving an expensive automobile, and decided to have himself a little fun."

"Maybe so," Michael said.

"On the other hand, it might—just might—be somebody who was waiting for you. You have any trouble with anybody recently? Anybody got reason to go after you?"

Sheri looked up from the wrist Emma was bandaging and waited for Michael's answer. The deputy caught the inquiry in her eyes as Michael shrugged in pretended confusion.

"You say it was a station wagon, sir?"

"Yes."

"Recognize the make or year?"

"I'm not much good at that sort of thing," Michael said.

"You, miss?"

"It was a big wagon. Not one of the compacts. Not a late model, but I can't be more definite than that."

"Color?"

"Tan," Michael said.

"Off-white," Sheri said.

"You know anybody who owns a station wagon?"

Michael gave a helpless laugh. "I must know dozens. I guess a lot of people do."

"You couldn't see the other driver's face?"

"He had the panel lights off," Michael said quickly. Sheri glanced at him expectantly again. "We were running at top speed and were scared half out of our wits."

"I can understand that," the deputy said. "I can surely understand that."

"Is it busted, Emma?" the older deputy asked.

"Sprained, I think."

"Better get her to Doc Porter's for an X ray. Stay on the safe side."

"We'd rather drive on into Los Angeles," Michael said. "I'll take the lady to her own doctor."

"We'd feel better if you came into town with us. Besides, I don't think that car of yours will drive."

"Won't," August said. "Tie rod's busted."

"See?" the cop said.

"Anything I can rent?" Michael asked Mr. August.

"This girl ought to be in bed," Emma said.

"No," Sheri protested. "I want to go home."

"I've got a car you can rent," Mr. August said.

Michael stood up and took out his billfold. "I'll see that you get it back sometime tomorrow."

He went off to the side with Mr. August and completed the transaction. He held out an extra twenty.

"I'd rather the papers didn't get hold of this."

"You don't have to pay me to respect your privacy, Mr. Nordland," August said, "but there'll be a police report, and Willy Bester—he owns the weekly— checks the blotter every morning and night. He'll phone it in to the city papers for sure. Extra money."

"I'll pay him."

"That's a lot of trouble. I mean, you can't pay everybody, can you? When you're famous, everybody's interested."

Michael drove the old rented sedan along the desert road that climbed into the cool mountains. Dawn was breaking in the east. The emptiness seemed threatening, not soothing. Sheri, unable to sleep, slouched against the corner of the seat, her eyes heavy and grainy.

"It was that joker Harry Smiley, wasn't it?" she said.

"We can't be sure of that."

"It looked like him."

"We only got a flash."

"Why does he hate us?"

"Me," Michael said.

"Why?"

"I don't know." The rising inflection of his voice suggested there was more, or that he was puzzled. "I guess I do know, in a way."

Sheri waited quietly.

"The newspapers, the magazines, most of all the

165

TV, pounds it into everybody that there are winners and losers. Some people turn a card and have it all—instant fame, respect, more money than they know, sensibly, what to do with. Some other poor bastard works his ass off all his life and comes up with a busted straight. Out of the money. Out of the game. There's not a hell of a lot of difference between them. At least the guy holding the dirty end of the stick doesn't think so."

"But why you out of all the world?" Sheri asked.

"It happened that Smiley and I were in the same place at the same time. At Century City when that woman tried to kill the President. The difference was that I was in the scene and Smiley was just watching it. But then he yelled out and—for a little, little while—he was getting some of the attention I get too damn much of. For just a minute Smiley was pointed out in the crowd, became a character player in an act of history, was somebody.

"But when it came down to feeding it to the public, he was shoved aside again by more important people and—as far as the attack was concerned—somebody not really so important as the plain citizen who cried out. I was somebody famous, and events made it pretty clear that Smiley was nobody at all."

They drove in silence for several miles.

"I'll talk to Smiley," Michael finally said.

26

There was a short alley at the back of the cottages on Broom Street. The garages serving them faced it. Most of the tenants left their cars on the street and used the garages for storage, hobbies or other things.

Harry's was furnished with a tool bench, seldom used, and a scattering of tools badly in need of maintenance. He had no particular love for tools and was clumsy in their use.

Peewit and Bondi both had an instinctive affection for tools of all sorts. It took no time at all for Bondi to clear the bench of all but the tools that might prove useful. Peewit followed behind him, setting out his own carefully kept toolbox, a wide assortment of taps, dies, reamers, wrenches, and a vise for working metal. He brought along a metal lathe which was carefully bolted to the bench. When they were finished it couldn't compare to the setup in the gun shop, but it was enough for what they had to do.

One by one they filed free the bead of metal that welded shut the machine guns at barrel and receiver. They both found pleasure in the work. Harry looked in once or twice, rubbed his hands together, and went away looking pleased. The last time, he ran into Hush walking across the court from her place to his, a newspaper under her arm. She followed him into his house and tapped the front page.

That conscientious newspaper editor and publisher, Willy Bester, had called in the story of the automobile attack on the famous movie actor Michael Nordland and his female companion. It must have been a fairly slow news day, because the item got first-page treatment in the *Times*. It reported the facts clearly enough and, in a final paragraph, deplored the random violence that threatened citizens everywhere and anywhere. Hush read it aloud to Harry.

"You, Harry?"

"I don't own a station wagon."

"Don't play games with me," Hush said tightly. "Bondi does. It's sitting right over there with a smashed-up fender."

Harry grinned. "That wreck's got three out of four smashed-up fenders."

"If you've got any brains at all, you'll get it the hell out of here. Tell that kid to hammer out the dents, maybe give it a paint job. But not around here."

"You're making one hell of a lot out of a coincidence."

"Just think what anybody else could make of it," Hush said. "Why?" she asked after a long silence. "What got you pissed off at Nordland this time?"

"The son of a bitch had me thrown off the location."

"So what?"

"So nobody treats me like a fucking dog."

"You keep pushing at that man and he's going to lean on you, Harry."

"He hasn't got the balls. He's a fucking coward, and he knows I know it."

"He'll find help then to get you off his back. He'll make waves. Just leave that man alone."

"Mind your own business," Harry said.

Hush handed him the refolded newspaper. "It's all yours."

"What the hell's the matter with you?"

"It's all yours, Harry. I'm stepping out."

Harry moved up close to her in the narrow hallway, backing her off a step or two until her hip struck the little table underneath the mirror.

"You're not going to do that," Harry said.

"Oh, yes, I am," Hush said, standing her ground. "You can play general without this soldier."

Harry reached for her wrist, keeping his eyes on her mouth and throat, but couldn't find it because her hands were behind her back.

"It won't look good to the others if you split," Harry said.

"That's right. Your whole damn scheme'll fall apart. They'll take it as a reason to quit. Armies break up fast when the troops start to desert."

"You're my executive officer, Hush. I can't let you run out on me."

His hands went to her shoulders, the thumbs lying along the slender collarbones, fingers curling around the back of her neck.

"I'd be walking, Harry," Hush said.

It felt as though she'd poked him with a finger. He looked down. His automatic was in his belly. He'd never heard the drawer open. As he watched, her thumb flicked the safety off.

"We'll consult." He smiled with some admiration.

"I'm going to put this gun down now, Harry. You get all over tough with me and I'll get mine back some other time."

Harry backed up, laughing, his hands raised in surrender.

"You'll have your chance at Nordland, Harry," Hush said. "The fucker's favored for an Oscar."

Metzler read the item on the "accident" involving Nordland out on the desert road. A light-colored station wagon, not old, not new. He remembered the vehicle driven by the big kid Arnold Bondi.

He checked the address he had obtained from DMV and took a drive to find out if the kid was still living there. He wasn't. His landlady told Metzler that her tenant had lost his job in some radio shop. She had a forwarding address, although, she said, Bondi had never received anything but bills and junk mail. "48 Broom Street."

He called Michael Nordland's home in Brentwood and was informed by a young woman identifying herself as Nordland's private secretary that the actor was at his beach house, but she wouldn't give out that number without express permission. She did give Metzler the number of Jim Truman, who, she said, might advise him further.

Truman wanted to know what the LAPD wanted with his friend and client.

"Just a few routine questions."

"I know that dodge. What routine? What questions?"

"Concerning the incident on the road from Valyermo."

"Some nut, drunk or crazy."

"Probably, but my assignment is Intelligence. That covers threats made on the lives of celebrities, politicians, and persons prominent in the news. Sometimes we spot the potentially dangerous crazies by incidents similar to the one that happened to your client."

"That sounds good," Truman said. "What's your badge number?"

Metzler gave it.

"Give me a telephone number where you can be reached in ten minutes."

"Right here," Metzler said and read off the number on his desk phone.

Eight minutes later it rang, and it was Truman.

"I called Lieutenant Jill. You check out. My client's at the studio. Three o'clock all right with you?"

"Yes."

"I'll have a pass left at the main gate for you. That's on Pico."

"I know."

Metzler went over to the forensic lab. Philip Waite, the technician assigned to the gun-shop murder, handed Metzler several sheets of paper.

"Can you tell me?" Metzler asked, trusting Waite to pare off the fat.

"Sure. Sixteen Thompson submachine guns, a Luger and a .38 Police Special were stolen. And a lot of ammunition."

"Any more on the two women?"

"What two women?"

"The one who left the lipstick on the back of the victim's neck. The one who left a fingernail caught in Geneva's sweater. The two women Roanoke told me about at the scene."

"Roanoke's a romantic. He reads detective stories. He thinks—hopes—we can take a fingernail and tell him age, sex, weight and color of eyes. He prays that somebody'll find ten perfect prints and a palm, an old calling card lodged in a chair cushion, or a corner torn off an envelope."

"Then what have you got?"

"Nothing except reasonable assumptions. Maybe a girlfriend kissed him on the back of the neck and he hadn't washed it off yet."

Metzler made a face.

"More than possible," Waite said. "The fingernail could have come from the girl at the place where he got the sweater cleaned. A lot more than possible."

"So you've got nothing?"

Waite picked up a glassine envelope with a pale blue cord coiled in it.

"That the garrote that was used?" Metzler asked.

"Yes. It's a nylon cord used by one manufacturer of lanyards."

"Military?"

"Could be. Could be used around sailing craft. Police. Private security."

"Can you pin it down?"

"Too much of it sold. I think it came from a whistle or a key ring. Something like that."

Metzler was quiet.

"Anything?" Waite asked.

"Suspicion."

"Not evidence?"

"Not if that blue cord's as common as you say it is."

"Common as dirt."

Metzler nodded and glanced over the sheets in his hand. The first was a typewritten inventory of the items found in Willard Geneva's pockets. The usual things—handkerchief, billfold, small change, comb and address book.

The next couple of pages listed all the names, addresses and telephone numbers in the book. Metzler's eye ran down the page, expecting to find it even before the name popped out at him: "Harry Smiley."

Metzler got up and started to leave. "Still, it's something," he said.

Michael Nordland didn't seem too pleased to be answering more questions, but apparently his manager, who sat there like his coach, had advised him to cooperate.

"There's nothing I can add to what I told the sheriff's deputies out on the road," Michael said.

"I haven't been in contact with them," Metzler said. "I'm acting on the information that was printed in the *Times*. Was it accurate?"

"As far as it went, yes."

"What do you mean, as far as it went?"

"The thing that scared my friend and me so badly was the crazy persistence of the guy in the other car."

"The guy? You could tell it was a man?"

"Yes."

"How?"

"The shape was bulky."

"Some women are pretty big."

Michael looked at Truman.

"I suppose so. I just got the impression that it was a man."

"Just from the silhouette?"

Again Nordland looked at his manager.

"I think you ought to say, Michael," Truman said.

"I don't want to blow this damn thing out of all proportion. I don't want to take the chance of getting a man in trouble for no reason."

"I'm sure Detective Metzler will act with discretion."

"I suggest you tell me whatever it is that bothers

you, Mr. Nordland. Every little bit helps, even if we can't act on it."

"When the station wagon was coming directly at us, the high beams on our car lit up the man's face for a second. I think it was a guard who works part-time here. But I can't be certain. I'd had some trouble with him earlier in the day and had him tossed off the set."

"Fired?"

"I don't think they'd go that far. Just tossed off the set," Michael said. "Maybe I had that in mind, felt badly about it and imagined it was this fellow trying to get back at me. But that'd be a crazy thing for a man to do over such a small matter, wouldn't it?"

"That's what the unit I work for is all about—crazy things. What's the guard's name?"

Michael hesitated, made up his mind with every sign of relief and said, "Harry—"

Before he was finished, Metzler said "Smiley" right along with him.

Michael didn't say anything more about it to Truman or Metzler, but he brooded about it afterward. He was trapped by the feeling that he was running on some fatal collision course with the Smiley character. There had been a quality of fateful evil and disaster about their relationship from the first casual beginnings, and now the man who so apparently carried around a great rage in his belly seemed to have come to focus that rage on Michael. He felt as though he were in a kind of combat filled with the fearful thought that killing might be done, yet leave no memory but nightmare.

Metzler sensed a similar fatefulness between himself and Smiley. Now he added Michael Nordland to the prophetic obsession with violence and death that altered his professional coolness and objectivity; made him emotionally partisan in his desire to bring Smiley to some uncertain justice for some unrevealed crime.

27

A search warrant is an order in writing, in the name of the people, signed by a magistrate, directed to a police officer, commanding him to search for personal property and to bring it before the magistrate. The warrant is usually quite specific. The police officer requesting the warrant must show probable cause and must support this by affidavit, naming or describing the person and particularly describing the property and the place to be searched.

After being duly sworn and deposed, a detective would, for example, state in writing that he had information based on his personal knowledge and belief and/or facts revealed to him that a crime had been committed; he would then disclose the results of his investigation before requesting permission to search for a suspect weapon in the apartment of the person suspected of the crime.

It is a damned difficult document for a police officer to obtain.

Metzler applied to his superior, Lieutenant Jill, for such a warrant to inspect the premises of Harry Smiley, residing at 48 Broom Street, West Hollywood.

"What have you got?" Jill asked.

"Berkley, the guy who hit Mary Margaret Masters's arm, thought he saw a gun in Harry Smiley's pocket."

Lieutenant Jill looked over his steepled fingers in a way meant to remind Metzler that he'd been there, and had disapproved, when that little bit of news had been remembered—or invented.

"Mary Margaret Masters knew Smiley. They attended some sort of political group together."

"What kind of group?"

"Well, a class at Santa Monica Community College."

"Scarcely a conspiracy."

"A close friend of Smiley's, a Marco Epstein, was also in the study group."

Jill said nothing in a very patient way.

"I've talked to the man without telling him I'm a police officer. He acted suspicious and fearful."

"Where did this conversation take place?"

"In Venice."

"Land of thieves and perverts," Jill said. "Next."

"A prostitute known to the police as Miss Marvel is also a good friend."

"So what?"

"She spends a lot of working nights at Smiley's."

"Oh, for Christ's sake," Jill said in unconcealed disgust. He straightened up in his swivel chair, ready to dismiss Metzler.

"The actor, Michael Nordland, had a little trouble with Smiley. He figures it started over some small show of temper on his part that escalated to a full-scale attack against himself and his girlfriend on the road from Valyermo."

"Is Nordland ready to file a complaint?"

"No. He can't be positive, and he wants to be sure he's not doing anyone an injury without being dead certain."

Lieutenant Jill shrugged and held out his open palms.

"Maybe I'm a little surer than Nordland is that Smiley was the character who tried to run them down. The car was a beat-up light-colored wagon," Metzler added.

"And does Smiley own such a vehicle?"

"Another one of his funny friends does—a kid named Bondi. I checked him out and found that he'd been fired for suspicion of stealing. He's moved in with Smiley and a woman named Alice Belmont."

"Any record?"

"No."

"Any on the Belmont dame?"

"No. It's Smiley I'm—"

"I know what *you're* trying to do," Jill cut him off. *"I'm* trying to find a scrap of due cause."

"Smiley's name is in the address book of the man named Willard Geneva who was killed in the Valley gun-shop burglary. There was no breaking and entering. Geneva must have known the killers and let them in."

"Any other names in Geneva's book?"

"Sure."

"Everything circumstantial."

"The cord that choked Geneva to death—"

"He was knifed, wasn't he?" Jill interjected.

"And choked. It's a lanyard used by private guards and police forces. I called up. Twentieth guards are supplied whistles on lanyards that are identical."

"Everything circumstantial," Jill said again.

"But there's enough of it."

"Not enough to get a magistrate to sign a warrant."

"Shit," Metzler said in defeat.

"How heavy's your case load?"

"Medium."

"All right," Jill said. "Dig a little more, if you want

to. Question this Smiley if you think it'll shake him up, worry him. I don't see anything here, but you're the one on the scene and feeling the shivers.

"But if we get busy, drop it. We can't hope to shag every screwball."

Metzler went to the door, anything but satisfied.

"Metzler," Jill said, stopping him for a moment, "in our particular specialty you get to see conspiracy everywhere."

"Maybe there is," Metzler said.

"That's what scares the shit out of me," Jill agreed.

Harry grinned easily and stepped back from the doorway, holding the screen door open with his fingertips.

"Come on in, Metzler," Harry said. "Get you a beer?"

"Why not?"

"None of that bullshit about drinking on duty, huh?"

"I won't tell if you won't," Metzler said.

Harry waved him to a chair and left the room. Metzler heard the tops pop on two cans; the muffled sound of Harry speaking. When he came back, Harry handed Metzler a frosted can and sat down.

"Well, what else can I do for you?" Harry asked cheerfully. "Want to see that gun?"

"You alone?" Metzler asked.

"No. What's that got to do about anything?"

"Nothing. I just heard you talking."

Harry laughed. "I don't talk to myself. I'm not nuts."

"You know a man named Willard Geneva?" Metzler asked.

"Yes, I do."

"How well?"

"What's the matter? He get his ass in some kind of trouble?"

"How well?" Metzler repeated in the same tone of voice.

"I just knew the guy in a casual sort of way. Met him at a gun shop, I think. At least that's where I got to be pretty friendly with him. He works in a place out in the Valley. He's a full-scale gun nut. That what's got him into trouble?"

"Were you very friendly? Did you see a lot of each other?"

"Hell, no. We weren't even drinking buddies."

"When was the last time you saw him?"

"What the hell is this all about?" Harry demanded angrily. "He get himself into some trouble?"

"He got himself dead. Haven't you read about it in the paper or seen it on television?"

"Would I be acting dumb if I did? I tell you, I haven't seen or heard from Geneva in over a year."

"That's funny," Metzler said softly.

"Now just what in the hell does that mean?"

"There's no reason to become belligerent, Mr. Smiley."

"You bug me. You really do bug me. What is it that's so funny?"

"Geneva had a new address book in his pocket when he was killed. You were in it."

"So?"

"Just seems funny to copy out a name from an old book to a new one if you haven't seen the person in over a year."

"Maybe he didn't want to forget me. How was old Willard killed?"

"In the course of a robbery," Metzler said. "There's

180

someone else who remembers you, Mr. Smiley," he added.

"Yeah? Who?"

"Mary Margaret Masters."

"Now I know as much as I did before you told me."

"The woman who took the shot at the President."

"How the hell would she remember me?"

"She says you were in the same discussion group at Santa Monica College."

"I'll be damned. Yeah. I thought that old broad looked familiar. I remember her now."

The screen door opened. Marco Epstein walked into the living room from the bright sunshine, through the dark hall into the gloom. He blinked his eyes.

"Sorry, Harry, I didn't know you had company."

"That's O.K.," Harry said, standing up. "I don't think Detective Metzler's got any more questions to ask me. Have you?"

Metzler stood up and smiled first at Harry, then at Marco.

"How do you do," he said politely to the old man.

Marco's lip trembled. He looked scared half to death. "How do you do, Detective Metzler," he said.

28

Selecting the showgirls for the spectacular was a very quiet sort of process. No tap dancing and not a hell of a lot of energy were required. All the girls had to do was walk in a fashion that was considered beautiful but which in any other context might more aptly be described as awkward and ludicrous, though admittedly provocative. The stiffness of the arms and back was matched by a corresponding placidity of feature. The ideal showgirl could easily be mistaken for a wax figure when standing still, a rack of bones designed to display tits, ass and legs to best advantage.

But under the mask of asexuality there must also be a certain glimmer, a promise that the proper word would melt the ice, a smile ghosting the lips, a lift to the eyebrows both questioning and aloof. Hush was a perfect example of that dichotomy of invitation and refusal.

"What a gorgeous broad," Eddie Barnes said.

"That's my girlfriend," Alice said. "That's one of them."

Eddie lay back against the theater seat, his knees up against the back of the seat in front of him, like a small boy at a Saturday matinee. Alice was scrunched up in the same way and her ass was getting numb. She turned her face to Eddie, and her cheek touched the stubble of the seat back. It reminded her of the stubble on Harry's face in the morning, and she turned her cheek away.

"You didn't have to ask a favor for that one," Eddie said. "You done me one."

"I had a feeling you'd like her. Guys flip over her all the time."

"Drop like flies," Eddie said. "That's a winner," he yelled out.

Alice smiled and straightened up in the seat. She'd been bothered by the strangest feeling all morning, as though her movements were not connected to her somehow; as though she had to be very careful or she'd get hurt and find herself fatally wounded. Every once in a while the thought went through her like a scream: "They killed a man. Hush choked him with a cord. Assy stuck a knife in him." Then she'd look around, afraid that she'd shouted the thought out loud.

Beautiful girls paraded across the stage, walked up and down a short double flight of stairs, posed arms, heads and bosoms, and walked off into the wings.

Evelynn appeared as languid as ever. She was very beautiful even under the glare of practice lights but, even among the professionally lifeless, so without inner life as to be off-putting. She seemed to drag her feet when she walked, and looked down at them when she negotiated the steps.

"That one's about to fall asleep," Eddie remarked.

"That's Evelynn," Alice said.

"Another friend?"

"Yes."

"No, Alice, no," Eddie said.

"What's the matter, Eddie? She's beautiful, isn't she?"

183

"Best-looking corpse I ever saw," Eddie answered.

"Put her in the back. You said it was a favor bringing Hush along," Alice said. "So you owe me one."

"Do I owe you, Alice?" Eddie asked, not smiling even a little bit. "How's it go? I been asking you to go out with me some night. Nothing expected. No strings. Just a few laughs and a few memories for old times'. . ."

"I know, I know," Alice said, trying to stem the tide of his accusation and soothe him at the same time.

"Just a date," he said, raising his voice. "Two old friends out for a few laughs. So today you tell me yes, you'll go out with me. You'll do me the favor of letting me buy you a great dinner and some drinks. Now you let me know you got three girlfriends coming in looking for jobs. O.K. Fair enough. I mean your first friend's got a job. This bitch had anything on the ball, I'd say O.K. Anything at all. What the hell do I care?"

"No need to carry on, Eddie," Alice said. "Please."

"I just want to know. Is going out with me hanging on whether or not I load the stage with your sorority sisters?"

"I don't belong to any sorority," Alice said, trying to break his tirade with a little laugh, but he wouldn't be diverted.

"Is that the deal, Alice?"

"No," she said sharply. "No, Eddie, it's no bargain. You think I'm going to pay off on my back for giving my friends a job, you're way out of line."

"Did I say that?" Eddie protested.

"Because if that's what you think . . ."

She left the threat hanging between them in the air. He could choke himself on it if he wanted to.

"I don't think that. I'm sorry." He snapped his head back to the stage. "Walk it through again, will you, girlie?" he called out.

Evelynn went through the motions. Eddie snorted softly through his nose. "I can't do it."

Alice shrugged. "All right."

"We still got a date?" Eddie asked.

"Sure."

When the girls had finished parading, Hush and Assy had jobs. Eddie picked the girl he'd known as Miss Marvel and wondered if the hooker remembered him from a couple of years back when some friends of his had given him a trick with her as a birthday present. She was far from being the cool and perfect showgirl type, but she had a sensational pair of legs and great buns, and maybe a little vulgarity wouldn't hurt the general feeling of the number.

The night on the town for old times' sake didn't work out very well. None of the old places were around anymore; everything had changed. Sunset Strip, Hollywood Boulevard and Beverly Hills were swinging to a different bunch of tunes.

Eddie drank sparingly, Alice scarcely at all. Trying to remember the fun they'd shared in the past proved to be hard work. Touching hands didn't help. Playing kneesies under the table at La Scala just made them both feel stiff and awkward. Eddie smiled into her eyes, trying for that mixture of cockiness and little-boy impishness that once had been his stock in trade, but on his aging face it looked more like pain than passion.

Alice tried. Not because she wanted the night to end in his bed, but because she was feeling so scared and sad that she wanted to cry, and maybe if they fucked and it was no good, she'd have her lost youth to cry over.

In the end they just talked till quite late. When he drove her to 48 Broom and parked the car, she kissed him good night and there was a little rocket of real passion. Not nearly enough to ride to the stars on. They smiled into each other's eyes, knowing exactly what had happened and grateful for at least that much.

Harry took the opportunity, with Alice out for the evening, to try it on with Hush again. Public intimacies had awakened a fierce appetite in him for private games. He requested a strategy conference. She could scarcely avoid that, since he consulted her in everything concerning the plans for the attack on the Dorothy Chandler Pavilion.

When Hush entered the living room of Harry's cottage, she chose to sit on the floor at Harry's feet when she saw he was seated on the couch. It was a subtle thing to do. She knew it would please him for her to so place herself in an attitude of subservience. At the same time it gave her greater mobility than he enjoyed and placed him in the position of being impossibly awkward if he tried to make amorous advances.

They touched on small speculations concerning the members of the group: a pre-battle assessment of the troops.

"Things are shaping up very well," Hush said.

"Yeah," Harry agreed, his eyes fixed on her mouth.

"We've got a chance to pull off a perfect magic trick," she went on.

"Yeah," Harry said, then asked her what she meant exactly.

"Assy and I will be up there on the stage with all the celebrities, making like entertainers."

"And Alice," Harry said.

"Sure, and Alice," Hush said offhandedly, as though Alice's contribution would be of small account.

"I'm thinking that we can pick up the hostages to cover our escape, just as we planned."

"And Janet backstage," Harry said.

"Yes, yes," Hush agreed. "We can pick up the hostages without any show of guns."

"Why?"

"We should make it look as though you've taken us captive along with the stars."

"What the hell good would that do us?" Harry asked suspiciously.

"Don't you see? It's sleight of hand. While everybody's got their eyes on you, they won't be watching us. We'll have the captives in hand and no one will know it."

"And I'll be out there on the line all by myself!" Harry said with rising anger in his voice.

"That's just the point. If they try to take you—if anything goes wrong and there's even a chance they can manage that—we'll be there to protect you. You can bet your life we'll show ourselves for what we are if that happens."

"I will be betting my life," Harry said pointedly.

He was staring at her, a hard fixed grin on his mouth. She regarded him calmly, lowering her eyelids a trifle.

"I know," she said softly. 'I've been thinking something else."

"What?"

"I've been thinking that you and I could cut loose from the others. We could use the hostages for more than a shield. We could score some big money and go away together."

Harry was silent for a long while, still staring into her eyes, trying to read them.

"You mean that?" he finally asked.

"I mean it, Harry."

"What about Evelynn?"

"Since this action started I've lost a lot of interest in that sort of thing, Harry."

His grin grew wider.

"What about Alice, Harry?" Hush murmured.

"I could do without her," Harry said.

He started to bend over toward her. Suddenly a thought hit him.

"Hey, that magic trick."

"What about it?"

"That cop Metzler knows we're all friends."

Hush laughed. "I don't think that cop thinks much of you, Harry. I don't think that cop thinks you're a very loyal person."

Harry started to laugh with her.

"He's right, Harry. You're not a very loyal person. You're going to double-cross everyone, aren't you?"

Harry grinned. "Yeah."

"Everybody but me," Hush said and allowed him to kiss her just once.

29

Las Virgines Road runs from Ventura Freeway, across the Santa Monica Mountains, to the sea at Malibu. There are several ranches butting on the two-lane blacktop that winds its way through the hills, a plant nursery or two, a picnic ground, the old Twentieth Century–Fox movie ranch, a few day and summer camps, horse stables, dog kennels and, scattered on the hillsides and in the canyons, the homesteads of loners who treasure solitude.

One of them was Warren Tregaskis, wrangler, stunt man, property director and expert powder man. At the age of sixty-eight he had pretty much given up everything but working with explosives. He was a master of the squib and the shaped charge. It was said that he could explode a charge on a man's shoulder without disturbing his dandruff or shave a lady's crotch without damage to her tender skin.

He was an acquaintance of—but no particular friend to—Peewit, who'd been a visitor more than once and knew Tregaskis kept an assortment of explosives in a shack close to his house in the hills.

He was known to have a supply of Composition C-2 and C-3 on hand. Both compounds were detonated by electric caps.

Harry was ready to go on the raid with the same party that had taken the gun shop, but Hush convinced him that Bondi might prove a liability again and that Assy had been blooded. It was her idea to test the nerve of Alice and Janet. Janet was eager for the adventure, but Alice took ill—or pretended to— throwing up all over the place when the day arrived. Peewit had to go along because he knew the dogs and the lay of the land.

They walked the half mile or so from the dirt road to the gate. Peewit carried a plastic bag filled with pieces of meat meant to pacify the old man's curs. The dogs came in a rush when Peewit removed the chain from the gate. There were four of them, big rangy brutes of no particular breed, three shag-coated, one slick as a pig. He was the barker. The others ran silent. They came up fast and quiet, stopping just outside of arm's reach. They tucked up shoulder to shoulder and faced the black-clad figures with the strange smells about them. The greenhorn hound blasted on through and leaped at Janet, barking and carrying on to show his buddies how brave he was.

Janet brought her knee up instinctively and he fell back, startled, the wind knocked out of him. Harry saw Janet pull the knife from her belt. He moved in and closed his hand around her wrist. Her whole arm was trembling uncontrollably.

"No," he said softly.

The slick-haired dog stayed back but started yelping worse than ever. Peewit took the scraps from the bag and scattered them on the ground. He reached in close, and the three old-timers smelled the back of his hand, stood up, wagged their tails, then went to gobbling up the gift.

There was a faint sound from the dark bulk of the house.

"Who the hell's out there?" Tregaskis called out in

a strong voice. The old man hadn't turned on a light, but there was no doubt in anyone's mind that up there in the darkness he was standing with a shotgun cocked and ready.

At the sound of his voice the slick dog had gone quiet. Now he started up all over again. One of the older dogs, impatient with the youngster's bellowing, turned quick and easy, nipped the new dog on the lip and silenced him.

The whole hillside seemed to hold its breath. Two of the shaggy dogs trotted up to the house. A moment later there was the sound of a door closing.

They went to the tool shed. Peewit cut the padlock with a pair of bolt cutters as the two remaining watchdogs watched. He identified and removed six packages of Composition C-2.

Hush gingerly carried three of them. Peewit smiled and told her they could play baseball with the stuff without fear. They carried the explosives away down the dark road toward the car on the blacktop.

As they walked along noiselessly they felt invincible. Janet touched the knife she'd been so ready to use against the dog. She held it in her hand. It slipped from her fingers and fell softly to the dirt. She knelt to pick it up as the others walked on.

"Stand still, you sons of bitches!" Tregaskis roared from out of a dark stand of trees beside the road. Harry, Peewit and Hush stopped in their tracks.

"Turn your asses around. Do it easy. No quick moves."

They turned slowly and stared into the dark. Tregaskis stepped clear of the trees. He was wearing slippers and corduroy pants, sagging in the crotch, over long grey underwear.

"A bunch of black-shirted thievin' assholes, is it?"
He laughed shortly.

"Little meat for the dogs and all's well, is it? You damn fools. A quiet dog's a warning just like a noisy one."

A beam of light flashed from his hand. The electric torch shone in their faces one by one.

"Don't I know you?" Tregaskis asked when the light fell on Peewit. "Don't I know your ugly face? Sure as hell I do. What the hell are you doin' here, Peewit?"

Her hand hadn't found the knife at once. Janet had crouched in the deeper shadows beside the road, groping about for it, and heard Tregaskis challenging the others. She found the knife and, silent as a shadow, stepped off the path into the brush and made her way around behind him.

In the distance an approaching police siren wailed.

"Cops comin'," Tregaskis said.

Janet stepped up behind him. Her mouth was sour with bile.

He passed the beam of his flashlight back and forth.

"Hey, didn't I see four of you back at the top?"

"You should have stayed in bed!" Harry yelled as Tregaskis started to whirl around, suddenly aware of Janet at his back. "Knife the bastard, Janet. Do it!"

She moved in a step, so close that the barrel of the shotgun couldn't be brought to bear. Holding the knife underhanded, she drove the blade into his side, slicing into his liver. She twisted the knife and, as he sagged, drew it out and struck at the heart. He doubled over and fell against her. She opened her arms and held him for a moment in a lover's embrace. The shotgun fell to the ground and went off. Janet screamed.

Blood soaked her pants at the hip. Hush dropped

the packages of explosives and caught Janet as she stumbled.

Peewit bent to gather up the packages that Hush had dropped. Harry moved to help support Janet.

"I've got her, Harry," Hush said and half-carried Janet down the hill as the siren came closer.

When the police arrived they found a discharged shotgun, a package of C-2 and old Tregaskis, dead.

The wound in Janet's flank wasn't as serious as it had first looked. Hush cut her free of the bloody black jeans and exposed the hip. The flow of blood had stopped. When the wound was cleansed, the flesh was seen to be fiercely bruised and dotted with small punctures. Hush gently probed with long-stemmed tweezers, removing the tiny pellets and washing the area with alcohol. Janet held Peewit's hand and didn't make a sound.

There was a brave spirit in the air. They were soldiers who had become true believers in their cause. They were nearly all caught up in a new fever of dedication and determination, except for Alice, who was afraid; Evelynn, who was insensitive to it all; and Marco, who knew that he was a prisoner of the mad or nearly mad.

The retooling of the Tommy guns went forward rapidly. Once the weld between barrel and receiver was broken, the chambers had to be reopened. It was painstaking work with files and reamers; hairline fractures could flaw the parts so that they'd become inoperable, perhaps cause the gun to explode in the hand. Then the barrels were placed in the metal vise, and, with the most careful application of a blow-torch, the lead was sweated out of them.

When the job was done, Harry decided that the guns and the plastic had to be moved to another place. The first visit from Metzler had nerved him up a little—all that business about the gun concealed behind an innocent interrogation concerning the assassination attempt. The second visit was something else again. Metzler acted as though he were really out to get Harry, trying to pin him to a conspiracy. Somehow the cop might get a warrant or even do a little nosing around on his own. Harry wanted the equipment out, but first the arsenal had to be tested.

They piled the guns and explosives into the secondhand Volks van which Bondi had taken in trade for the station wagon and twelve hundred bucks underwritten by Harry. Bondi had his radio repair kit and the parts from half a dozen radio-controlled model airplanes. They piled in two bales of hay.

They drove out into the Mojave Desert and the dry lakes beyond the Opal Mountain. Just the men; no women or old men allowed. They reached the barren shores of the dry lake as the first long shadows stretched out from their feet. A cool, almost chill, front seemed to power across the sand all the way from the Sierra Nevadas, meeting with the heat of the desert floor and creating shimmering illusions on the horizon.

Harry walked away from the others, planted his feet astride and raised his arms above his head, hands clenched in some terrible spasm of joy. He threw his head back and started to laugh. Peewit and Bondi looked at each other as though he'd gone nuts, then started to laugh too, feeling the power in themselves. Goddamn it! They were giants as big as their shadows on the land.

"It's going to happen!" Harry shouted. "Do you know that?"

"Yes, I know it!" Peewit yelled.

"I know it!" Bondi shouted.

"We're going to do it!" Harry shouted. "We're going to be *somebodies*."

Janet was at home, taking a nap. Assy leaned her hip against the counter in Harry's kitchen, chewed on a sandwich and laughed at what Hush was saying. Alice laughed too, but in a way that said she really didn't know what was so funny. Evelynn laughed because Hush seemed elated.

"These dudes," Hush said. "These tight-assed jocks on their power trips. Out there in the desert jerking each other off with their guns and firecrackers. Bang! Bang! Bang! Noisy sons of bitches." Big laugh all around. "Very large on bang-bang are the boys. Dynamite and guns and cocks. But it's the girls who slip the knife. Very big on muscles and macho, the boys are, but when it comes to killing, it's the girls who get it done."

Her eyes went to Assy, singling her out for honors, romancing her. Assy knew it and preened herself as she would before a man, feeling the power in Hush.

"We've got Assy and Janet doing the killing," Hush said. "We've got Alice setting it up for us at the theater. We've got me telling Harry what to do when he starts putting his foot into it."

"Harry's the leader, though, isn't he?" Alice asked.

Hush went to her and kissed her on the mouth. "You're cute. You're so damned innocent. Harry couldn't lead a raid of mice on a cheese factory."

Evelynn and Assy laughed. Alice was simply bewildered as Hush strutted around the kitchen, thumbs hooked in her belt, playing at being a man.

"Well, aren't we doing what Harry tells us to do?" Alice went on, her brow furrowed, trying to puzzle out what Hush was saying.

"Harry's crazy," Hush said flatly.

Alice gasped and looked around, as though expecting Harry to jump out of a closet to punish Hush for insulting him, punish them all for agreeing with her by their silence.

"He wants to murder a bunch of glamorous damn fools just to make some kind of obscure protest, deliver some sort of abstract message to the world. The son of a bitch is mad."

"Aren't you going to do it?" Alice asked tentatively. Her face was suddenly soft. Her lips and cheeks began to tremble, her eyes wide like a child's hoping to hear a fairy tale in which ogres and monsters were merely creatures of the imagination.

"Shoot a lot of bloody actors for no reason?" Hush crowed. "Not likely."

"What, then?" Alice asked eagerly, ready to hear that the nightmare was over.

"While Harry and the boys are at their noisy murders, we're going to lift a couple of those valuable bodies and whisk them away. We'll get them right back here and hold them until somebody pays us a million dollars apiece."

"We won't have to kill anybody?" Alice said, and started to cry.

Hush went to her and took her into her arms. Alice leaned her head on the taller girl's breast and allowed herself to be comforted.

"It might come to that," Hush said softly, "but we won't shoot anybody down for no reason. We won't do that."

She made it sound quite reasonable, made them sound almost charitable in their forbearance.

"We're going to be in charge of everything and make it look as though Harry's herding us around."

Alice moved fearfully in Hush's arms. Hush held the smaller woman closer.

"That's going to be your bonus, Alice. I'm going to set you free of Harry Smiley."

"What about Janet?" Assy asked. "Are we going to tell Janet?"

Hush released Alice and looked at Assy with something like admiration.

"Do you have reservations about her?" Hush asked.

"She complains about him, but I think, when push comes to shove, she'll stick with Peewit. If I hear you right, you're saying we're cutting everybody else out."

Hush glanced at Alice, who had seated herself on a kitchen chair and was drying her eyes with a napkin. She looked back at Assy.

"That's right. That's what we're going to do."

Assy met Hush's look. She knew Hush was flirting with her. Ever since they'd shared in the killing of Willard Geneva, ever since they'd joined in the ritual orgy, she knew that she and Hush would share something even more private and binding.

Before it got dark, Bondi and Peewit set up the bales of hay and pinned paper targets to them. Harry laid out the sixteen rebored, reblued and polished machine guns, ready to see if they would fire and kill. They tested the guns in short bursts. Bondi used the guns with a certain grace, Peewit was nearly expert, and it didn't take Harry long to get the knack.

Ten of the guns proved serviceable. For no reason they could figure out, the others wouldn't operate after firing a few rounds, but it didn't matter. They had enough.

The next morning they started on the testing of the Composition C-2. Bondi rigged an electric detonator to a small chunk of the plastic and hooked it up to a radio control unit, and Harry carried it off some distance away to place it on the desert floor. Peewit was in the van, trying to find something on the radio, unaware of the fact that it was a CB.

Harry put the plastic down gently, let go, and had started to straighten up when the explosive went off with a blinding flash. Harry fell backward on the sand, not from the force of the explosion but from tripping over his own feet at the surprise of it.

"Son of a bitch," he screamed, high and shrill like an impaled animal. "If I was two inches closer to that fuckin' thing it would've blown my hand off."

When his rage had drained away, Harry went to sit on a water can. A shiver went through him; he looked at his right hand and flicked it back and forth as though testing it. Bondi dropped the little control box and ran to the camper to get some ice cubes from the little portable fridge for Harry's flash burns.

"Ice'll keep it from gettin' a blister," he told Harry. "It'll take the pain away."

"How'd you get so smart?" Harry demanded. "How'd you get so smart that you nearly blew my hand off?"

"I don't know what went wrong, Harry."

Harry looked at Peewit, who had hurried over.

"You hear that? The big electronics expert doesn't know what went wrong."

"These things are tricky as hell," Bondi said.

There was a squawk from the cab of the van.

"Oh, Jesus," Bondi said. "The CB. Peewit was fiddlin' the Citizens Band and tapped the frequency."

"What the hell you talking about?"

"Peewit thought he was going to get some music on a regular AM, but he was dialing a CB. Some broadcaster might be heaping power on and triggered the radio control in the plastic."

"You mean these gimmicks can be set off by just any damn signal?" Harry asked.

"If there's enough juice behind a signal, it slops all over the place. It can fuck up the whole parade."

"Any damn trucker beepin' along the street down in L.A. could blow up the bombs we're going to plant in the auditorium?"

"That's what could happen," Bondi said agreeably.

"All right, let's get the hell out of here," Harry said.

"Can we stop for a beer, Harry? I'm thirsty as hell," Bondi said.

"After we get all this shit back to Marco's hotel in Venice."

"Marco's?" Peewit said.

"That's where we're going to stash them until we need them," Harry said. "I want that old bastard in it all the way."

Assy's bedroom was splashed with red. Red flocked Victorian wallpaper covered all four walls and the ceiling. The rug, bedspread, satin sheets and pillowcases were all red. The shades that were pulled down, obscuring and filtering the hot afternoon sun, turned to rose color the light that fell on the naked bodies of the two women standing beside the bed.

The clothing that Hush and Assy had removed from each other's bodies lay in crimson, stained puddles around their feet. They explored each other's mouths with their tongues, their breasts and inner thighs with their fingertips.

Hush gently pushed Assy down on the bed, then went down on her knees on the scarlet carpet and placed her mouth on Assy as Assy spread her legs.

Assy began to moan softly after a time, her hips moving in small circles. No man had ever been so expert as Hush. She possessed a woman's sense of pace and timing. She drew Assy up and up the slow spiral of arousal. When Assy was at the very top, going into the first wave of her orgasm, Hush stiffened her tongue and held it in Assy without motion, allowing her to finish herself off gently.

Assy lay still, only her hands moving through Hush's hair, along her neck and shoulders. When she was recovered, she sat up, took Hush's wrists and drew her onto the bed. Her soft feminine hesitancies gave way to masculine manipulations of the English girl's limbs. Assy arranged her, went down on her with a certain fierceness.

Hush understood. It was clear to her that Assy felt lost in the role thrust on her by society and circumstances. Assy wanted dominance. She wanted to be the user, not the used, for a change. Wanted her own center of power. That's why she'd grabbed so hard at Harry's crazy scheme, had been ready to pull the trigger on Marco, had wielded the knife on Geneva readily and with apparent relish. Her appetite for killing was strong.

Hush stroked Assy's flank. "You're the best damn soldier in the outfit," she flattered.

Assy purred and cuddled.

"When this is over," Hush said, "it's going to be just me and you. Just me and you."

Assy smiled into Hush's shoulder. She had known from the very start that it would one day end up being this way. She hadn't understood it with the front of her mind, but she'd known it somewhere deep inside.

30

About two weeks before the night of the Oscar presentations, Michael's nomination was announced along with those of Warren Beatty, Jack Nicholson, Al Pacino and Steve McQueen.

He experienced a momentary but powerful surge of elation and triumph. Somehow he'd done it. Out of a casual childhood and a shabby beginning he had made a name for himself. He had literally manufactured it from the scraps of other lives and made it count for something.

Reaction set in. He worried at the fact that the Oscar was another honor created by men for their own vanity. Had he really achieved anything so notable in his craft to warrant being named a candidate for such a championship? Was there any more purpose and deliberation in what he'd done than in his charge up a nameless hill after seeing a friend fall that had brought him a medal declaring his unremembered valor?

He was left high and dry between the summit and the valley, and suffered a certain dullness of spirit.

Sheri offered congratulations. He accepted the congratulations of many more in cables and phone calls. The official notice of the nomination arrived with a flood of social invitations.

"There was a time when I wouldn't get a single

invitation to anything for months." Michael smiled. "Now I'd rather not even go."

"Let's not," Sheri said.

"We'll have to go to Jim's. He makes me feel guilty as hell if I miss one of his parties."

"Well, it might be fun."

"At least crowded."

It proved every bit as crowded as Michael had predicted. He and Sheri were dragged into the heart of the party, kissed, hugged, pinched and provided with drinks and congratulations.

Michael was stared at by even the sophisticated and the famous, as though they wondered what bargain he'd made or secret he possessed to be fortune's darling. He smiled so often and long that his face began to ache. He looked for a corner near a bar and drank more than was usual. When Sheri found him again it was almost two in the morning and the party was thinning out.

"Having fun?" she asked doubtfully.

He didn't answer.

"Are you all right?" she asked, and he grinned strangely at her. "Just drunk," she said.

He stopped smiling and said thickly, "Get me out of here." Sheri saw that he was terrified, barely holding on to himself.

She helped him stand and placed his arm about her shoulders when he stumbled. They threaded their way among the considerable number of die-hards who patted and poked them, hugged them and covered them with damp kisses. Michael smiled pleasantly enough at first and then grimaced as though he were in great pain. He began to whimper like a small child, finally screamed out in terror. Ghosts were walking out of his nightmares.

Truman kept that out of the papers, though the town buzzed next morning with speculations about what kind of "dust" he was on. The expert gossips finally agreed that he'd been plain drunk, maybe a little nuts or just overcelebrating the nomination.

Harry was in the gatehouse glaring at Michael's picture in the paper when Charlie Clabber came buzzing up on the golf cart.

"Still running around on Gus's baby buggy, I see," Harry said.

"Permanently. I'm going to have my name painted on it. That bouncing around took something out of old Gus. He's retiring."

"Making you the assistant chief?"

Funny, Harry thought, how his whim had set Bondi on the old man and got him out of the way; how his old buddy Charlie had ended up in a position where he could do Harry a lot of good.

Harry smiled. "Lucky you."

"What the hell's that supposed to mean, Harry? You said that once before. Don't make a hit tune out of it."

"Hell, I'm just trying to say congratulations."

"Well, sharpen up your act," Charlie said.

"Any chance of my getting full time now that you're a man shy?" Harry asked.

"What's it worth?" Charlie speculated.

"Bribery?"

"Well, come on now, Harry. Make me an offer."

"A week's salary."

"No good."

"My undying loyalty and devotion."

"I can get that from a dog."

"Will you or won't you put me on full time?" Harry flared.

"Come on, now, that's not the way to play the payola game."

"Say again?"

"Payola. Viggerish. Grease. You know."

"That's just what I don't know, damn it," Harry said.

"Disc jockeys want one of three things."

"Yeah?"

"Money, publicity or broads."

"You won't take money."

Charlie grinned. "I'm about as well known as I want to be."

"Which leaves broads."

"Give me a present, Harry. You're always saying what a big cocksman you are. Buy me a little action. You pick up the tab for a pussy hunt."

"Hell, I don't have to do that. I've got it right in my pocket."

"Sure, sure," Charlie scoffed. "You got a stable. You got a harem."

"That's just what I got. Want some?"

Charlie squinted at Harry, trying to figure out whether or not he was pulling his leg.

"You mean it?"

"Can you get away from your old lady?"

"When?"

"Friday night?"

"Hell, yes."

"O.K. Take a bath Friday and come over to my house. I'll see what I can do for you."

"If you're putting me on, Harry, I'll have your ass."

"Don't worry."

"You really mean it?"

Harry gestured in disgust. "Ah, hell, you don't want a piece of ass, you want an insurance policy."

204

"All right, all right," Charlie said hurriedly. "Friday night."

"No charge," Harry said.

But you'll pay for it all the same, he thought.

Charlie Clabber arrived looking the way he imagined a suave fellow should look when invited to a party that promised action: brown slacks and a boldly patterned sport shirt worn outside his pants to hide his belly, a bottle in a brown paper bag under his arm.

Ten minutes later Charlie found himself in the middle of the foxiest-looking broads he'd ever seen gathered in one room for private purposes. He sat in Harry's easy chair with a glass in one hand, taking his toke from the dope when it was passed around.

In two hours he'd forgotten all about trying to hold his gut in; the bottom buttons of the shirt were opened and his belly was exposed, as white as the belly of a flounder. He was sitting splay-footed and spraddle-legged, giggling practically without pause and trying to look down Assy's dress.

Assy was sitting on a cushion on the floor at his feet, her elbow resting on his knee. Alice seemed to be forever asking Charlie if there was anything she could get him, do for him. He took his eyes away from Assy's tits and looked at Alice's long dancer's legs with bouncy little calves. He wanted them both on their backs. Where the hell did that lucky son of a bitch Harry scare up this kind of action? What was his ace? He felt Janet's lips on his cheek.

"You are a cute old billiken," she said. Charlie reached out for her ass, looked sharply at Peewit because he'd heard all about the jealousy and the strength of the propman, and saw Peewit smiling at him. He cupped Janet's ass; she laughed and spun away as if it were all fun and games.

Over in the corner of the sofa some girl named Evelynn dropped her sleepy eyes to his crotch. Jeeeesus! What if I could have them all? he fantasized. What if I could get this monstrous fail-safe hard-on that wouldn't say die? Suppose Peewit and Harry and the big kid with the muscles gave him the nod, gave him the old "be my guest"? Then suppose he took these broads one after the other into the bedroom and— Jesus Christ, it was happening! Assy was still at his feet, smiling up at him, but now she was clutching his stiff cock.

"What's that you got there?" she said.

He felt Janet's tongue in his ear. He wanted to tell them both to stop because he'd get his gun off before it was pointed anywhere. He looked across the room and saw the old man staring at him from the shadows. Why did the old man look so scared?

Assy massaged his cock, and he knew there wasn't a damn thing he wouldn't suffer for what that promised.

Assy stood up and leaned over him, never letting go. "Come into the bedroom, lover, unless you want to join the circus."

All at once Bondi was looming over him, grabbing at Assy's hair, pulling her head back, telling her to keep her goddamn hands off the old pig. Harry jumped across the room and dragged the kid away. Peewit got to his feet, fists clenched, looking around for an enemy. Janet was still behind Charlie with her arms around his neck.

"Get away from him, Janet," Peewit yelled. "This ain't your goddamn job; it's Assy's."

"Shut up!" Harry shouted. Then he punched Bondi in the gut as hard as he could. Bondi went

"Oof!" like a balloon bursting in the funny papers. Harry faced Bondi with his hands dangling at his sides, daring the huge kid to hit him back, forcing something that Charlie couldn't understand.

Charlie pushed himself up from the chair, feeling trapped in its soft depths.

"You don't own her," Harry said very softly. "None of us even own ourselves." He raised his voice a bit. "Assy? Why don't you take our good buddy Charlie somewhere for a little chat?"

"Sure, Harry," she said. She took Charlie's hand, walked past a tense Bondi and headed for the bedroom. Bondi started to go after them, brushing Harry's arm aside.

Assy hesitated, looking at Bondi with some concern.

Hush moved in front of Bondi and placed her hands on his chest.

"What the hell's the matter with you?" she grated.

"I don't want Assy making it with that pig," Bondi said.

"We agreed," Hush whispered. "We all agreed to show this man a good time. We'll need him. Harry's got to have him owing a favor. You understand?"

Bondi nodded dumbly.

"That Charlie Clabber's not one of us," he said weakly. "It makes what Assy's doing with him different. Like she's a whore."

Harry closed his eyes against his friend's stubborn stupidity. "Don't think about it," he said.

He nodded at Assy and she started to lead Charlie toward the bedroom again.

"There's just one chief honcho around here," Hush went on. "And that's—Harry.

"Go ahead, Assy," Harry called after the departing couple. "Show old Charlie a good time."

She showed him the best time he'd ever had in his life.

Later on, before Charlie left to wend his unsteady way home, he took Harry aside to tell him just how much he appreciated all that Harry had done for him.

"Old Harry Smiley, the fucker's friend. I'm going to owe you for life."

"You don't owe me," Harry said.

"Yes, I do, goddammit. And if there's ever any-thing—*anything*—I can do for you, all you got to do is ask."

"Well, there's something—"

"What? What? Tell me."

"You'll laugh the way you did about the movie magazines."

"I won't laugh. I'd cut my throat before I'd laugh at anything my best friend wanted."

"It's crazy, but I really get a boost when I see one of the really big movie stars. You know?"

Charlie patted Harry's chest judiciously. "A rea-sonable desire. A sensible request. You want to see movie stars?"

"Yeah, I do."

"Well, I'm gonna see to it that you rub assholes with the biggest. At the Academy Awards I'm gonna put you right in the same room with 'em. They'll shake your hand, Harry, each and every one. What do you say to that?"

"I'd really like to get close to them," Harry said. "I really would."

31

Hush clearly meant her smile to be threatening, but the showgirl named Thessaly hadn't the wit to know it.

"What would you take to step out of the show?" Hush asked.

Thessaly seemed dumbfounded by the idea. "What would I want to do that for?"

"I'd pay you what you're getting. You'd be getting paid for not working."

"Well, what about the social security? What about Equity health and welfare contributions?" Thessaly asked, having the wit for that.

"I'll pay you something for that too," Hush said patiently.

Thessaly narrowed her eyes a bit, the better to think. "What's in this for you?" she asked.

Hush leaned forward very confidentially, one woman of the world to another. "I know you'll understand. This girlfriend of mine has lost her confidence. A boy friend she had kicked it all out of her. She just mopes around crying the blues at me. I want to get her wound up again, you know?"

"Sure, I know," Thessaly said a little angrily. "I got the same goddamn problem. I got no self-confidence. I want this job so I can strut my ass up there and see if some bastard will spot me and give me a break."

"I'll pay you double," Hush stated flatly.

The suspicion really rose in the girl's eyes at the offer.

"Now, something's crazy here. How do you know your girlfriend will get the gig even if I step out?"

"I'll take that chance," Hush said and leaned forward in the chair.

"It's crazy. It's really crazy. I'd sure like to know why you want her to be in the show so bad," the girl repeated with heavy suspicion.

I want Evelynn right by my side when the action starts going down, Hush thought. I want her there with me and not watching the whole damn thing at home on the television set. I want her with me because she sure as hell won't cry for me if I don't survive the killing. If I die myself, I want her to die with me. I won't go alone without her.

Hush opened her mouth to speak. She wondered what the girl would do if she said flat out, "I want my lover to be with me when I pull off the biggest rip-off in the middle of one of the most sensational murders in history." Instead she said, "I really wish you'd think it over."

"There's nothing to think over, kid," the big man said. "I've got all the maintenance crew I can use."

Bondi smiled shyly at Mr. Fermi in his friendliest, big-pawed, puppy-dog way. Fermi smiled back because he liked what he saw in the big kid's face and was sorry he didn't have a job for him.

A truck pulled up to the loading platform of the Music Center where Bondi and Mr. Fermi stood talking. The driver got out with a clipboard in his hand and greeted the superintendent.

"Lights," he said and unlocked the double doors,

opened them and dropped the short ramp. Inside the big van were a dozen assorted big ten-kw spotlights. The trucker loaded two of the lamps on a pallet with dolly wheels.

"Where's your helper, Ed?" Fermi asked.

"Flu."

Without saying anything, Bondi went into the truck and single-handedly pushed the heavy lamps out onto the loading platform, got the nod from Fermi and wheeled them in onto the back of the stage.

A small man emerged from the shadows, blinking at the sun, and stood bemused on the platform.

"Help with these, Sharps," Fermi said.

Sharps took a step and stumbled. He looked down at his feet and peered all around the concrete for the thing that had tripped him up. There wasn't anything.

"Get back inside, Sharps," Fermi said.

"I help," the man said thickly and nearly fell over sideways.

"Keep your hands off the lamps. You're drunk."

Bondi was picking up the lamps one by one, not even bothering with the dolly.

"Look at that kid," the trucker said.

Fermi shook his head in appreciation of Bondi's strength. He looked at Sharps. "Kid," he called out, "I'm really sorry I've got no job for you right now. But I tell you: keep checking with me every couple of days if you don't get anything else, and maybe something'll come up."

Bondi carried in the last lamp, smiled, waved a casual hand at Fermi and the trucker and went back to the car, where Harry was waiting. He told Harry what the super had said and about the worker who was drunk.

Harry smiled and said, "We'll come back tomorrow."

Hush renewed her offer to Thessaly the next day, doubled it, but got turned down all the same. She maneuvered the girl into a corner and threatened her, but either Thessaly was too dumb to understand, or she was one of the stubborn types who wouldn't let go once she'd set her mind on something.

Harry and Bondi went back to the Chandler Pavilion. Bondi wandered over to the loading dock. He didn't see Fermi, but he did see Sharps running around sober as a judge, bright-eyed as a squirrel and busy as a beaver. Harry grinned when Bondi told him about the worker's reformation. He went off to a nearby liquor store and came back with a pint concealed in a paper bag. He wandered over to Sharps at the lunch break and traded a slug out of the pint for half a sandwich. Before too long Sharps had consumed nearly all of the pint and was as drunk as a skunk. He got the feeling that Harry was the best friend a man ever had and invited him to a local gin mill where he could repay just a little of Harry's hospitality.

Bondi was talking with Fermi when Sharps came weaving his way back to work an hour late and piss-drunk. Fermi handed him his notice, checked with the union shop steward, and signed Bondi on.

Harry had his electronics technician on the inside.

Hush and Assy, in stocking masks and heavy anoraks, concealed themselves in the bushes outside Thessaly's apartment house. They caught her coming home from a laundromat well after dark and inflicted enough damage to make certain she wouldn't be present for the next day's rehearsal and costume fittings. When Thessaly didn't turn up, Evelynn was sitting there quietly watching her girlfriends. Eddie hired her on the spot.

Janet was helping with the fittings; fussing around Assy, Hush and Evelynn; placing bits of ribbon here and there; handing out the huge fur muffs which would suggest nudity beneath and which would be the principal concealment for the showgirls.

"Perfect," Hush remarked softly. The problem of bringing the Thompsons on stage had been neatly taken care of. More importantly, as far as Hush was concerned, the trick of making Harry believe his three tigresses were armed, while everyone else who saw them would think they were not, had come to pass as though planned by a perfect fate.

32

Preparations for the rapidly approaching Academy Awards were going forward on all fronts at a quickening pace. Presenters were being named nearly every day in the press and on television or radio. It was from these—celebrities certain to be onstage at the finale—that Hush, Assy and Janet would pick their special targets according to the plan forming in Hush's mind.

When everybody was together, Harry talked about the whole crowd of them—presenters, nominees and audience alike—as victims indiscriminately marked for death. Alice listened but took no part in it.

"Harry," she finally said, "can we do anything to leave Eddie Barnes out of it?"

Marco felt a terrible need to cry. Even Alice had accepted the madness of it.

"Sure, Alice," Harry said. "We'll save the midget's ass."

"Thanks, Harry. It's just that Eddie's an old friend; and, after all, he has done us some favors."

Bondi spoke up then. "The Duke's gonna be there. That bothers me, Harry. He's always been my idol, sort of. You know?"

Harry just sat staring at Bondi.

"I mean, we don't have to shoot John Wayne, do we? Couldn't we at least try not to hurt the Duke?"

Harry suddenly smiled at the kid fondly. "Sure, sure. We'll leave the Duke. But nobody else—you hear? We can't go around picking this one or that one to keep from shooting. It'd drive us all crazy."

Marco felt as though he'd fallen down the rabbit hole, but there was blood, pain and death at the bottom of this pit, not fantasy.

But still he carefully kept the journal of their campaign, which Harry read each evening like a general reading battle orders. He'd laugh and look up at Marco, terrifying the old man, who feared that Harry could read his thoughts. He knew now why the detective, Metzler, had struck up the conversation with him on the bench, told him his name and suggested that Marco tell it to Harry. The man suspected something about Harry but had no proof; he was trying to warn Harry off and prevent a crime. But Marco hadn't passed the name on. Now he wished he could find the courage to call the detective and put this nightmare behind him. He was afraid that Harry somehow knew all that he felt, because he hadn't been allowed to go home for several days.

He slept on a makeshift bed on the floor of Harry's living room and awoke each morning feeling brittle in his bones. His tongue felt harsh and the rims of his eyes grainy. Small stabbing pains bothered his ears, and the very end of his nose hurt too. He hoped for some illness, dramatic and obvious, to strike him.

On Friday he got up from the floor, stumbling with dizziness. He put on his trousers, offended at the old smell that rose from them, and removed his flannel pajama top to replace it with a shirt that showed stains at collar and cuffs. He put his bare feet into his shoes and shuffled to the bathroom, eager for its privacy.

This enforced stay with Harry, Alice and Bondi

was as much a problem to his sense of order as the terrible future that was rushing toward him. Once in the bathroom, he began to cough and produced a rattling of phlegm in his chest. He showered, letting the water run cold, then stood in the draft from the small open window. He cupped his genitals in his gnarled old hand, molding their weight in such a way that they offered him the illusion of youth.

He shaved carefully with the razor from his Dopp kit. The smell of souring washrags rose unpleasantly from the line of them flung over the rod on the wall. He rinsed his own cloth, folded it and placed it carefully in a plastic envelope.

He left the bathroom just as Alice, sleepy-eyed and domestic in her chenille robe and fuzzy slippers, reached the door. She smiled and said good morning, reminding him of his own wife when he was young.

"Breakfast in a little while, Marco," she said, and he was warmed by the simple kindness.

He put the water on to boil for the coffee, then sat at the kitchen table, staring at the end of his nose, making himself dizzy all over again.

"You feeling all right?" Alice asked when she came into the kitchen with her hair freshly combed, her robe replaced by a crisp housedress and sunny apron. Her sandaled feet made padding sounds on the tile floor.

"I think I've caught a cold," Marco said and was happy that there was a convincing raspiness to his voice.

Bondi rattled in, his hair wet and dark.

"What's the matter—you sick?" he asked with genuine concern.

Marco looked at the boy with thankful, mournful eyes. "I think I am. Thank you for asking."

"You better not get sick. Harry'll get mad as hell if anybody cops out," Bondi said.

"An old man can't help it if he gets sick," Marco whined, working up a store of self-pity.

"Who the hell's sick?" Harry asked, charging into the kitchen.

My God, Marco thought, this is turning into a vaudeville act, and I'll begin to laugh; then Harry will never believe I'm really sick.

"I am, Harry," he said. "I feel terrible. There's this pain in my chest and I have a cough." He coughed.

"Probably the pains came from sleeping on the floor. An old man shouldn't sleep on the floor," Harry said with bland good spirits.

No one remarked that he was the cause of an old man sleeping on the floor when he had a perfectly good bed in his room at the Cadillac Hotel.

"That's all right, Harry. I don't mind. I didn't want to crowd anybody. But a sick old man shouldn't be sleeping on the floor."

Harry took his eyes away from Marco's face and looked at Bondi pleasantly. "You got to get to work, don't you, kid? Let's not blow the job by being late."

Bondi nodded and wolfed down his eggs and toast, gulped his coffee.

"You know what to do about the wall sconces and the overhead lamps?" Harry went on.

"Hell, yes," Bondi said. "It was my idea to rig the charges to the rheostats, wasn't it?"

"You know what to do about the wall sconces and the overhead lamps?" Harry repeated with exactly the same inflection.

Bondi stood up. "If there's no other way for me to get the job of checking the bulbs, Fermi will have an accident."

"No, dammit!" Harry nearly shouted. "Don't you

arrange no goddamn accident on your own. You call me and I'll figure a way."

"All right, Harry, all right," Bondi said and, passing Alice on the way out the kitchen door, kissed her on the cheek in the absentmindedly affectionate way of a small boy kissing his mother goodbye on the way to school.

"You got to get going too, don't you, Alice?" Harry said.

She glanced at Marco. A little spurt of fear for him started in her eyes, and then she blinked and looked quite stupid and insensitive again.

"Sure."

Harry turned to Marco and grinned at him. "Have some more coffee, Marco," he said.

"Maybe too much coffee won't do me any good, Harry."

"Hot coffee's good for a cold. That what you got?"

"Perhaps. Perhaps a cold."

"Maybe the flu?"

"Maybe."

"All kinds of flu." Harry grinned. "Asiatic, pig, Australian. Yellow flu. Yellow flu's a pisser, Marco."

"I don't know I've got the flu . . ."

"Maybe pneumonia. Maybe you got galloping pneumonia. Maybe you're a really sick man, Marco."

"I don't feel well, Harry. That's all I know."

"What you want to do about it?"

Marco shrugged. "Perhaps I would feel better if I went home. A familiar room. You know?"

"Don't you think you need a doctor?"

"No. No doctor," Marco said hurriedly.

"No doctor," Harry repeated thoughtfully. Alice came through the kitchen in slacks and blouse, a sweater thrown over her shoulders in a girlish way. She touched Marco's cheek with her lips. She kissed

Harry on the mouth, then looked at Marco again as though concerned for his health and went on about her business. The silence between Marco and Harry stretched out.

"No doctor," Harry said.

"I think I'd feel a lot better if I could just go home to my own bed for a few days. Have a little rest, a little fresh air, make some tea, sit out on the benches in the sun. Sun is good for a little cold."

"Out on the benches in the sun, huh?"

"Yes."

"With your friends."

"What do you mean, Harry?"

"To maybe talk to your friends about things that don't concern them."

"I would never do that, Harry," Marco said, placing his hand over his heart.

Harry was staring at him, his mouth twisted in one of his puzzling but vicious grins. "Wouldn't you, Marco?"

"I feel terribly ill, Harry. You must let me go home." Marco started to stand up, but his legs were too weak to support him. "I'm very sick, Harry." Suddenly he threw up all over the table and floor with a violence that shocked them both.

Harry drove Marco home. He went to the closet and checked the stash of guns and explosives.

"I'll be sending Bondi and Peewit for these Friday night," he said.

"That will be a relief," Marco said. "It makes me very nervous having them in there."

"I'm just taking them away for a couple of days so the girls can get used to firing them. They'll be back." Harry smiled.

"Whatever you say, Harry."

Harry stared at Marco for a long while.

"What is it, Harry?"

"You know how to use a movie camera?"

"What?"

"I'm sorry I didn't think to get all this down on film. Sort of a documentary, you know?"

"I can't use such a camera," Marco said.

"Too far along anyhow, I guess," Harry said regretfully. "You take care of yourself now, and I'll see you when we get back from the desert."

"I will, thank you, Harry."

Harry nodded and left, closing the door behind him.

Marco went to the door and placed his ear against it, listening to Harry's footsteps fading away on the worn carpet. He sat down weakly on his bed and stared at the telephone, but he couldn't find the courage to call for help.

A knock sounded at the door, and his heart leaped in his chest like the fist of a devil. He hurried to open it, expecting that Harry had returned.

Metzler stood there.

33

"What can I do for you?" Marco asked with the shrillness of panic sharpening his voice.

"Not a thing. Just wondered where you've been."

"That's not true. You know where I've been. You followed me here."

Metzler walked over to the window and glanced out on the line of storefronts on the other side of Dudley Court. Marco couldn't afford a room with a view of the sands and the sea.

"Just checking on you from time to time." He turned and gestured to the straight chair. "May I sit down?"

"I don't want to be rude, but I'd just as soon you didn't. I haven't been feeling very well." A small inspiration came to Marco. "That's why I've been staying with my friends," he added.

"Uncomfortable as hell, isn't it?" Metzler said, sitting down anyway. "Four people in a one-bedroom, one-bathroom house. Sit down, Mr. Epstein."

Marco sat on the bed again.

"You're afraid of this character Smiley, aren't you?"

"No. Why do you say that?"

"Why didn't you tell him I approached you down here and made up that story about living on Broom Street?"

"Why did you do that? What purpose did it serve?" Marco asked.

Metzler smiled and picked at the fraying arm of the stained old chair. "I couldn't lose, handing that story out. Least it could do would be to shake old Smiley up. The best it could do would be to test your action with him."

"Suppose I just forgot to tell him."

Metzler nodded in disbelief. "Yeah, suppose. Mr. Epstein, you're a mess."

"What?" Marco said, shocked at the casual insult.

"Look at yourself. Now I figure you to be a very neat man, Mr. Epstein. Very much concerned about how you look. If you were off to your friends' for a while, how come you didn't take enough clothes?"

"I'm not a rich man. I haven't got a closet full of suits," Marco said lamely.

Metzler got up and walked to the closet. He put his hand on the knob.

Marco's heart plunged in his chest. "What are you doing?" he protested. The words scarcely passed the fullness in his throat.

"Just going to have a look."

"You have no right. You have no right," Marco said and nearly fell to his knees as he tried to rise from the bed. Metzler moved fast and grabbed his arm, settling him back down on the thin mattress.

"You've got no right to shame me," Marco said.

Metzler backed off and sat down again. "If you're still feeling bad, why didn't you stay at Smiley's?"

"They're going away for the weekend. I didn't choose to go with them," Marco lied, feeling trapped and harried.

"All right. I suspect that something's going on. Something criminal. I can't prove it yet, but I really do want you to tell Smiley that I called on you this time. Tell him I don't mean to let go. I want you to tell him that, if you really mean to hang in with that crowd. But if you'll tell me what's going down, I'll put it on the record, right away, that you're cooperating with the police."

Marco felt a surge of hope, followed at once by a new terror. At the very moment Harry might be outside the door listening to all that was being said; might have seen the detective and returned to catch Marco in a traitorous act.

"I haven't got the faintest idea what you're talking about," Marco said loudly. "I go to Harry's because he's my friend and is kind to me. He knows that I'm a lonely old man and takes pity on me."

"I'm trying to take pity on you too," Metzler said. He handed Marco a card. "If you change your mind," he said and left.

They all went out into the Mojave in the van and two cars.

The girls were given instruction in the use of the handguns and Thompsons. Surprisingly, Alice seemed the most adept in their use after only a little instruction, for no reason anyone could figure. Harry hugged her and praised her.

Bondi devised a new way of detonating the C-2 with the use of the rheostat that controlled the dimming of the houselights at the Pavilion. When they were raised full, the voltage would become critical and would explode the rigged bulbs.

"Electrician up in the booth rides gain on that dial," Peewit said.

Bondi nodded. "I can get into the booth easy and block the dial from going all the way to the top with a little plastic shim, so when the electrician tests the gain, it won't peak."

"So how do you blow it when you want?"

"The main box is backstage like it usually is. The master switch overrides the booth."

"You're one smart soldier," Harry said, not understanding much of what Bondi said but trusting the kid and wanting to prevent any quarrel. Peewit was clearly jealous.

Metzler was breaking and entering. If he was caught, his ass would be in the vise, but he was taking the risk while Harry's place was empty because he needed a handle to support his hunch or else he'd have to give it up altogether. He had already examined the house and hadn't found a thing. Now he was in the garage at the back.

He flashed a light around, noting the metal lathe, the vise, the taps and drills. Nothing condemning about that. He spotted an oily sheen on a piece of heavy paper about as big as a cigarette pack. He picked it up and saw that it had been torn from a larger piece. The paper was waxy and somewhat translucent, bearing the slightest odor of clay and something acrid. It was the only clue he found and was probably not worth a double damn, but he took it to the police lab all the same.

Waite rubbed it between his fingers, smelled it and said, "It's the kind of paper used to wrap certain types of plastic explosives."

Metzler smiled.

"Evidence in a case? Shall I tag it and work up a report?" Waite asked.

"Check it out against any stolen explosives in the last couple of months, but don't tag it. I can't use it as evidence the way I got it."

"No warrant?"

"Breaking and entering."

"Metzler, you've got to learn not to abuse the law."

Marco had fought with and mastered a good deal of his fear over the weekend. The bright sunshine, the company of his friends, and things familiar seemed to make the terror created by Harry Smiley unreal and distant, manageable.

He lay on his bed, watching the dusk fall in the alley beyond the window. He lifted the phone and dialed police headquarters according to the number on Metzler's card. He asked for the detective by name and was switched to Intelligence. Metzler wasn't there, and he was asked to leave his name.

"I'll call back another time," he said, suddenly frightened. He heard footsteps in the hall outside his door. He got to his feet, took a step and felt his legs give way. He reached for the side table, and it crashed with him to the floor. The door opened and Harry came in carrying a paper-wrapped bundle. Peewit and Bondi carried guns and explosives wrapped in blankets and coats. Harry put his stuff on the bed and reached for Marco.

"I'm still not well," Marco nearly screamed.

"If you're as sick as you seem to be, I'm not going to let you stay here alone," Harry said.

"I'll be better alone!"

"You're coming with me." Harry wrapped his arm heavily around Marco's thin shoulders. "You're coming back to the house and have some nice chicken soup."

"No, Harry."

"Yes, goddammit!"

He grabbed Marco's jacket with one hand, his

shoes with the other and shoved the old man out the door.

"Put these on," he said, dropping the clothes. Marco sat down on the landing and did as he was told. Then they walked down the stairs, Harry's hand tightly gripping the old man's elbow.

34

The showgirl named Thessaly, at home nursing various injuries done to her rather beautiful face and body, found that the fear that had haunted her for ten days had diminished and had been replaced by a deep and insistent anger. She was pretty certain Hush was behind the attack, because she'd wanted her girlfriend to have the job for a reason that seemed crazy at the time—and still did. Thessaly wasn't too bright, but she was no coward. She called the cops.

Her complaint was duly recorded, and she was asked if she wished to file a charge against the person or persons she suspected. Thessaly was afraid to go that far without absolute proof. The police said they were sorry, but there wasn't much more they could do except file the report.

It was, in fact, duplicated and added to a file labeled "Academy Awards Presentation, Dorothy Chandler Pavilion, March 16." It was the policy to compile a dossier on any major public event expected to attract large numbers of celebrities. It included all complaints, crank calls, threats and suspicious circumstances even remotely connected with the affair.

The complaint of a girl who'd been a member of the production and beaten some days before the gala evening was suspicious enough to be added to the dossier but not strong enough to warrant investigation on its own merits.

It was added to such matters as an anonymous phone call warning the police that John Wayne would be killed if he attended the awards. It was two days before the event, and such threats against the lives of celebrities were coming in with increasing frequency.

On the stage of the Dorothy Chandler Pavilion, the final rehearsals were in progress. Television technicians were swarming about backstage in the area of the scene lifts, instructing a crowd of carpenters and electricians about the construction of a temporary glassed-in television booth from which the director would command the signal sent out to the American public.

After the dress rehearsal the following day, Hush gathered with all the others in Harry's living room to go over the details of his plan. She thought it shoddy and amateurish but pretended to believe it was all most professional and certain of success.

Bondi showed the plastic shim he'd made to insert in the slot of the master gain switch so it couldn't be run up all the way in a test and explode the bulbs prematurely.

"All right, hold up on the rest of your orders," Harry said like a briefing officer. "What about you, Peewit?"

"What about me?" Peewit asked, staring at his hands.

"Tell me what you're supposed to do."

"I know what I'm supposed to do," Peewit said angrily. "I'm supposed to sit around outside in the

228

van while everybody else is inside where it's all happening."

"Now, Peewit—" Harry started to placate him.

"No," Peewit interrupted. "I'm a propman. I'm a powder man. I know as much as that punk kid about wiring up. But he gets to be inside, and I'm out in the alley playing 'chickie' with an eye out for the cops. That's a job for a kid. I don't carry no spit buckets."

"Why now, Peewit? Why do you start complaining now?" Harry asked. "Why at the eleventh hour?"

"I don't know anything about hours," Peewit said stubbornly. "I'm saying I ain't gonna hold everybody's coat while the fight's goin' on."

Harry shook his head in disgust. The whole thing was stupid, but he knew Peewit was as stubborn as he was dumb. He looked at Janet for some help. She shrugged her shoulders. Harry looked to Hush. She was smiling one of her sarcastic smiles at him, practically saying that he couldn't handle his own people. Harry turned back to Peewit.

"Who's going to drive the goddamn van?" he shouted, manufacturing vicious rage in one instant. "Just who in the hell can we depend on to drive that van?"

Peewit shrank back into the chair despite himself. Harry bent over him, thrusting his face close, modulating his voice now.

"Who's good enough to drive that big-assed van at speed through the streets with half the cops in the county out to stop him?"

Peewit glanced at Janet. She smiled at him, and he shrugged his shoulders almost the way she had done.

"You're the best wheelman we've got," Harry said.

Peewit smiled. "Well, O.K., Harry. Just so everybody knows I'm not gonna be on the inside because I have to be behind the wheel."

"Everybody knows. Now tell me," Harry said.

"I'm gonna drive the van right up to the stage entrance on Grand. The guns'll be in back under a pile of dirty clothes."

"What about the sign?"

"The sign?"

"The sign we made to put on the side of the van."

"Oh, yeah. First I put up the sign that says ACE CLEANERS; then I go to the stage entrance."

Harry coached Peewit through his recitation.

Each of the women detailed how they'd place themselves with the other performers in the show, who would be lined up in a long rank behind the celebrities. Evelynn was the last one to speak, agreeing with everything the others had said in the same dull, passive way she did everything.

Harry frowned at her.

"You know what's going on here, Evelynn?" he asked pointedly. "You understand any of this? You know why we're doing this?"

She looked at him expressionlessly. "Sure I do. You're unhappy," she said with stunning simplicity. "You're going to kill a lot of people so you won't feel so bad all the time."

Harry stared at her quietly for a long moment. He didn't seem angry. Finally he blinked his eyes several times and turned away from the softly smiling girl.

He asked each one of them to review his assigned task again and again, as though the plan he had devised was one of dramatic and significant complexity.

They huddled about like bad playactors trying out the roles of conspirators. Peewit, Harry, Bondi, Assy and Janet were dead serious. Alice and Evelynn were only somewhat interested, mostly confused by it all. Marco was clearly terrified, if anyone cared to read the fixed stare correctly, and only Hush seemed aware that this band of assassins was as amateurish and inept as most of those who have placed a bloody hand on history. She made no comment, merely pursed her lips judiciously and nodded when Harry glanced her way, and appeared to underwrite the strategies with her silence.

Harry, through Charlie Clabber's good offices, would be able to roam about backstage at the Chandler Pavilion pretty much at will. It would be simple enough for him to allow Peewit to deliver the real Thompsons at the scenery dock. Peewit was to arrive with the weapons well before time and take a parking space that would be saved for him by Bondi, who would have arrived for work early in the day. At the proper moment it would be simple enough to drive around to the dock without fear of traffic delay.

Janet in her capacity as a wardrobe mistress would help conceal the machine guns and would even pass them to Assy, Hush, Evelynn and Alice in the dressing rooms. Alternatively, Harry would attend to the switching of the real and prop weapons, depending on the location of the stage manager's table.

Peewit would remain at the dock, ready for the getaway in the van. He would discard the cleaners' sign at the proper moment.

When the grand finale of the show arrived, with all the winners and presenters and entertainers gathered for the traditional singalong, the bulbs would be exploded, and in the resulting chaos Harry's killers would fire at targets of opportunity.

Only when it was all over would the declaration of their protest be announced from hiding.

When all the recitations were done, Harry smiled.

"We've got to stay loose," he said. "Most bank robberies and assassinations go wrong because the perpetrators get too detailed in their planning and try too hard to stick to it. We'll stay loose and take advantage of whatever comes our way."

No one asked Harry where he'd come by that particular intelligence about bank robbers and assassins; they simply nodded like a bunch of puppets.

Hush tipped Assy the wink when no one was looking, and when she invited Assy over to stay at her cottage, Assy told Bondi she was too nerved up to sleep with him. They'd really celebrate when it was all over.

Janet and Peewit were already assigned to sleeping on Hush's pulldown couch. Peewit decided to stay at Harry's when Hush suggested the men have their own pre-battle drink without the women, but Hush maneuvered things with sympathetic concern for Alice, so that Alice was sent off to bed and didn't join the rest of the women.

Hush faced Evelynn, Janet and Assy in her own living room.

"That fool went through his ridiculous little charade guaranteed to get us all killed and nothing accomplished. Now I'm going to tell you the way it's really going to go down."

35

Michael awakened at 6:06 on the morning of the day of the Academy Awards. He felt a momentary thrill of expectation, a sudden desire to win the golden statuette. The feelings were instantly replaced by reluctance and an actual sense of fear. He closed his eyes, drew up his knees as he lay on his side, and pretended it wasn't time to get up.

Ever since the night he lost control at Truman's he had been avoiding everyone except those he couldn't avoid. He had the terrible feeling that he must hold on tightly or lose his sanity.

He got up.

At 6:15 Charlie Clabber got out of the bed he had shared with his wife for twenty-seven years. He looked at her sleeping on her back, mouth open, gasping like a beached whale, and compared her to Harry's women.

A charge went through his groin as real as a jolt of electricity. A smile tipped the corners of his mouth. He clacked his tongue, testing the memory of that incredible Friday night. I got to have another crack at those broads, he thought.

"I'm going to give Harry a spot right up against Jane Fonda's ass. I'll drown him in celebrities. I'll make him owe me," Charlie murmured.

"What are you mumbling about?" his wife complained.

"Go fuck yourself," Charlie scarcely whispered and went out to make the coffee.

Sheri was awake at 7:00. She watched Michael as he padded about the bedroom getting dressed. She saw the fullness of his waist and realized that her lover was no longer a boy.

Alice wasn't thinking about loving Harry as she watched him moving about their bedroom. Instead, her mind was on fear. It created the sudden hope that Harry would be struck down dead. But he left the room, and she heard the water running into the pot in the kitchen.

Marco heard Harry and wished as fervently as Alice for his death. What had happened to make his angry but really rather commonplace friend into a monster? How had he managed to corrupt a handful of apparently ordinary people? Marco looked at the telephone, touched it, but didn't try to lift the receiver to make the call to Metzler again.

Metzler had a second cup of coffee at his desk, then put through a call to 20th. Charlie answered the phone. Metzler identified himself and asked about the use of 20th guards for the Awards.

"Everybody'll be at the Chandler Pavilion except the regulars on duty at the studio," Charlie said.

"Part-timers, as well?"

"Everybody except men out on vacation or sick leave. What's up?"

"Nothing. Just a routine assessment of what force will be available to us from all sources."

"That all?"

"That's all," Metzler said and signed off.

Like hell, Charlie thought. Why'd he ask about part-timers? Who had his ass in hot water? "Harry," he said. "I wonder what that son of a bitch is up to."

Janet woke up feeling uncomfortable as hell on the pullout couch in Hush's cottage. Peewit lay beside her, his hard muscles crowding her in the narrow bed. He was on his back, staring at the ceiling.

"What's wrong?" Janet asked.

"I was thinking," he said and was still.

After a long time she asked him what he was thinking.

"What about after?"

"After what?"

"After tonight. We'll have to run away."

"I know," she said.

"We got a nice house."

"Yes," she said.

"We got that little cabin up to Arrowhead."

"Yes."

"I work pretty good."

"I know."

"You want to do it, Janet?"

"Do what, honey?"

"You want to kill all those people?"

She thought about it for a minute. "I do, baby, I do."

"Why?"

"I'm tired of being nobody."

He was silent again, and she watched the clock on the mantel tick off a minute: 7:21.

"All right," Peewit finally said.

Eddie Barnes awakened in his small apartment overlooking the Sunset Strip and wondered where all the good times had gone. He lay there in his jockey's body imagining that he was seven feet tall. Then he bounced out of bed and into the shower, singing, cutting capers and telling the world that he was the king of the hill on this big night coming. He dried himself off and hit the alarm button to keep it from buzzing off at 7:45. The phone rang.

Hiram Evers glanced at his Patek Philippe watch. "Hello, Eddie. Sorry if I woke you. Couldn't sleep myself. Been up for two hours. Details. Details. Want everything to go off without a hitch. Want this to be the best Academy Awards show ever." He hung up at 7:47.

At 8:00 on the button Bondi arrived at the Dorothy Chandler Pavilion's employee entrance. Fermi was at his desk double-checking a maintenance list for the day. This night was of, by and for professional theater people. It had to be perfect.

He smiled at Bondi.

"I want you to go into the Founder's Room and—" he started to say.

Bondi interrupted him. "I'm supposed to change the lamps in the auditorium. You said I was to check every one of the bulbs and make sure—"

"Take it easy, kid," Fermi said. "Plenty of time for that this afternoon. I just want you to do the same thing in the Founder's Room."

"Oh," Bondi said as though the information were being slowly digested. He smiled broadly. "Oh."

By 8:30 everyone who was to have anything at all to do with the ceremonies at the Music Center was up and about.

Every actor, actress, singer, dancer, electrician,

photographer, police officer, set mover, usher, parking lot attendant, maid, chauffeur, and killer was ready for the day.

Hush and Evelynn sat at the kitchen table; Janet had already gone to the Music Center with Bondi. Their faces were devoid of makeup, hair skinned back and concealed with kerchiefs. They were dressed in pants and sweaters. They were, oddly, never more beautiful in each other's eyes.

"We'll be all right, won't we?" Evelynn said.

Hush felt a wave of love pass over her. She held out her arms.

"Oh, baby," she said.

Evelynn moved off her chair and went to her knees between Hush's legs, where she could be held and comforted.

"You just do like I say and everything will be all right," Hush reassured the girl. "No matter what happens—ever—we'll be together. That's never going to change. No matter what anybody else thinks. No matter what I've told them," she murmured into Evelynn's hair.

Evelynn raised her face and Hush kissed her, so tenderly that it was a wonder even to herself.

"I love you, baby," she said. It was the first time she'd ever said that to anyone and meant it since her sister died.

Jim Truman called Michael at 9:03.

"Remember to wear your dark glasses in the auditorium. Don't take them off until you go to the stage to accept the award."

Michael laughed sharply. "You seem pretty sure I'll be getting it."

"You'll get it," Truman said.

Assy went into Alice's bedroom and got dressed in the black jeans and sweater she'd worn on the nights of the killings. She padded around in the black tennis shoes, watching herself in the full-length mirror hung behind the door. She liked the look and feel of the sinister outfit and regretted that she'd be half naked when the big action went down.

At 9:25 she heard Harry leave for the studio, and moments later Alice came into the bedroom.

"What did the girls talk about after I went to bed?"

Assy hesitated, wanting to tell her friend that Hush had decided she was too weak a straw to be included in the real conspiracy she'd designed, wanting to tell Alice to convince Hush that she was wrong, that she was strong enough to stand with them. But Assy kept her mouth shut, because Hush had described Alice as a dog that had given its loyalty to Harry and couldn't be expected to switch allegiance so quickly.

"Did anyone say she was scared?" Alice finally asked when Assy didn't reply.

"Everybody's scared, Alice. There's nothing wrong with being scared."

"I got sick the other night because I was so scared."

"I know. You going to be sick again?"

"I'd like to be. I'd like to be so sick I might die," Alice said in a whisper that had the quality of a scream. "Oh, my God," she suddenly cried out, "I'm not mad enough at anybody to kill them."

She stared at Assy as though she'd given herself away. Assy put her arm around her.

"You'll be all right."

She led Alice into the kitchen and poured her a cup of coffee. Hush and Evelynn came over and joined them. They sat around like four housewives having a coffee klatch.

Marco shuffled in, looking ill. Alice made a fuss over him and insisted that he get into her bed to rest.

The day grew warm. The smog started to build up.

At 10:03 Metzler was looking through the file of threats, crank calls and complaints having to do with the Awards. He noted the report on Thessaly Copley and her claim that she had been beaten by two persons dressed in anoraks, stocking masks and black trousers. He noted that she suspected another showgirl of the attack. Her name was Hazel Bostock.

Harry arrived at 20th at 10:10 and went to Charlie's office.

"What you been up to, Harry?"

"What do you mean?"

"Some cop named Metzler called up asking questions," Charlie said, trying it on. He noticed a slight tightening of Harry's jaw. "You know this Metzler?"

"He questioned me about the attempt to kill the President."

"That all?"

"How the fuck do I know? What did he ask about me?"

"Well," Charlie drawled, "nothing specific."

Harry grinned. "Then stop pulling my chain. Having a little party next Friday night, Charlie."

Charlie showed his teeth as well.

"What's my assignment?" Harry asked.

"Wherever you want to be, Harry. Consider yourself my deputy at large. Roam around and rub asses with all the celebrities you want, wherever you want."

"Rubbing asses, rubbing asses," Harry said and they both laughed.

By 10:55 Metzler had reached the Music Center and the cool, busy gloom of the Chandler Pavilion. He was challenged by a Center security guard togged out in a maroon jacket. Metzler flashed his badge, took the nod and walked along the corridor from the artists' entrance to the foyer that contained an elevator to the third-floor security command post. He entered the small office and greeted Sergeant Sloan of the LAPD and Freebody, the head of Music Center Security.

"Do you know where I can find Evers, the producer, or Eddie Barnes, the dance director?" Metzler asked.

"Looking for a job?" Sloan said.

"I'm already a star."

"Barnes is onstage, I believe," Freebody said.

"Everything cool?" Metzler asked.

Freebody wagged a hand in the air. "Running easy."

Metzler went down to the main stage access. He found Eddie Barnes and obtained a list of the performers, dancers and showgirls who would be on the stage that night.

As he scanned the roster, his heart started up the way it did at the track when he looked over the racing form and spotted a horse he just knew in his bones had to be a winner.

There they were. Alice Belmont, Hazel Bostock, Mara Courtney and Evelynn Shafter. The stage was practically filled with Harry Smiley's friends.

Metzler crossed the stage to the wings at the right, heading for a way out and a cup of coffee, someplace to sit down and think it out. Head down, he strode along and nearly collided with a woman rushing along with her arms filled with costumes. He lifted his head to apologize and said, "I'm sorry," to Janet Peewit.

Bondi sat in the Founder's Room, having checked out all the bulbs in the lamps, sconces and overheads. He lounged in one of the great leather chairs and pretended he was having a highball and smoking a two-dollar cigar. It must be a good feeling to be rich, he thought in a vague, unfocused way, and then he smiled. "But not tonight," he said aloud. It was 11:30. He went off to take his coffee break.

At 11:40 Metzler sat down at the counter in the coffee shop and saw Bondi having pie and coffee three stools away. His stomach started to churn with excitement. The arm of coincidence was getting too long by a mile.

He dawdled over the coffee and then walked the entire block around the Music Center complex. He had no reason to notice the van parked on the street, but he did have reason to notice the man who was feeding a coin into the parking meter.

Metzler stared at Peewit, wearing white coveralls with ACE CLEANERS on the back. It was just noon.

Metzler drove back to Headquarters but didn't get to see Lieutenant Jill until 1:30. He was moving around the city checking out security at all seven of the public gatherings in his book of possible trouble areas. Metzler might have done better standing still and waiting for Jill to come around again, but he chased after him and finally caught up with him at a television media convention being held at the Pan-Pacific Auditorium.

He sketched in the extraordinary gathering of Harry Smiley and his friends.

"What do you think it means?" Jill asked.

Metzler made a face of frustration. "I don't know," he said, "but I've got the biggest hunch of my life."

241

"Couldn't it be that these people know one another because they're all in the same business one way or another?"

"Mara Courtney's a whore."

"That's how a lot of performers pay the rent."

"Alice Belmont's a waitress. Gave up dancing years ago."

"So she picked up a one-shot gig and some extra money."

"Hazel Bostock and her roommate don't work at all."

"Don't they have to be in the union?"

"They aren't. I checked that. Somebody's doing favors for somebody. Janet Peewit is down as a wardrobe assistant. She hasn't got a union card either."

"Everybody can work a job one time without being union."

"Arnold Bondi is inside working on the maintenance crew, and a fellow named Peewit is outside with ACE CLEANERS sewn on his back. He *is* union—a union *prop*man."

Jill was silent for a long while.

"I have to tell you, I don't see a damn thing in your speculations. There's not going to be any money in the till. The statues aren't worth anything. They can't hope to hold an entire auditorium full of people hostage long enough to rob them or make demands we can only imagine. And after all's said and done, they could just be friends helping one another out with jobs for extra money any way they can," Jill summarized.

Metzler nodded hopelessly through it all.

"Well, what do you want to do?" Jill asked.

"Let me pick up a few of them on some pretext."

"What?" Jill nearly shouted. "Illegal arrest? Harassment?"

242

"Just Smiley, then. Let me lift him out of there."

"Out of the question. I want to back your hunch. I know the feeling, and I've had them pay off, but I can't have you shooting from the hip. We're out to protect all the citizens, and like it or not, that includes Smiley."

Metzler shut his mouth.

"All right," Jill said. "This is what I'll give you. Go back to the Pavilion. Keep your eye on Smiley. If he so much as spits on the floor, lift him."

At 2:00 Bondi drove Peewit's car from the employees' lot to where his van had been parked and took the space so that it would be available when Peewit returned. The ex-fighter made a big deal about Bondi's remembering to keep feeding the meter and drove off toward Broom Street to get Marco.

Sheri went out for some last-minute shopping at 2:12. Michael went to lie down to rest his eyes for a bit and fell deeply asleep.

Bondi moved the tall cherry picker ladder from place to place, changing the bulbs in the sconces and wall washers. He wore a large apron with two big pockets, one for new bulbs and the other for discards. Among the new bulbs were some marked with little blue smudges. They were the ones that had been rigged with C-2. He screwed them into chosen sockets where they'd spray the most glass when they exploded.

At 3:00 the security officers from the studios were called in for a short seminar on the conduct expected of them. No one paid much attention. It was fairly routine. Harry filtered out of the room in the middle of it.

At 3:05 Peewit arrived at Broom Street. The three showgirls and the chorus girl, looking not at all like such glamorous creatures, were ready to leave for the Music Center.

Hush was nervous, impatient, irritable; she turned on him as he walked through the kitchen door.

"What the hell took you so long?"

Peewit looked at her in surprise. "What the hell's eating you?"

"We've got to be getting down to the theater," she said.

"Who's stopping you?"

"I don't want to leave Marco alone."

"Why the hell not?"

"I don't trust him. He's about to lose what little nerve he ever had. We've got to watch him. He might go on the run. He might decide to yell 'Cop.'"

"Where is he?" Peewit asked.

"In the bedroom."

Peewit grinned accusingly. "With nobody watching him. You're not as smart as you think, are you?"

"The door's locked and the window's nailed half shut."

"Oh," Peewit said in a vague way. He went to the bedroom and unlocked the door.

Marco was still lying on the bed, clothed but with his shoes off, sheet drawn up to his stubbled chin.

"Get up," Peewit said suspiciously.

"I don't feel well," Marco tried a last time.

"You just get up, you old son of a bitch!" Peewit shouted in a sudden rage.

Marco hurried out of bed. He sat on the edge of it, swaying from real vertigo. He retrieved his shoes from under it, his face ashen.

Alice pushed past Peewit, bent down on her knees and put Marco's shoes on for him.

"Why"—he said, meaning to say one thing but finishing the sentence differently,—"are you helping me with my shoes?"

"I used to do it for my father," Alice said, as though that should explain everything.

"Let's get the hell out of here and get them guns," Peewit said.

36

The Pavilion was filling up with people. Some wore ribbons that said, "Photographer," "Academy Official," "Press," "Security," and any number of other words meant to authorize the wearer's presence.

Each was a different combination. White and blue buttons identified a "Program Participant." White and black said "Music Center." There were red badges with black letters and numbers, blue with black, yellow with green, silver with red and gold. There were so many different badges that nobody paid any attention to anybody's badge. Sensible security would have suggested one combination of colors so that all others would have been easily spotted and casual forgery made difficult.

Harry wandered around the place, noting that too much security seemed to mean no security.

He went outside and strolled around the plaza for five minutes. When he came back through the same entrance, there was a city cop on duty instead of a Pavilion guard. He glanced at Harry's uniform and cap badge, smiled, nodded and waved a casual hand as Harry went past him.

A twenty-five-dollar costume rental was the price of admission, Harry thought.

Metzler sat in the auditorium at the back, watching

Bondi as he moved the ladder and changed the bulbs. Metzler cleared his throat. Bondi jerked his head around, and the bulb he held slipped from his fingers and shattered on the arm of one of the aisle seats below. He quickly screwed another bulb into the empty light socket, hurried down the ladder, picked up the pieces and brushed the residue away with a rag.

At 4:20 Peewit and Marco arrived at the Cadillac Hotel. Peewit parked the van at the front entrance.

"It's not allowed," Marco said. "No parking here."

"The hell with it."

"The police are giving out tickets all the time."

"I don't give a damn. I'm fed up being the donkey in this operation. I ain't lugging those guns all over hell and back."

"Suit yourself. But sometimes the police do more than give tickets. Sometimes they search vehicles," Marco said with unusual spirit.

Peewit set his jaw stubbornly.

"I could wait here while you carry the goods down," Marco suggested, holding out his room key.

Peewit snatched it away. "All right. You stay right here."

"Right here," Marco agreed, scarcely able to speak around the excitement that was thick in his throat.

Returning from her shopping trip, Sheri heard Michael thrashing about crying out in his sleep. She ran into the bedroom, dropping her packages along the way, and took him into her arms as he awakened.

"Jesus Christ," he said. "I'm a wreck."

"We'll go away for a while," Sheri said, and Michael nodded.

"After tonight's over."

Marco stood by the open van doors, trembling like a wet cat. The guns lay on the floor wrapped in paper and old blankets. Peewit had gone to get the rest. Marco cursed himself for being a coward. Why couldn't he go to a public phone and make the call to the police or simply run away?

He turned at the sound of his name to see Bertha Isaaks waving at him. He started to run away from his friend, from the van; away from everything.

"What's the matter?" Bertha screeched after him.

Marco ran on. He heard feet pounding behind him but was afraid to look over his shoulder. His breath sharpened in his throat, honed to a cutting edge. Each gasp cut his lungs. Up ahead, along the walkway, a police car was on the prowl. It began to accelerate toward him just as he felt a heavy hand on his shoulder.

He was glad to stop. He turned to look into Peewit's face, angry and puzzled.

"What you trying to do?" he asked, putting his heavy arm around Marco's frail shoulders. They walked back toward the van. Marco was amazed to see how close they were to it. He thought he'd run a long way, but he hadn't run very far at all.

The police car was at their backs. Peewit led Marco off to the side to let it pass, but the black and white pulled up in front of them. The van was only yards away, its side doors open, the bundles exposed.

A big cop got out of the prowl car.

"Hold it," he said.

Hush watched Evelynn languidly change from her street clothes into a blue robe that seemed to accent rather than hide her nakedness. She had a momentary wave of feeling that wasn't at all carnal but sensual in the way she imagined a mother might feel at

248

the sight of her child. She wondered idly if that might be called love.

The dressing room was filled with chattering beauties putting on their makeup, fitting their elaborate wigs.

Evelynn sat down at a table and allowed the robe to slip from her shoulders, baring herself to the waist. She spread liquid base over her face, neck, shoulders and breasts. She was the most beautiful of them all, Hush thought.

"What's this all about?" the cop asked.

Marco was breathing too hard to answer.

"Kidding around," Peewit said.

The other cop got out of the car and came around to join his partner.

Bertha Isaaks stood some distance away, watching curiously. There was a little frown of concern between her eyes, but she was too timid to interfere.

"Your idea of kidding around is running footraces with an old man?" the cop pressed.

His partner wandered over to the open van and leaned into it, about to have a look around. Peewit turned his head sharply to watch.

"Jesus, Marco, tell him we was only kidding around."

Marco watched the officer reaching out to the bundles. The matter was being taken out of his hands. Fate had intervened to save him, to save them all.

The police radio squawked.

"Six twenty-two in progress. Main and Hill. See the man. Officer needs assistance. All cars."

"Let's go, Marty!" the interrogating officer shouted. Marty moved away from the van and raced to the squad car. The doors slammed and they sped away, siren rising above the sound of the peaceful surf.

Marco felt tears come to his eyes. Bertha Isaaks approached tentatively, looking Peewit over.

"It's all right, Marco?" she asked.

"Yes. Yes."

"Let's go," Peewit said, grabbing Marco's arm. "Jesus, this is a dangerous neighborhood. You really ought to move someplace else."

Marco began to laugh hysterically.

Peewit and Marco arrived at the Music Center at 5:56. Bondi was standing by his car, jiggling from one foot to the other. When he saw the van, he jumped into his car and pulled away, making room for Peewit. Then he double-parked and came barreling out to confront the ex-fighter.

"Where the hell you been?" he demanded.

"Shut your mouth. Don't go yelling at me, kid."

"I'm asking where the hell you been. You're late."

"A few minutes, maybe."

"I been standing out here half an hour."

"So what?" Peewit shouted.

Bondi took a step, hands held at ready. Peewit turned his left shoulder, ready to dump Bondi on his ass.

"Hey!" Harry said. They turned to face him as he approached across the sidewalk. "That's enough. You two crazy?"

"This kid's got a big mouth," Peewit said.

"Hell, we know that, but we know he's a good man, too," Harry soothed. "Bondi, get your car off the street. Some cop'll come nosing around if you let it stay there double-parked."

"That's why we was late, Harry," Peewit said.

"What the hell you saying?" Harry asked as he watched Bondi drive off to the employees' lot.

"Some cops held Marco and me up."

"What for?"

Peewit was going to say it was Marco's fault, but he saw that the old man's face was screwed up in naked terror. Something touched Peewit. "Parking in a no-stopping zone. Those cops in Venice are hustlers," he said instead.

"That's all?" Harry asked.

Peewit nodded.

"O.K. No harm done. Open up."

Peewit unlocked the van.

Harry got inside. He strapped a police holster with a .38 Special in it around his waist high up and buttoned his Eisenhower jacket so that it was concealed.

Hush sat outside the dressing room in a straight-backed chair. Beneath her robe she wore a G-string and flesh-colored tights. Two small cups covered her breasts.

Marco sat next to her, wearing his best black suit. It was only a short time ago, he thought, that he'd been with this beautiful girl in this very theater, out in the audience listening to a concert of rare excellence.

Hush looked at Marco and smiled. "You look nice," she said.

"So do you."

She laughed softly.

"I like your button."

He glanced down at the badge Harry had given him to wear. It said "Security."

"Suppose somebody asks me who I'm with?" Marco asked. "Suppose someone asks me for identification?"

"They won't. Don't you worry."

"You don't have to sit out here in the corridor with me," Marco said.

Hush smiled at him. "Oh, yes, I do, luv."

The crowds massed in the plaza were eager for the first glimpses of the arriving celebrities. Early comers were already stepping out of expensive cars and hired limousines to be herded like prize cattle through alleys fashioned of velvet ropes toward Alan Alda, who greeted them before the television cameras, doing a rather thankless job with considerable grace and the help of Farrah Fawcett-Majors, herself no small obstacle to overcome.

Eddie Albert, with his heavily lined grin and careful eyes, paused to agree that it was going to be a mighty fine night. "Mighty fine."

Michael Learned, immediately recognized by the crowd because she'd been the mother on the Waltons long enough for the youngest characters to have grown and have children of their own, allowed that it was to be a grand evening. "Just grand."

Raquel Welch was thrilled at the prospect of a "thrilling" Awards Presentation; William Holden shyly admitted the possibility that it might be the best in years; Shirley Jones was sure she'd love it; and Lee Grant smiled her crooked smile and said she was happy to be there when clearly she was not.

Harry walked past the line of fire doors along the side of the stage area. They were marked with red and white alarm warnings. If one of them was opened with the use of a special key, a warning bell would go off.

A big man wearing the maroon jacket of a Music Center security guard strolled toward Harry. They met just as they reached one of the fire doors. The guard stepped aside and, throwing his weight against the push bar, flung the door open and glanced outside. Three television technicians stumbled in under the weight of their equipment.

"Thanks," one of them said, and the guard nodded.

"Hey," Harry exclaimed, "how come the alarm didn't go off?"

"What?"

"You turn it off to let those guys in?"

"No. It's getting close to show time. We can't take the chance some sucker opens one of these doors somehow and sets the alarm blasting off all over the place."

"Makes a hell of a racket, huh?" Harry said, not believing his ears.

"That's why we turn the system off."

"Isn't it supposed to keep unauthorized people out of here?"

"Crazy, isn't it?" the security guard said smilingly as he walked away.

Harry decided they'd bring the guns in through that door and went out to tell Peewit he'd found an untrafficked spot to make the transfer.

Metzler saw Harry open the fire door. He walked up behind him.

"Hello, Smiley," he said.

Harry snapped his head around.

"Glad to see me, Smiley?"

Harry closed the fire door and stared at Metzler without saying a word.

"You protecting the people, Harry? You protecting us?"

"What the hell you want with me?"

"Maybe *I'm* protecting *you*—from yourself. Maybe I've got proof—not trial proof—but proof enough for me—that you and some of your crazy friends were at the gun shop out on Ventura the night your friend Geneva was offed. Maybe I got proof—scientific proof—that you were up in the hills the night an old man named Tregaskis got his."

A pulse was beating in Harry's throat. He bared his teeth savagely.

"You know what I think?" he asked.

Metzler stared at him silently.

"I think you're full of shit."

Metzler smiled. "Well, I've got my eye on you, turkey. And don't you forget it."

He walked over to the curtains, slapped them, found the parting, and disappeared from sight, leaving Harry trembling with rage.

"You look like you're going to have a heart attack."

Harry whipped around like a scalded cat to face Charlie Clabber, who reached out to give him a steadying pat on the gut. His face froze. His eyes dropped to Harry's waist. Charlie ripped down the zipper and opened Harry's jacket.

"What the hell you got there? Just what the hell you doing carrying a piece? You're no goddamn cop. You got no authority."

He reached for the .38. Harry snatched it from the holster before Charlie could touch it. The sounds of the gathering audience drifted in from the auditorium. Harry was afraid that Charlie's voice could be heard.

"Shut your fucking mouth," he whispered fiercely, pointing the gun at Charlie's belly.

Charlie slapped at the gun. "You son of a bitch—"

A shot went off. It sounded like a door slamming.

Metzler had crossed the stage apron and gone down into the auditorium. He had started up the aisle, pausing to make way for people looking for their seats. As he'd come up even with the row where Bondi had dropped the light bulb, he'd seen a sliver of glass glittering on the carpet. He stooped down to pick it up just as a sharp crack sounded at his back.

He stood up fast, putting the glass shard into his pocket and listening very carefully. He thought he recognized the sound but wasn't quite certain. No one else seemed to have noticed anything. He hesitated, staring at the curtains from which the sound seemed to have come. He decided there'd be nothing lost in taking a look and started backstage.

It's not all that easy to kill somebody with a bullet from a .38, but pointblank, up against the belly, angled just right so that the slug enters the heart from below, it can be done. Charlie slumped into Harry's arms, his mouth falling open and his eyes staring with a look of outrage. Harry staggered under the sudden weight and looked around desperately, his mind racing like a jet. There was no one in sight; only a knot of people down at one end of the backstage area, and they were absorbed in themselves.

A few yards away, he saw a big green prop box. He sort of waltzed Charlie over to it, set him down against the wall and opened the lid. It was only partially filled with some pulleys and coils of rope which he cleared out in a jiffy, piling them neatly along the wall as though they were meant to be there. He hefted Charlie's heavy body into the box, closed it and sat down on the lid just as Metzler reappeared on the stage. They stared at each other across the space.

"I got my eye on you, sucker," Metzler called before disappearing through the curtain again.

37

Alice came out of the dressing room looking like a kewpie doll, her lips painted like a little valentine cinnamon heart, her hair puffed out from beneath a velvet cloche. Her dress revealed knees tinted with rouge.

"You are the bee's knees," Marco said and tried to smile.

"Evelynn wants you, Hush," Alice said.

"You sit here and keep Marco company," Hush said. "You understand?"

"Yes, I do," Alice replied and looked at Marco as though he were a patient in distress and she a nurse. She sat beside him, and together they watched the arrival of the celebrities.

"It doesn't have to be, Alice," Marco said without looking at her.

"What doesn't have to be?"

"Any of this madness."

"I don't know what you're talking about," she said.

"This killing."

"I don't want to listen," Alice said.

Marco turned to her and took her hands in his. They were cold.

"Are you trying to fool yourself that you don't really know what's about to happen?"

Alice's painted-doll face screwed up as though she were about to cry or scream.

"You know that the young man in the gun shop is dead. You know that the old man in the hills is dead."

"Don't talk to me!"

"More people are going to die."

"I don't want to think about it," Alice begged.

"It's going to happen." He dug into the pocket of his vest and removed his heavy old watch. "In something over two hours it will happen. It's half past seven."

Alice stood up.

"I'm going to get mad if you keep talking to me, Marco."

He stared up at her. "Listen to me. I know you're afraid. I've been afraid. I am afraid."

"There's nothing I can do about it," Alice said.

"There's nothing you have to do. I think I'm finally able to act."

"I'm not listening to you."

Marco rose, never taking his eyes from her. She kept her head averted.

"Will you excuse me?" Marco said. "I would like to go to the toilet."

She nodded and he began to walk away, suddenly feeling a real urgency to empty his bladder. He saw Metzler coming toward him and glanced toward the door of the rest room.

"Where are you going, Marco?" he heard Hush call at his back. He walked faster.

Metzler saw the look on Marco's face and knew the old man wanted to talk to him in the privacy of the toilet. Was he ready to finally blow the whistle on Smiley? Metzler wondered. He heard Hush call the old man's name and saw the look of terror appear on

Marco's face. She began to run after him, and Metzler ran too.

Hush grabbed Marco's arm. "Where are you going?"

Metzler reached them, taking Marco's other arm. "Something wrong here?" he asked, looking into Marco's face.

"Who the hell are you?" Hush demanded. "Get your hand off my friend."

"She your friend, Mr. Epstein? Is she really your friend?"

"I just want to use the toilet," Marco said piteously.

They all became aware of the sharp smell of urine. Marco looked down at his shoes in shattering humiliation.

"Now do you see what you've done, whoever the hell you are?" Hush cried. "You've made him embarrass himself."

Alice finally joined them, clucking her tongue like an anxious mother, drawing Marco away. Then Harry was with them, taking it all in. Marco wouldn't look at him for fear that Harry would read his mind, know that he'd tried one last time to accuse them.

"See if you can dry his pants out, Alice. See that he looks presentable again," Harry said tightly.

He nodded to Hush, who left with Alice and Marco; then he turned to Metzler.

"Got my eye on you, sucker." He grinned boldly.

Michael arrived with Sheri at 7:46. She was breathtakingly beautiful in a gown the color of deep water. He was wearing sunglasses to hide the ravages of sleeplessness. They had talked of going away for a while after this was over, but Michael had come to realize that he must seek more than a change of scenery to get over the terrible nightmares, the sense that his carefully nurtured identity was slipping away from him, that the frightened, quivering creature inside would finally be exposed.

They found their seats next to Truman. At one minute to eight Truman leaned across Sheri and said, "Remember to take the shades off when you go up there to collect the award."

Harry stood in the doorway of the performers' lounge, which was crowded with celebrities. A table with the Oscars and another with the prop machine guns were taking up a lot of room.

Freebody from Music Center Security looked in. He was greeted by Bob Hope, Rock Hudson, Shirley MacLaine and other actors who'd been through this routine many times before. Freebody glanced at Harry.

"You're with 20th. Right?"

"Yes, sir."

"Where's your boss, Charlie Clabber?"

"I don't know. I haven't seen him around for a while."

"I told him to move these tables out of here so these people can have a little room."

"I'll do it," Harry said.

"I'll get somebody to give you a hand," Freebody said.

"The hell with that. We can help," Bob Hope offered.

He tapped Gene Hackman on the elbow, called out to Walter Matthau, enlisted the help of Clint Eastwood and Ryan O'Neal. He made a joke of it, about Harry having the highest-paid moving men in the world working for him.

They smiled at Harry. They kidded with him as

though he were one of them. Harry glowed. Then the moment was over and they moved away from him, back to their own kind.

The rattle of the dancers' taps sounded like gunfire to Harry's ears.

38

The President of the Academy of Motion Picture Arts and Sciences stepped up to a plexiglas and chrome lectern and delivered an admirably brief welcoming address before introducing Bob Hope. The show was ticking along and running.

The obligatory introduction of the accounting firm of Price-Waterhouse was given.

The all-too-familiar repartee between beautiful pairs of successful people went on, punctuated from time to time with renditions of nominated songs.

In the glass booth the director chose his images from among the seven cameras watching the proceedings from various vantage points. It was rolling along as smooth as glass, even the occasional fluff made to look slick and shiny.

Harry watched with envy that burned like acid in his gut as the famous handed each other the golden lollipops.

At 9:35 he glanced at his watch, left his vantage point and went to the fire door along the walkway. The dancers and showgirls moved past him on their way to the stage for the big production number. Out came the chorus boys in their wasp-waisted striped suits and grey fedoras. The propman handed out the Tommy guns as they hurried by.

Harry opened the fire door. Peewit was waiting. They brought in the real guns.

Peewit wanted to hang around, like a kid delivering ice cream to somebody else's party. Harry told him to get out to the van before some cop came nosing around.

Eddie Barnes was in the wings, following the number with little movements of his feet, trying to convince himself that the show could lead him back into the big time.

The music came up, the last taps clattered out, and the girls danced off the stage. Alice's heart jumped and she nearly tripped when she saw Eddie. Her old friend was right there where he could get hurt, even killed, when the guns opened up, and she didn't want that to happen.

"You shouldn't be here!" she yelled at him.

"What the hell do you mean?" Eddie frowned.

"Just that you should be out front. You got a good seat right in the center, haven't you?"

"I'll be there for the finish. What's this all about, Alice?"

"Nothing. I just want you to have a good seat," she called back softly as she ran on toward the dressing rooms.

A hush came over the audience as the stage was cleared. The big awards were coming up. Harry walked over to the table where the fake Tommy guns had been replaced by the male dancers. He put his hands underneath the rim of it on one side and hissed between his teeth for the propman's attention. The guy hurried over.

"What the hell you think you're doin'?" he whispered harshly.

262

"Help me get this goddamn bunch of junk out of the way. There's going to be one hell of a lot of traffic through here in a little while, and we don't want anybody knocking this damned hardware on their toes."

"O.K. O.K.," the man said soothingly and picked up the other end. Harry backed off to the place where the blanket- and paper-wrapped guns were piled on top of the prop box that contained old Charlie Clabber.

"Thanks, chief," Harry said and touched the bill of his cap.

The propman smiled, waved and hurried back to catch the rest of the show. In a matter of seconds the prop guns were replaced by the real ones, loaded and ready to kill.

Janet came over to him. "It's going to happen soon, isn't it, Harry?" she asked nervously.

"Pretty soon." He could see how edgy she was. She needed something to do. "Keep an eye on these pieces, Janet. Can you do that?"

"What?" she said as though startled. "They the real ones?"

He winked.

She stared at them, fascinated. "I'll watch them, Harry."

The presenter's voice onstage said, "And the winner is . . . Vivian Lennox for *Mute.*"

The theme music from the film rose up with the applause.

Metzler stood at the back of the house with his hands in his pockets. His fingers played with the sliver of glass he'd picked up from the carpet. It was sharp and he pulled it out, wondering, for a moment, what the hell it was and how it had gotten there. There was an oily sheen to it. He rubbed his thumb in the shallow of the shard, then lifted it to his nose.

He recognized at once the smell of plastic explosive. He looked toward the sconces and realized that some of the bulbs in them were unlit. All at once he flashed on much of what Smiley and his bunch intended to go down.

They were going to blow those bulbs filled with explosives, probably with some sort of radio triggering device. The bursts would turn the sconces into crystal grenades, blowing them up into a million deadly points that could slash, pierce, maim and even kill. There would be instant panic, people rushing to the doors to escape the danger, and only adding to it, crushing one another. Under cover of that terrible, bloody confusion, Smiley intended to—what?

That would have to wait. Frantically Metzler looked around for security guards or police, but there was no one in sight. Up on the stage Goldie Hawn and Peter Fonda were cracking jokes.

Then, "For the best actor in a supporting role, the nominees are . . ."

Metzler started moving down the aisle to the far right of the auditorium. He bent over the richly dressed people and smiled.

"I beg your pardon. A special event's been planned immediately following the announcement of the best picture."

"What the hell—" a grey-haired man started to protest.

Metzler scarcely raised his voice. "Please, there's nothing to be alarmed about. Just leave your seats quietly and file out the side door to the lobby."

The young blonde with the grey-haired man got wide-eyed, opened her red painted mouth as though about to scream. Her escort sensed it. He gripped her wrist.

"Heidi, it's all right," he whispered fiercely. "Be quiet and let's do what the gentleman says."

"But what—" she started to speak again.

The man stood up, dragging her along, drawing her close to him. He leaned down and across her.

"Come on, Joe. Margaret. Some sort of ballyhoo going on."

Joe looked afraid, glanced at Metzler, nodded.

"Sure, I get it," he said, standing up swiftly. "Goddamn bomb scares."

"Well, for God's sake, don't let anybody hear you say it," Metzler hissed into his ear.

People in the vicinity turned around in annoyance at the activity.

Metzler hurried along, giving the message that there was danger in such a calm and smiling way that no one gave in to panic. He made them all party to a conspiracy of silence and courage. They'd read enough to know that uncontrolled panic would send the whole place rushing madly to disaster. Metzler moved, bending down, whispering, straightening up. The steady emptying of the seats was causing wider and wider attention. People farther and farther away were craning their necks to see why so many of the audience were leaving.

A Pavilion guard moved down the aisle. He grabbed Metzler by the arm. Metzler pushed him back against the wall out of earshot.

"Whatever you've got to ask, keep your voice down," Metzler said.

"What the hell are you doing?"

"I'm Metzler, LAPD Intelligence."

"I don't give a fuck—"

Metzler struck him sharply with his fingertips just

beneath the breastbone. The guard coughed and grimaced with pain.

"Bombs, you stupid son of a bitch. I'm not pushing these people out because I don't like the show. Now you go get some of your buddies—anybody with authority—to start moving the people along the aisles near the crystal fixtures the hell out."

The guard's face was white. He nodded.

"Smile, stupid," Metzler said.

That was more than the guard could manage, but at least he didn't scream out "Bomb!" and start the panic. He hurried off, and Metzler patiently kept on telling his little fiction to one person after the other, begging them by his manner and the subtle urgency he put into his voice to obey him without argument or discussion.

Up on the stage they were just about to announce the award for the best male performance in a leading role. Elliott Gould was making the presentation. As he tore open the envelope, he very frankly watched what was going on at the side of the auditorium.

"I get a feeling the friends and relatives of the losers have already decided to take a powder."

Practically everyone was rubbernecking the action now, so he wasn't drawing undue attention to it. When Metzler glanced up at the remark, he caught Gould's eyes upon him, and he had the idea the actor was shrewd enough to know something was going on. Tensions were growing in the place.

Let's hope you do a good "Yankee Doodle Dandy," Elliott, Metzler thought, just in case somebody starts the stampede.

Freebody and a few of his maroon-jacketed security men were moving back and forth in both aisles now. There was a rising murmur in the crowd.

Harry had come up as close to the stage apron as he could get. Something was going on out there on his left. His view had been obscured, but the attention of the people onstage was clearly taken with something going on in the auditorium. Now he saw Freebody and his men clearing both sides of the house. He knew at once that somebody had discovered a bomb threat, but he had no way of knowing whether the danger discovered was that of his making. Bomb scares had become that common.

"The winner is . . . Michael Nordland for *Mute*," Gould said.

The music came up.

Michael rose from his seat, surprised that he felt no elation or pride. He felt he was being given an honor once more that he didn't really deserve.

"The glasses," Truman hissed as Michael went past his knees.

Michael didn't remove them, afraid that people might see the terror in his eyes. Out in the aisle, he came face to face with Metzler. Deep in the eyes the cop looked as scared as Michael felt.

Metzler watched the actor go to the stage to receive the golden statuette. He looked up at the control booth, wondering if that was the vantage point from which the bulbs would be exploded. Everything seemed all right in the booth. He started for the stage, knowing that there were ancillary master controls in the wings. As he approached he saw Smiley at the edge of the proscenium. They stared at each other for a moment.

Something seemed strange about Smiley, Metzler thought. He dropped his eyes to Smiley's open jacket and saw the gun. His eyes flashed back to Harry's, but he'd already given himself away. Harry's hand dropped to the holster.

267

Harry looked into the wings and saw Bondi standing by the master switch, just where he was supposed to be. He pumped his arm up and down. Bondi smiled stupidly.

"Pull the switch!" Harry shouted and started to run across the stage.

Michael saw Harry coming at him with a drawn gun. The fear he'd been concealing exploded in his chest.

People were screaming and shouting.

"Pull the switch, Bondi!" Harry yelled again.

From the corner of his eye Michael saw Metzler diving for the stage, jerking a gun from the holster beneath his armpit. He turned his head to see Bondi fumble at a knife switch for a moment, throw something aside and slam it home.

The crystal sconces exploded all at once, the glass shattering with a singing sound. Millions of tiny barbs sprayed out forcefully into satin and velvet, gold lamé and silk—into flesh. Eyes, powdered cheeks, slender necks, bare arms and half-exposed breasts were laced with blood. Several hundred beautiful people were dappled with it like victims of a plague.

Michael saw the blood and had a clear memory of Carter Nordland at the moment when a bullet took his voice and his life. He remembered what it was that Carter shouted at him in contempt:

"Trying to find a hole to crawl into, you yellow son of a bitch?" he had screamed, even at the end refusing to forgive Michael for not backing him in the stupid fight against the Limeys.

Connections flashed through Michael's head. He remembered that night long years ago when he'd made no move against his aunt's assailant, and that ridiculous confrontation with Smiley in the bar after the hockey game. Now he saw Harry running at him. He tried to step aside but became entangled in the confusion of the presenters, Metzler and people who seemed to be appearing out of nowhere. He raised the Oscar to strike at Smiley. He looked straight into the fury and terror in Harry's eyes and read an accusation there as well. He couldn't complete the blow. Smiley hit him in the chest, knocking him into the charging Metzler, who shouldered him away and knocked him to the floor.

When the explosions went off, Evelynn and Hush and Assy were in the showgirls' dressing room, waiting for the last call to go onstage for the big sing-along. Hush understood right away that the gun had been jumped. She grabbed Evelynn by the arm and dragged her to her feet.

"Oh, no," Evelynn said.

"It'll be all right. Just do what I told you. Get a gun from Janet and hide it in your muff," Hush ordered.

Assy had kicked the spiked heels off and was already racing barefoot out the door and toward the table where the machine guns lay.

"Take one. Take one just the way I told you!" Hush shouted after her. Then she went to her makeup box and removed the two small Barettas. She intended to be the least conspicuous and encumbered of them all.

39

Harry was on the run. Things had gone off prematurely. The glittering, beautiful celebrities were not lined up like so many figures in a shooting gallery along the length of the stage singing "There's No Business Like Show Business." He'd have no opportunity to face them with his soldiers, armed with machine guns, his own Tommy gun in his hands spitting out his rage and frustration.

There was only a scattering of the famous on the stage. He scarcely saw them. His big plans were nothing but rags that encumbered his escape. His desire to be a somebody could only delay him now. With indelible clarity he saw who and what he was. He was "spit in the wind"; a never-was; a second-stringer with a game leg to excuse the fact that he had never been able to run the race; a fourflusher; a fugitive from bust city. He was a man on the run, and he couldn't even go that alone; he had to have Alice. He had to have somebody to crawl with him into a hole—if he could ever find one deep and dark enough—and she'd have to do, for lack of anything better.

He ran past Assy, who was standing at the table of guns, tucking one away in the concealment of the huge muff she carried. Evelynn stood near her, hands tucked into a similar muff, holding a gun and

270

looking at Assy with dull eyes, waiting to be told what to do next.

Personalities had gathered in the wings, ready to go onstage for the finale. They were in confusion now, screaming and crying in terror. Harry bulled his way through them, Metzler in pursuit.

Janet saw the detective stop and take a shooting stance, revolver pointing at the running Harry.

Janet picked up a machine gun and slammed home the cocking mechanism. She screamed Peewit's name, wanting him near her suddenly. She stepped around Assy and Evelynn to get a shot at Metzler. Her violent actions and the scream had drawn Metzler's attention. He reacted immediately by running headlong into her, grabbing the barrel of the weapon she held.

Assy grabbed Evelynn and drew her toward the stage. They'd been told to go to their assigned places even if one of their number got boxed in. Assy looked for a shot at Metzler as she ran but couldn't risk one for fear of hitting Janet as well.

Metzler, encumbered by his handgun, was having more trouble than he had bargained for. Janet let go of the Thompson all of a sudden. She clawed her fingers and went for Metzler's eyes. One hand raked four tracks, immediately bloody, along his cheek from eye to chin. He threw the automatic weapon away but held on to his revolver as he tried to grab her wrists and subdue her. She kicked at his shins and tried to knee him in the groin.

He heard someone shout a warning at his back. He twisted around, flinging Janet with him, to see a young cop moving into a shooter's stance and dropping a .38 right on line with his heart. The kid was nervous and ready to shoot anybody who looked dangerous. Metzler raised the hand that held the gun to indicate his surrender, trying to hold on to Janet at the same time. She almost got away, and he instinctively used his gun arm to help him hold her. The cop fired just as Janet jerked around in front of Metzler. He could feel the impact shudder through her body into the hand that grasped her wrist.

Someone screamed her name, and he felt a shattering blow on the back of his neck.

Harry felt a weakness in his bowels and legs. He was so tired he wanted to weep. Everything had gone wrong again, as it had always done. Smiley, the second-rater, had been kicked in the ass by fate again. Things and people always let him down.

They'd be sorry.

He passed Marco huddled in the chair outside the dressing room, a man with no place to go and no will to get there.

"It's over, Marco. It's all over. Get the hell out of here," Harry said. "Take care of yourself."

Marco looked at him uncomprehendingly and continued to sit there as Harry went into the dressing room.

After a moment Marco straightened up. He thought about running away now that there was nobody to stop him. He saw Hush approaching. She was half-naked in the showgirl furs and feathers. The thought came to him, startlingly, that he'd known that beautiful body intimately. He started to smile at the thought. He stood up as Hush came close.

"Harry says it's all over," Marco said.

Hush removed a small automatic from the depths of the muff. Marco could and would tell the police of her involvement.

"I'm sorry," Hush said. "There might have been a time when we'd have traveled the world together."

The little gun coughed three times, like an apologetic old man. Marco fell back dead into the chair.

Hush knew that Peewit and Bondi would keep quiet if they were taken. She wasn't so sure about Alice.

40

Assy walked up to Vivian Lennox, the winner of the best actress award, Michael Nordland's co-star in *Mute*. The actress was standing in curious isolation amid the turmoil, holding her small, slender body very straight, motionless except for her head twisting from side to side like that of a mechanical toy, eyes wide and brimming with unshed tears.

"It'll be all right, Miss Lennox," Assy said. "You better come with me."

Vivian allowed herself to be led over to the glassed-in television booth. Assy tried the door but it wouldn't open. Someone inside had wedged a chair underneath the handle at the first sounds of the explosions, apparently believing it would afford some protection from whatever danger was outside.

There were four technicians at the console trying to make some sense from the signals received on the monitors from the abandoned cameras and the two manned ones, all of them sending pictures. The director was behind them, trying to sort out anything of significance and value, shouting orders to anyone, telling them to get all they could on tape, as though he were an old-time news cameraman risking life and limb for the story.

Assy kicked at the wooden bottom half of the door

274

with the toe of her rhinestone slipper. The director's assistant looked at her, startled, stupid-eyed.

Assy pointed to the blocking chair. She saw the girl speak to the director and tap him on the arm. When she spoke to him a second time, he turned and looked first at her, then at Assy and Vivian Lennox with a fishlike stare. When recognition of the motion picture star finally came to him, he motioned his assistant to take the chair away.

Assy gently pushed Vivian before her into the glass booth and caught the tail end of what a video mixer was saying.

"—don't know what the hell good it'd do. Any gunmen want to get at us they'd just off us through the goddamn windows. Still nothing on number seven camera. Shit."

"The crew left it long ago, Marty," one of the other men at the console said.

"I know that. I got eyes," the director said.

"What the hell, Marty, we got two out of seven running."

"But I want to see what's going on in the performers' lounge. It's loaded with stars. If there's any kidnapping going on, that's where it'll be happening."

"Kidnapping? Who the fuck's said anything about kidnapping?" the technician nearly shouted. "Excuse me, Miss Lennox."

"Could be," the director said.

"You've been watching too much television, Marty. What we've got here is your everyday terrorist bombing," his assistant said, as though such atrocities had become commonplace, even predictable.

"Shut the fuck up, Marsha," Marty said. "We're on to a big story here. Kidnapping. Half-assed political protest. Mad bomber. Whatever. And I'd like to have as much goddamn coverage as I can get. I'd like to have camera seven taking the pictures of all those celebrities in the lounge. I want that all on tape if I can get it."

"You want a fucking Pulitzer," the talkative technician said and rose from his chair. "O.K., I'll help you get it."

One of the other men on the console stood up. "I'll go with you," he said without emphasis.

They went to the door, smiling politely at Assy and Miss Lennox, with the air of battle-hardened veterans.

Evelynn watched Assy take Vivian Lennox in hand like a child seeking instruction. After they had gone into the control booth, she looked around for someone she could take in tow. She walked out nearly to the center of the stage. Almost naked, she looked as beautiful as a witch from a hedonist's paradise—or from hell. She watched the audience, screaming and clawing in every direction, as though they were curious migrating creatures.

Michael, still half-stunned, was getting to his feet close by. It caught her attention. She walked over to him and said, "Mr. Nordland, I've always admired you. Will you please come with me?"

"Are you all right?" Michael asked her, looking into her spellbound eyes.

"Oh, I'm perfectly all right, thank you. I just think you should come with me."

"You'd better find someplace to hide." He turned to the audience, hoping to find some glimpse of Sheri. "There are things I have to do," he said, starting to move toward the stage apron.

Evelynn put her hand on his arm.

"Please come with me," she said in the mildest of voices.

He shook her hand off and started to tell her that she'd best look after herself. Then he saw the barrel of the machine gun protruding just a few inches from the big fur muff.

"I said please," Evelynn murmured, so softly that Michael only knew she spoke because his eyes had returned to her face.

"Are you crazy? Are you in shock? Put that play gun away."

She smiled a bit and pointed the muzzle of the gun at the stage floor. It chattered briefly, like a jackhammer. A long splinter of wood flew up and traced a bloody line along his cheek.

"I'll kill you if you make me," Evelynn said loud enough for him to hear.

Peewit had rushed in from the outside at Janet's cry. Now he struck at Metzler again and again. The young cop had finally sorted everyone out and was now ordering Peewit to stop and raise his hands.

Metzler managed to get to his knees, scrambling away from the full fury of Peewit's powerful punches. He swung his fist blindly and managed to knock the old fighter aside for a moment, got his feet under him, straightened, half-dragging the clutching man with him, then struck at Peewit's head, pounding him behind the ear with the butt of the gun until Peewit's scarred hands let go of him.

Peewit fell, rolled away, struggled to maintain consciousness, reached out for Janet as he collapsed. He touched her arm. The cop closed in, grabbed the dazed and bleeding fighter and hauled him to his feet.

Metzler stumbled across the area toward the back

of the stage. He arrived behind the back curtain just as Assy opened the door to the control booth to let out two men and let in Evelynn and Michael Nordland.

He heard a shot and felt a lancet of pain slice into the flesh of his thigh. Instinct and hours on the firing range dictated his twisting move, the set of his legs and body as he brought his gun hand up, steadied it with his other hand around the wrist, and fired off four shots in rapid sequence at the instantly identified shooter facing him dead on.

His four bullets made a tight pattern that could be covered with a silver dollar right in the middle of Bondi's chest.

Alice was putting on her coat while Harry stood by, looking curiously like an impatient husband wanting to be off for the evening and forced to wait on a dawdling wife. The gun was back in his waistband, the flesh of his gut pillowing around it as he slouched against a dressing table.

Hush walked in and Harry looked at her with unnatural calm.

"Are you coming with us?" he asked.

"Running out on it, Harry?"

"I'm being smart. It started to fall apart before we really got rolling. Before all those royal bastards were set up in the shooting gallery."

"Are you deaf?" Hush asked.

Harry frowned, trying to grasp her meaning.

"Can't you hear those people out there screaming their rich, gaudy heads off? They're running around like chickens under the ax. We can still drop it on plenty of them and make a fortune to boot."

"Hush, didn't you hear what Harry said?" Alice

278

asked, as though a neighbor lady had failed to understand that her husband had called the party off.

"Shut up, Alice," Hush said.

Alice was about to get indignant. Hush took two steps and slapped her across the mouth. Alice looked at Harry, waiting to see if he'd come to her defense. When he didn't, she began to cry softly with her hand over her mouth.

Hush watched Harry as well. What he did right now would decide things. Had she pushed him back in line? He looked from Alice to her.

"Take a good look, Harry," Hush said. "It's time to spend your thruppence. You can't have both sweets."

Harry hesitated, straightened a bit as though growing a spine.

"You can have the cookie, Harry, if you're ready to go all the way."

Harry nodded. "Stay out of the way, Alice," he said sharply. He was taking command. "Let's go," he ordered Hush, taking the gun from his belt and walking fast. Hush followed.

At the door she stopped and fired two bullets into Alice, whose sobs became a single scream. She fell to the floor and was quiet.

"For Christ's sake," Harry said.

"No excess baggage, Harry."

Out in the auditorium, much of the pandemonium was dying down as Harry and Hush crossed the stage. They passed Metzler, on one knee beside the fallen Bondi. No one seemed to notice them. When they reached the control booth, Assy let them in.

Harry's eyes met Michael's. Neither spoke, but Harry grinned as fiercely as he knew how. Hush palmed the little Baretta as she preceded Harry inside, hurrying with little steps like a driven lamb, playing her role. As if on cue, Evelynn and Assy backed off as though frightened of Harry.

Good God, Michael wondered, was this a Manson affair? Did Harry have control over these women?

"Who knows how to work a camera?" Harry suddenly demanded.

Marty, the director, looked at him curiously. "Why do you want to know?"

"I think you should bring a camera up to this booth so you can send a picture of what's going on out to the public."

Hush moved away from Harry to the corner of the booth, still acting cowed. Assy and Evelynn looked at Harry wide-eyed. Michael wondered if the women would intervene if someone tried to take Harry. He felt the sudden desire to test the idea. He took a step. Assy raised the muzzle of the machine gun hidden in the muff. She smiled, and Michael settled back. He was satisfied that the women were simply playacting, making it appear that they were as much hostages as he and Vivian Lennox. A little insurance in case anything went wrong.

Michael was pleased to find himself thinking so clearly. He felt cool and centered, very much in command of himself. The way heroes are supposed to be?

"Do it," Harry said and touched the gun he'd tucked back into his waistband.

"Marsha, you know how to work a camera, don't you?"

"I'll stay with you, Marty."

"No, you won't. Go with Jack and bring camera five over here."

Marsha hesitated but finally followed the technician called Jack out of the place.

Four minutes later camera five was rolled over to a

spot twenty feet from the front of the booth, its cables snaking behind it. Jack and Marsha put on earphones, Jack got behind the camera, and the red light above the lens went on. At the same instant the captives and captors in the booth saw themselves on the monitor. Harry's lips moved. The director, sitting at the console, reached to touch a button, and the monitor shot was duplicated on the sending monitor. Marty touched another button and flooded the glass cage with the sound of an excited commentator's voice describing what everyone could see.

"Give me a mike," Harry demanded.

Marty pointed to one on the console, and Harry sat down in front of it.

At 11:17 Harry Smiley introduced himself to the television audience and presented his demands for the safety of Michael Nordland and Vivian Lennox, the reigning king and queen of the movie world. Ten million dollars and safe transport to Uganda.

41

The entire nation was witness to the scene of a man in a rumpled studio guard's uniform, gun at his belt, menacing three half-naked showgirls, a television director, a technical assistant and the two stars who'd just been awarded the highest honor the motion picture industry could confer, before Lieutenant Jill, taking the responsibility upon himself while jurisdiction was being sorted out, ordered the television station to stop transmitting anything from inside the Dorothy Chandler Pavilion.

Within fifteen minutes not only the contracting network for the Academy Awards Presentations but both rivals and the four local stations had sent crews to take up positions on the plaza. The educational station was to send crew and cameras sometime later.

Within twenty minutes they were announcing that three starlets, Evelynn Parsons, Hazel Ronstock and Mary Court, and the television directors Marty Goldaber and Warren Swift were the ordinary people who'd been scooped up along with the real targets, Michael Nordland and Vivian Lennox, by a part-time 20th studio guard by the name of Larry Wiley.

It was reported that the LAPD Intelligence Division had taken control of the situation and were investigating the possibility that Wiley's act was one of personal revenge despite the fact that he'd publicly demanded ten million dollars for the release of his multimillion-dollar hostages.

It was reported that a wardrobe lady, one Janet Peewit, had been critically wounded and had been transported to the hospital, where at first report she was not expected to live.

The deaths of Arnold Bondi, a new Pavilion maintenance employee, and one Marco Epstein, some sort of security expert, were also announced.

The names of the casualties in the auditorium were not yet available, but it was announced on good authority that dozens of the foremost entertainers and celebrities in the country were among the fallen.

The wounded were reported as being anywhere from fifty-five to one hundred seventy-five in number. The dead were counted anywhere from twenty-eight to eighty-seven.

Coolidge arrived with a contingent of FBI. Secret Service men, experts in the fields of hijack, kidnap and terrorism arrived on the scene. In the absence of the mayor—who was in the East on a speaking tour—the deputy mayor came with his special assistants.

The chief of LAPD arrived, officially took jurisdiction from the deputy mayor, and handed it over immediately to Lieutenant Jill, who kept on about his business.

Jill ordered all the lights in the auditorium to be turned off and all the doors entering into it closed. Men of two SWAT squads, armed with high-powered rifles equipped with telescopic sights, silently and invisibly took positions in the Founder's Circle and the first balcony.

In the glass cage Assy and Evelynn, pretending to be frightened and under orders, walked back and forth by turns, as though protecting Harry.

Metzler stood off in the wings, watching the people illuminated within the glass cage. Harry looked up once and seemed to stare at him, but Metzler knew he was lost in the shadows.

The commentators from the various television stations continued reporting to the public, reiterating what had already been said over and over again when there was nothing new to offer. Some emendations were made. Assy was correctly identified as Mara Courtney by Channel 13, but no mention of her true profession and police record was made because it was not yet known. Hush was properly renamed Bostock by CBS. NBC broke the news that an ex-fighter, Walter Peewit, currently working as a freelance property man in Hollywood, had been subdued by force and taken into custody. They were trying to find out whether or not there was any connection between him and the wounded seamstress of the same name. It was a reasonable guess, the commentator said, that two people with such an uncommon name might well be related. New and different estimations of the casualties were offered by each station.

Metzler was called into Freebody's office to confer with Lieutenant Jill.

His superior was sitting alone behind the desk, hands clasped behind his head in a pose that seemed rather casual, considering the circumstances.

"Well, you were right about that character Smiley," he said to Metzler. "Sit down."

There was a television set on a cabinet off to the side. It was a black and white monitor and was receiving the picture of the brightly lit control booth transmitted over a closed circuit by camera five. Jill glanced at it. He straightened up and began to reach for the phone just as it rang. Metzler looked at the TV set. On the screen a tiny Harry Smiley held a phone.

Jill put the handset on a speaker after saying "Hello" into it.

"Who am I talking to?" Harry's voice said through the small amplifier.

"Lieutenant Jill of the LAPD."

"You in authority?"

"That's why they switched you through to me. What do you want?"

"I want you to take those rifles out of the auditorium and turn the lights back on."

"You've got it," Jill said immediately.

"Are they getting the money?" Harry asked after a pause.

"Working on it," Jill said.

"How long is it going to take?"

"How the hell do I know? Ten million isn't sitting in one pocket."

"All right. All right," Harry said and hung up.

"Are you taking those snipers out?" Metzler asked Jill when he'd cut off the phone, then started dialing a number taken from an internal list taped to the desk.

Jill didn't answer directly but looked at Metzler, indicating that the instructions he was about to give were the answer.

"Control booth," the speaker said in a startled voice.

"Give me the lights in the auditorium again in thirty seconds. Got it?"

"Yes, sir. Hey, wait a minute. Who is this?" the engineer at the light console asked.

"Lieutenant Jill, LAPD."

"How do I know that?"

"Can you see the officers in the auditorium from up there?"

"Yes."

"I'm going to call their squad leader on the walkie-talkie. I'll tell him to stand up and wave to you."

Jill picked up the miniature transceiver.

"This is Jill in command. Who's the SWAT leader inside the area?"

The little radio coughed and stuttered. The tinny radio voice came through with startling clarity.

"Sergeant Fukuda here, sir."

"Smiley wants the lights on in the theater and the riflemen cleared out."

The radio itself seemed to contemplate the remark. Finally it spoke. "Sir, with your permission may I remind the Lieutenant that first principle insists on containing the situation with firepower."

"Thank you, Sergeant. I want you to make a clear show of evacuating the area when the lights go on. How many men are in place?"

"Two squads. Ten men, sir."

"Thank you, Sergeant. Leave the two in concealment that have the best angle for a shot. Wave to the overhead booth."

"I understand, sir," the sergeant said with a trace of glee in his voice.

Jill spoke into the speaker phone again. "Got all that, you up there in the booth?"

"Yes, sir."

"Count to thirty and put on the lights."

Jill got up.

"Let's walk down to the lobby," he said. "Now tell me any ideas you've got. Smiley's your baby, in a way. How can we get the edge on him?"

286

"He's got a short fuse. He can be pushed into get-ting mad," Metzler said as they walked to the elevator.

"That'd be fine if we could get up close, but he's got glass between us and him and seven people under the gun."

"Three of them are friends of his," Metzler pointed out. "Those showgirls are his friends."

"Didn't you say his friend Alice was a dancer in this show?" Jill asked.

"Yes, sir."

"She's dead in one of the dressing rooms. Eddie Barnes, the dance director, identified her. He says he saw Harry Smiley come out of there with a gun in his hand. Barnes was on his way to see if she was all right. He found her dead."

They entered the elevator.

"He may have some hold on the women," Jill said, "but I think he'd off them in a wink."

They crossed the lobby swiftly and went through one of the side doors into the auditorium. The lights were up full, starkly illuminating the bloody ruin so much of it had become. The last of the SWAT men were just leaving the balconies.

Jill and Metzler looked up as a young Japanese officer casually saluted and went out one of the doors.

"That Marco Epstein's been killed too," Jill said as he resumed his march down the aisle.

"Smiley's going to have a lot to answer for," Metz-ler said.

"Let's not give him any more. I want you to stay right with me, Metzler. We're going to fake this bas-tard into a hole."

"If we can."

"If we can."

Jill reached the stage and jumped up onto it nimbly. Metzler followed.

"Get us a couple of chairs, will you?" Jill asked as he walked toward the glass booth. He stopped a dozen feet away and waved a greeting.

"Hi'ya, Harry," he said.

42

If containing the situation with firepower is a first principle among the experts in a field that would seem to defy expertise by its very nature, the second principle would be to set up proper contact with the captors who are holding human beings and society up for ransom.

The body of the great Pavilion designed for the cultural edification and entertainment pleasure of a vast city had been made a battleground. It was filled with enough personnel from enough branches of law enforcement to mount a small war, but the conflict was actually focused within a comparatively small area—the glass booth and the stage area immediately surrounding it.

Jill and Metzler were covered by directional shotgun microphones so that everything that transpired from their side of the transparent wall was taped. The end of the conversation that originated inside the cage was taped via the microphone that enlarged Harry's voice monstrously in the echoing cavern of the empty theater.

Beyond that, two men dressed in black crouched in positions of increasing discomfort among the balcony rows.

Dennis Bryan was born to be a cop. It was a family

tradition. His father, his grandfather and half his uncles and cousins were cops. He'd done his Nam duty in an MP outfit. He'd graduated in the top ten percentile of his academy class. He'd applied for the SWAT team the moment his probation was finished. He was an overachiever. Some of his superior officers had already noticed that but were certain that proper seasoning would calm him down. Had Sergeant Fukuda had another option he probably would have pulled Bryan out with the others and left someone else on the line. But Bryan was perfectly placed if a clean shot presented itself. He'd been instructed to do nothing on his own initiative. He was to take no action unless given a clear-cut order. He lay awkwardly, preferring flawless concealment to comfort. The position was becoming painful, but he never moved an inch or took his eyes off the lighted booth at the end of the rifle barrel.

"I'm not sure it's the best idea for you to be here after all," Jill said to Metzler. "The book says to try to cool any emotional tension and try to create trust between the negotiators and the terrorists."

Metzler made a snorting noise through his nose.

"I don't think Smiley would trust anybody. He's out of it. A loner. He gunned his girlfriend. He's using these other friends as shields."

Behind the glass Harry frowned. He leaned toward the microphone, pushing Assy aside where she sat with Evelynn and Hush as though making a cordon of flesh around him.

"What're you bullshitting about, Metzler? Telling your boss what a smart-ass you were? How you had your eye on me?"

"Lieutenant Jill was just saying that my presence might be upsetting to you."

Harry laughed. "Hell, no. I want you right where you are. I want you to see me collect the ten million. I want you to sit there with your fucking hands in your pockets while I walk out of here free as a bird."

Metzler smiled easily. "Well, you'll be flying," he said. "What made you pick Uganda?"

"Why not? I read the papers. Amin would like the chance to put one over on a bunch of arrogant white bastards."

"Getting a little messy, isn't it?" Jill said casually. "Amin's considered crazy at best. He might just decide to kill you and cop the ten for himself."

"Don't shit on my parade," Harry said angrily.

"I don't give a damn about you, Smiley. You know that. I'd be a fool to suggest anything else," Jill went on, "but I am concerned about any hostage you take along with you to insure yourself against a broken bargain. I'm concerned about the crew of the aircraft that's being prepped to take you out of here."

"So?"

"So let us examine the possibility of dropping you in some other nation that's proven safe for hijackers. The Middle East, perhaps. Some other third-world nation. Let's see if we can't make a contribution to somebody who will play straight with you and keep the people we care about safe."

Harry shook his head. He glanced at Hush, but she quickly turned her eyes aside so that he wouldn't seem to be conferring with her.

"Well, he's certainly not going to put any trust in me to help him," Jill said, "but I think he'll buy the fact that we're willing to help him to save our people and the innocent hostage." His lips scarcely moved as he spoke to Metzler.

"I don't think the stupid son of a bitch knows what

the hell he's doing. Something's all out of kilter," Metzler murmured back.

Harry peered at them sharply again.

"You got anything to say, you pick up that mike and let me in on it too."

Jill took the mike from Metzler.

"What do you say? Shall we start investigating possibilities?"

"We'll just go ahead the way I planned it," Harry said. "It better be damn fast. I'm getting impatient. Tell them to hurry up or somebody's going to die right in here."

"Don't do anything foolish," Metzler said.

Harry blew his top then, suddenly, unexpectedly.

"Who the hell you think you are, Metzler? Who the hell you think you are, telling me what to do? You're the sons of bitches better watch out you don't do anything foolish."

His eyes shifted to Michael Nordland, who regarded him with extraordinary calm.

"What the fuck you looking at? You waiting to see if I do anything foolish? You got that superior look in your eye. You think you're better than me, you yellow son of a bitch? Stop looking at me like I was something crawled out from under a rock."

Michael thought it might be prudent to drop his eyes in a show of subservience and fear, to get Smiley's venom directed elsewhere again. On the other hand, the thought came to him that to show weakness to this man on a power rampage could send him out of control altogether. Smiley might kill if Michael broke the confrontation.

He felt cool and well-centered and a bit surprised. He wondered if this was the way naturally courageous men faced danger or if he was just acting out a role. Whatever the case, it felt good.

"Stop staring at me, I said!" Harry screamed and started toward Michael, raising the gun to strike at him.

"Step back, you crazy bastard," Michael said in a voice that was almost conversational.

Harry stopped with his arm upraised. He even retreated a half step.

"What the hell did you say?" Harry asked Michael, not believing the effrontery of the man. "What did you call me?"

"A crazy bastard."

"I got a gun on you and you're calling *me* a crazy bastard?"

Michael smiled pleasantly. "Were you in a war, Smiley?"

"I told you once I served in Korea."

"You never faced the guns."

"You're facing a gun right now and still you're mouthing off," Harry said. "You're the one who's nuts."

"I'm facing *guns*, Smiley. Maybe you are too. Perhaps you should be afraid."

Harry made another move toward Michael, who didn't budge. Harry slammed the mike switch closed.

"What the hell do you mean? These are my soldiers," he said fiercely.

Michael felt a little motor of tension start up and start racing.

"Don't you know that these are my soldiers?" Harry nearly screamed.

Michael held Harry's eyes with his own, keeping him talking, getting him to doubt, planting a small seed of confusion.

"That's a stupid thing to say, Smiley. Look at those girls. What have you got to offer them? Look at yourself."

"Shut up!" Harry shouted. The grin on his face pulled back the corners of his mouth so hard his face seemed split with an ax.

"You're a pig, Smiley. An old man with a gut. Which one of them said she'd go away with you?"

Harry's demands for silence grew incoherent. The veins of his neck pulsed with the charges of fury in him.

"What are you trying to do, Nordland?" Hush demanded. "You trying to get yourself killed? You trying to get him to run wild?"

"Don't worry, miss." Michael smiled with curious politeness. "He knows he's got nowhere to go. You'd better tell him so."

"Nobody's telling me anything," Harry raged. "I'm running this."

Michael smiled ruefully and shook his head.

"They're using you, Smiley. Can't you see that? You're nothing but the cat's paw, you damn fool."

Harry looked at Hush. He knew that what Michael was saying was the truth. He lifted the gun, throwing Assy aside with one arm.

Bryan squeezed the trigger when he saw Harry about to shoot. Squeezed the trigger as Jill started to shout something, anything, to deflect Harry. Squeezed as Michael dove for Harry, angry as hell, afraid but attacking all the same.

The slug caught Harry between the eyes, taking the back of his head out. He was dead before the gun his hand released dropped to the floor.

Michael slammed into the body, sensed the death, saw Evelynn automatically lifting the muzzle of the machine gun concealed in the fur so that it pointed dead center on Vivian Lennox. He reached out desperately for her ankle, lunging across the floor.

Evelynn was spun around as she fell. Her finger

closed on the trigger, and the Thompson fired a short burst. Assy was flung away. She sat on the floor against the wall, staring at the brief green satin panties that were turning red with the blood from the wounds in her naked belly. Then she toppled over.

Hush reached into the elaborate wig she wore and removed the little Baretta concealed there. Her attention was all on Nordland. She felt the kind of hate that Harry had felt for the actor. Harry's focus of frustration and rage had become her own.

Metzler had started running at the sound of Bryan's bullet, not toward the glass cage but away from it. He went as far as the edge of the stage, then turned back and drove hard for the gleaming transparent wall now spattered with blood. He passed Jill and leaped forward, turning his shoulder into the glass as he hit, shattering it, forcing entry. His momentum carried him in front of the muzzle of the little gun Hush fired. He felt the touch of fire at his shoulder, then had his forearm up, knocking her arms aside, getting into her throat, bringing her down.

Jill was right behind Metzler. He grabbed Evelynn before she had a chance to recover. She made no attempt to struggle.

Vivian Lennox began to scream without pause in a high keening wail that was the very soul of human shock and grief.

Michael Nordland held his hands out in front of him. They trembled a little but not through any lack of courage. He felt a curious lightness in his chest and belly, the desire to laugh.

43

The sun was bright above the Los Angeles basin. The smog was beginning to build up, irritating the eyes, searing the lungs, bringing death a little bit closer for the citizens of the city.

Metzler and Coolidge walked out of County Hospital. Metzler's arm was in a sling.

"I'm here to tell you that you've got a job with the Bureau if you want it," Coolidge said.

"Why?"

"You've got an instinct."

"What the hell good did it do?"

Coolidge shrugged.

They stood on the corner waiting for the light to change.

"What's the score?" Metzler asked.

"They're still counting, but it looks like only thirty-one citizens dead, one hundred thirty-four wounded or seriously injured."

"'Only'?"

"It could have been worse."

The light changed and pedestrian traffic poured both ways across the street.

"It could always be worse," Metzler said bitterly.

He was looking at Coolidge. A man coming the other way, rushing against a deadline even he probably didn't understand, slammed into his bad shoulder. Metzler cried out in pain. The man didn't pause to say he was sorry, just glared at Metzler with naked fury and cursed him silently.

He was one of the faceless, voiceless millions. His name was Murray Bowzer. He knew that no one gave a damn about him. He'd known it since he was a kid, the smallest in his class, the one all the other kids beat on to prove themselves in the miniature rituals of manhood.

When Murray was in the seventh grade he had his first opportunity to be noticed. He'd been picked at random—as an act of charity, really—to represent his grammar school at a small conference of teachers and students concerned with the new math. He was to present a little speech about it to the assembly, but on that day he became sick with anxiety. His mother kept him home. That was to be the pattern of his life. He was never there when the goodies were passed out.

He read much about terrorists, assassins, hijackers and kidnappers. In his thirty-third year he read about the coming visit of a great ballerina. He knew something of ballet and the way things were conducted backstage. . . .